STARVENGER

CHRIS TURNER

Chapter 1

I drove the loaded flatbed with an itchy foot on the accelerator. I cursed every pile of rubbly shit that made me deke around and waste more time. Bad enough to have to maneuver through a war zone than to drive this claptrap two-ton shipment in to the rebel dropoff point. Why hadn't I allowed myself more time?

Hindsight, Rusco. Everything's easy in hindsight.

Many times I'd have to tell myself the same thing. This road was blocked like the last, sprawled with some building that'd caved, spreading across the pavement like a broken tower of Babel. The city was a shambles. Courtesy of dear old Mong, our friendly neighborhood warlord, Star Lord, whatever the hell, who had torn through every nook and cranny of this metropolis. Made an example of this rebel city with his Warhawks. The insurgents would certainly like our precious cargo, that tickletrunk of fiery, feral goodies in the back, everything a diehard, red-eyed rebel could ever want to use against a hated enemy—RPGs, land mines, R4s, death-dealing fire flares. Only problem was, I wondered if they'd still be there. We were late to dropoff with all this backtracking and I'd already been running far behind on the long haul from Uziles in *Veglos* where we loaded the stuff. Not to mention nursing a very bad feeling about this gig in the first place.

Too late to back out now. Too much invested. You're up to your neck, Rusco. You've a reputation to keep. Backing out has its price.

Wren was at my side in the truck's cab, calm as the quiet before storm, her shiny dark hair grown back from its ugly baldness when I had met her. Could smell the faint odor of her sweat. Three blond youngbloods hunched in the back behind us, breathing down my neck. A trio of hothead punks

I'd brought in on short notice. Breaking them in. Good training for their lot. Blest had potential, but Klane, well, dunno about Klane. Could go either way—something off with his logic. Tager, worth a chance, but I'd dump him if he messed up.

Sweat beaded under my brow, the grey showing to the discerning eye. I tossed back my faddish, purple-dyed pony tail kept tied as a nostalgic gimmick while I still had hair. I stretched my six foot frame in that cramped cabin, tired and yawning from the long space flight across the black gulfs, stewing over these zany last minute plans.

I looked around the terrain and shook my head. Too many worlds like this one, blown to shit. Wartorn prizes of space thugs and warlords, captains of disaster and ragged-eared dogs fighting over graveyard bones in a planet-wide slurry. The few pristine worlds left would be sodomized by warlords and gangsters before the decade was up. I knew it in my heart. The rest had fallen into corruption, decay, death. I'd grown up into it and it was no different now than it was say, ten years ago. If anything, worse.

Enough doom and gloom. Get on with the program.

After a brief recap of our plans, I screeched the tires to a halt on the warehouse asphalt and ordered my new recruits out. Wren sauntered out like a lioness, slinging her R4 rifle over her lean, but sinewy shoulder.

I squinted around in the opaque light. The sullen sky did not improve what I saw. A rectangular shitbox of a warehouse, steel refab beams leaning on drunken angles. The lot, strewn with crumbled concrete, was no better than the rest of the city: a write-off. Some wrecked vehicles and lift loaders to the side, nothing now but mangled junk fallen to the fire of warships. An overturned jeep sprawled with bent wheels and a jerry-rigged flamethrower mounted on overhead bars. Made to look like an abandoned base, I guessed. Ten to one there were assault vehicles tucked inside just waiting to burst out and wreak havoc. To the other side lurked a tangled thicket that backed out onto another yard and some open land beyond, here at the western edge of the city. Broken light-posts teetered around the lot's perimeter. Remarkably, one tall one still stood and its yellow lamp burned feebly by the warehouse door where some activity caught my eye.

Two sets of explosives I carried hidden in my breast armor, coin-size, not easily detectable. In case things went awry. Any arms dealer would have such. We wore fatigues, dirty grey and green-black, padded. All of us wore Kevlar vests underneath. "You know the drill," I grunted at them. "No embellishments. Everything to plan." I stared at Klane who'd already shown a tendency to waver from orders.

They growled at that. Two of them gave nods. These recruits still gave me cause for worry. Wren I needn't worry about. She was an asset: wiry, statuesque, a gutsy brunette. We'd worked together before and she'd gotten me out of a lot of jams. Big ones. Like the one where we were shipwrecked on Talyon when Baer and his thugs had pinned us down. We knew each other. I'd fight to the end for Wren.

Two armed men stepped out of the doorway and motioned us to a rusted side entrance while others poked the back of the truck with their rifles, lifting a flap to peer in with oily smiles. They didn't disarm us but I noticed they kept their sawed-off R4s well-trained on us—probably in case we were agents of Mong. The detail escorted us none too gently into the half bombed warehouse, down a stale-aired hallway reeking of kerosene and old cheese. From there, to a dim backroom with a rat-eaten table and two bulbs burning overhead.

The nearest man jumped up from a stool: Froy, our contact. He turned about with a scowl, impatient, surly, a half-chewed beedi leaning out of his tar-gummed mouth. "You're late."

"Yeah, well, it's a fucking far way from Veglos," I said. "We were told this is the place and that we should bring no others and here we are."

Froy grunted, unimpressed.

The man was cloaked in ragged brown fatigues, frayed at the edges, hair askew. He'd suffered multiple wounds recently, judging by the hackjob on his khakis. Looked as if he hadn't bathed in weeks. Pearly eyes were round saucers into nowhere as he blinked at us. I'd seen eyes like that on wartorn mongrels before. The enlarged whites gleamed—the mark of the *invinco* addict and crack hashish user if I've ever seen one, mixed with Myscol OD, floating in his blood. With nothing to lose, these war types remained volatile to the end. A chip on their shoulders as big as an anvil and an axe to grind. I looked at him in casual disinterest, hoping to disarm him. It failed. The situation would require careful maneuvering.

His henchmen who'd escorted us from the flatbed shifted, and one inclined his head with a flick of eyes. "They came in on a truck, Froy."

"A truck? You check it?"

"It's got the stuff."

"Good." Froy nodded, momentarily appeased, but still wound as tight as a prowling tiger. "I thought you were coming in on a ship, Rusco." His voice was a low, sinister monotone.

"Plans change."

"Yeah, and so does the price, smart guy. I just dropped it. Bad for you. Market's low today, as is my mood."

Klane surged forward. "What do you mean, dropped?" The gunman choked, licking his lips, gripping his R4.

Froy turned to him. "What does 'price dropped' mean to you, kid? You deaf or something?"

"Relax, cool it," I said, clutching at his elbow.

The idiot wriggled out of my grip. "Less profit for us, Rusco. We've got to get a profit out of this."

Froy gave a sour laugh. "Profit? Kiss your boss's ass for profit. This is wartime."

I suddenly felt a noticeable dip in our security here. The hothead lout, Klane, was all elbows and knees, clacking teeth, as if Santa Claus had denied him a toy. Too worried about losing his share of the spoils, dumbfuck. Made a move too fast which spooked Froy's nearest boy. The gunman's barrel came up and Klane took this as a threat and whirled his piece about, another stupid move. He had the butt end braced in his gut like a gangster. The clack of fire nearly killed our ears in that tiny place. Klane's innards spilled over the floor and his head exploded in a crimson mash like a melon bursting.

I jerked back, a warm sickness swarming my gut. "What the fuck—" I ducked, wiping the putrid slime of Klane's brains off my camos. "You stupid dipshit, Froy. Why the hell did you do that?"

"Get them to shut up, Garr." Froy stabbed out a fist at his men. "Bind these fuckers. Pissed me off enough today, and it's been a bad day. We won't be paying anybody anything today, Rusco. Mong's up our ass. My cousin and his brother, Joely, are jelly. They wouldn't have been corpses in the grave today if you bags of shit had showed up on time…if we had your RPGs in our hands and used them to cut down those pinkos. Cost us too many lives today. Too many valuable lives."

In any other scenario, we would be toast. But Wren and I had already acted. I pulled the pin on one of my coin-size bombs and chucked it at Froy's three minions. We dove for the exit just as gunfire raked the air where we'd been. Blest and Tager, likewise lucky, saved their heads from being shot off. We raced down the hallway, a motley misfit of four, me, lifting my weapon, blowing out the hanging bulbs. Wren bowled over a surprised guard at the door while we burst through the rusted exit and raced for the flatbed.

The seconds passed like hours in a nightmare. The first piff-paff of shells came spraying at us and I flung myself to my stomach, breathing tarmac. One of the goons came coughing out of the smoke, shooting blind. I pulled out the second flash bomb, and chucked it. Three of them disappeared in a cloud of smoke and blood splatter. Not before the first one had riddled our ride's tires to useless shreds. No getting away on this rig or retrieving the cargo.

"Fuck!" I breathed. "Out of here." I gave back covering fire while I pushed Wren and the other two toward the tangled thicket breasting the lot. "Move!"

We ran with fire flare eating at the foliage around us.

Blest's sweat-laced face was wide-eyed with terror, a curse on his lips. "Screw you, Rusco! I didn't sign up for this shit."

"What did you sign up for then? Tiddlywinks? Get your ass moving."

We struggled through the brambles, getting pricked like divers in a school of blowfish. The least of our concerns. More rebels must have buzzed out of the warehouse and swarmed after us while I felt the riffle of shots at my feet and a whizz over my ear. One grazed my thigh; not enough to damage me, but it hurt like hell. Bee stings soaked in vinegar.

"Fucking hot-headed rebels fueled up on rage, having their city sacked." Seems as if they'd forgotten who their friends were.

Chapter 2

A hail of fire blizzarded over our heads. We broke out of the scorched thicket, hopped the next yard and raced down a gravel path with the intent to loop back toward the city closer to where my ship was hidden. Froy's goons were somewhere behind us, shooting away. I caught muffled echoes of boot on gravel, stray shots, shouts.

Keep moving. That's your middle name, Rusco. Another botch up. How many more there going to be? I should kill you myself, put you out of your misery. The shell shock of the last blast had spun my head sideways. I did a quick scan.

Wren was in good shape. Tager had taken a minor hit, his left forearm grazed. Blest was ruffled but seemed okay.

Me, some cuts and scrapes and bruises here and there, nothing I couldn't handle, a wicked ache in my left thigh.

I shrugged, fingered my compact R4. Always liked the snug feel of the wooden stock in my hand and how it slipped so easily into killing mode. One of the older models. Trustworthy. The black, fast-action carbine sported an energy-pulse with good range and accuracy and unlimited shell action.

This wasn't what I had planned. But is there anything that is?

We rounded a curve in the road in a direction I roughly estimated led to our parked craft. I studied the ruined city below. Ugly as a mummy's crypt. I grimaced. I'd give Froy's screwball rebels dibs for spunk. So far they'd survived this hell. I'd promised them arms at a decent price because I have a hard on for that bastard Mong—well, okay, I like the money and the smell of it and I too have to eat. Getting too old for this shit.

We hustled down the slope into what was once a main boulevard in that concrete jungle of shattered shapes, keeping our heads down, our guns aimed in front, and alternating rearguard. We crossed the main street, past broken, burned-out vehicles. The rank smell of soot and charred flesh filled our nostrils. Our boots crunched over rubble. We passed a small pile of blown-out stone in the center of the street, something that used to be a monument. I could see the toppled marble head with a crown or coronet, some heroic figure of the past, with the eyes bullet-holed out.

Maybe not such a good idea to play hide and seek here with my ship

Bantam so far away now from the drop site. I'd landed it five miles at the edge of the city in case of treachery. Treachery we got, but now Bantam, my Alpha-Omega Beamer, wasn't here to help us out of this madness.

The instant they'd wasted Klane, we were running on borrowed time.

The biggest problem was how to get back to Bantam without getting our heads blown off. Froy's thugs seemed farther behind us than five minutes ago. With some luck, some more of these cross-alleys would help us lose them. But that tactic could backfire at any instant.

"Loop around past the old section," I directed, "more shelter there and less chance of getting bottled up in a narrow alley."

"Mines?" Tager croaked.

"We look for signs and watch our steps." I shrugged. Wren cast me a fugitive glance which I ignored.

Why was everything so dark on this miserable world? Was this a solar eclipse? Only a creepy, leaden light from Remus's sun. No, there was Arkades poking through the clouds like a timid widow. This world was downright eerie. Another dumbass decision to risk a quick venture on a backward planet. I ran through the rubble, breath rasping, clutching at the burning ache in my leg. No time to apply regen. Unless I wanted to get a pulse-burst in my guts. Wren labored at my side, breathing heavily like a winded mare. Blest ran a few paces behind, thin, wiry, the whites of his eyes darting back and forth from the broken structures ahead to the moving shadows behind. Tager, squat, burly, lumbersome brought up the rear, giving covering fire when he could, huffing and puffing like the Billy Goats Gruff. Was he trying to be a hero? The fool was lagging and going to get himself tagged. I dropped back. "Get up ahead, Tager. I'll take over as rearguard."

A rumble rolled across the sky. An enemy ship? Moving fast. Question was, what enemy, Mong or Froy's rebels? Likely Mong, the Star Lord.

I ducked. Shellfire rained at our sides. *Rat-a-tat.* The nightmare echo of my sweaty dreams.

"Get Noss the fuck over here," gusted Blest.

My fingers itched to do it, and call up our shipmate. But I held back, feeling a tingle in my wrist and hearing a little creak in the left finger of my prosthetic hand.

"Oh, for Christ sakes," cursed Blest, "I'll call him myself."

"Can't. They'll trace it. Then alert their scouts. If that's who I think it is,

Warhawks'll blow Bantam out of the sky. I can't chance losing that ship."

"He's right," grunted Wren. "Noss is neither tactician nor marksman. They'll make mincemeat out of him."

"Then we're screwed," cried Blest. "So what do we do?"

"Do what we're doing. Come hell or high water, we get to Noss and the ship."

"You should have had a backup plan, Rusco."

"Right, like it was obvious to guess that our business partners would be so kind as to turn wolf on us. What's with you?"

Blest bleated something unintelligible.

"Speaking of which, weren't you the one gave the all-clear after radar-scouting out the city and telling me Mong's forces were gone?"

Blest licked his lips. "They must have come back."

"No, you dickhead, you didn't look hard enough and they were hunkered down somewhere, tucked away like bugs. I should have done the scan myself."

The arguing was doing us no good. Blest had fucked up. I had fucked up. Klane had fucked up, and then he paid the price with his life. I wiped my sweaty brow then rubbed my eyes. All adrenalin and rage and frustration thrown in for fun. A lethal, toxic mix that needed an outlet. But now we needed to move on and concentrate on surviving.

Supposed to have been only a simple drop off, for shit's sake. A hundred crates of R4s and various land mines and fire snares. Everything set up by our contact Romos and his gang of scumbags. Nice bunch of people to work with.

It's never simple, Rusco, you should know that, you dreamer.

If that idiot Klane hadn't shot off his mouth, we wouldn't be in this jam. Didn't he know that shortchange was part of the whole package? I'd allowed for it, factored in the slippage, that's why I charged 20% more. Something I'd been expecting. I should have briefed Klane better though. Hindsight. All this fled through my mind as we ran. Move on, Rusco, the boat is leaving the dock.

Some brief gunfire flashed from the side, startling us as we scooted across a vehicle-sprawled square. Tager dropped as a slug slammed him high in the shoulder. He gave a hound's yelp as another smacked into his temple. I looked back, saw blood gushing from his mouth. No saving Tager now.

With a choked gurgle, Blest dropped down behind an alley's corner.

"What are you doing? Blest, get up, you fool!"

He ignored me.

Two figures burst into the square, one covering the foreground while another offered covering fire.

Blest's R4 spat out a vengeful burst.

The figure flopped like a ragdoll. Wren tagged the other.

"Nailed the bastard," croaked Blest.

"What do you want, a kiss?" I hissed. "Pipe down, there may be more of them."

Wren mumbled, "Good shot." She touched Blest's arm and he gave her a terse nod, working his lips and struggling on ahead.

A sour wave of nausea hit me. I pushed on through the empty streets, shaking my head like a dog, herding myself along.

I stared down at the gash in my leathered thigh. More blood was trickling where the shell had grazed me. My nine lives were running out.

The distant rumble of ship's engines coursed above. Closer now. Much closer. Made more menacing by the low cloud cover. The explosion in the warehouse must have alerted Mong's imperial scouts.

The endless maze of streets was disorienting. More and more squares with shelled fountains, toppled statues and broken buildings and fly-ridden bodies, young, old, short, fat. Death did not discriminate. At one time it looked as if this city had been built in an elegant baroque, the style probably deliberately copied from Earth by some high class types, but with cathedrals dedicated to a new, modern-day savior.

Stone bridges ran over the canals; blown out now, so we had to wade through rank, brown-scummed water. Grey sluggish streams dotted with bloated bodies; animals too, what looked like kangaroos crossed with mastiffs.

These insurgents, I knew the type, had their noses ground in the mud too often. They'd been fighting this guerrilla war for months now. Turned red devils into savages. I hadn't realized how far they'd regressed until I snatched a look at Froy back there. I caught a flutter of movement in the arched ruin of a church.

Swore it was Froy, cloaked in his ragged brown khakis, loping like a tiger. Wild eyes gleamed with a special something of vindictive madness. The squad was far enough away for me not to be shitting bricks. He and his goons'd lost sight of the cause, chasing us like rabbits. I mean, who in their right mind would go after their supplier? Were we their enemy, or Mong? I looked over and saw the Warhawk T-wing roving the sky in the low-scudding cloud, the roar of its heavy-duty engines polluting the desolate silence over the doomed city, drowning out the raucous croaks of strange, oversized crows. The ship's homely green and brown prow thrust out like the beak of a bird of prey.

A sudden sound broke behind me.

I aimed behind me and shot a spray of death. A rebel with full beard and a fuckboy cut fell clutching his leg as one of my fire bursts hit home, knocking the feet from under him. His two lithe partners hopped over him like gazelles.

We ducked into a culvert that curved under a shell-pitted road. Puddles of water pooled at our feet, the echo of our boots sloshing through stagnant water. We scrambled out the other end then down another ruined alley, our breaths hissing ragged rasps in our throats, lungs pumping.

Still another mile or two to the ship, if my bearings were correct. Everything looked the same in this wreck of a city. Piles of rubble and dead bodies feasted on by carrion birds. Feral kangaroo creatures foraging for scraps and rooting amongst the dead. I kicked one of them out of the way that snapped and growled at me, defending its turf like a guard-dog of the dead. Most of the people who'd survived this holocaust had fled, but there was the odd hobo or old coot hanging around.

We'd taken a wrong turn and gotten jammed up in a dead-end alley. Shelled buildings rose to either side, the windows blown out. We were just about to backtrack when a ragged transient lurched out, scared out of his wits. A bottle of whiskey or rubbing alcohol lay clutched in his hands. "Don't shoot me, misters, don't shoot—"

The cry died in my throat as he staggered for a few steps then exploded in scarlet spray, his head blown clean off. I winced as the corpse fell in a ragged heap, the head pumpkin jelly. I flung myself to the ground behind a rubbled heap. I pulled Wren with me. Blest dove the other way into the shelter of a debris pile, broken dolls and a human foot.

A voice called out from the silent rubble, "You're a dead man, Rusco."

Froy.

The sound of my name bounced off the battered walls.

"Kill my men, will you?" Froy taunted. "We've got the arms. You've lost your payout."

"You killed my man first, Froy."

"Your boy was out of line," Froy called. "What I want is your ship, and you can throw in the woman as a bonus. Come out with her and I may spare your asses. We'll take your little raven tail for a ride or two." He chuckled, a sleazy echo answered by one of his henchmen.

I ground my teeth. Yes, they'd turned into savages.

I tried to make sense of it. Distorted perceptions. Any stab at a perceived enemy made a logical target. Too many loved ones snatched away in too brief a time. Too many pent-up hopes shot down in flames. Froy, half-baked on *invinco*, a hair-trigger finger on anything that moved, friend or foe. Now his goons' communal libidos were jacked up to rapacious pitch— maybe some god-awful side effect of the *invinco*.

"We've got to keep that bastard talking," I muttered at my two team members.

Wren gave a fierce nod. Blest gazed at me with resignation, his belly hugging the damp dirt. His curly blond hair was covered with dust and a blood smear to the side where he'd bashed his head on something.

The first pangs of desperation crawled over me. I called Noss on the com. Things were desperate. No answer. Where the fuck was Noss? Deserted? Stolen my ship? Sorry bugger'd get a rude surprise if he tried to leave this planet's gravity without authorization. I'd rigged something up to deter all such adventurous forays from pilots who didn't know how to disarm the sequence. The electro-force would kill him if it kicked in and would bathe his world in hell.

My red eyes roved above the cracks of the apartments and blackened stone where Mong's forces had taken out a whole block. Monstrous crows, a threesome, or what looked like a threesome, flapped out of the gaping windows, their dissonant croaks echoing down the alley of shell-blasted stone.

"I'll sit tight, draw them in," I wheezed. "You go up there, Wren, sniper them down."

She tensed. "They'll kill you. Why sacrifice yourself?"

I shrugged, gave my usual clown's grimace of a smile. "We're already dead, Wren. Trapped here. Go!" I slapped her on the back. She shook her head, her lip downturned.

Shots echoed from up the alley. Covering fire ricocheted as her weapon leaped out while they tried to pepper her.

I crouched, whipping out shots, laying into the moving figures with everything I had. Blest picked up on her cue and beetled down the alley to purchase a sniper position.

I debated taking the building on the right versus closing in after her. I risked a peek past the crumble. I saw four bogies in black suits, heavy-set, crabbing forward from pile of debris to debris. High-powered R4s. They must have taken them off the flatbed.

The gunmen blasted my shell hump of refuge with heavy fire. Enough to rattle my teeth. I pinched my eyes shut, and prayed not one of them would see me.

Fire flashed from overhead. Two of the enemy went down. I took the opportunity to poke my R4 out and spray anything in sight. One burst caught the closest not twenty feet away, tagging him in the shin and he hobbled with a curse. I heard the *rat-tat-tat* above me and Wren blasted the other bitchdog to kingdom come.

More were crawling out of the woodwork. How many of them were there? These last bastards were not so easy. Froy'd survived this long and he knew where we were and what our capabilities were. He might have even known that I was injured.

Come up with a winning plan, Rusco, or you're all dead. This Froy fucker's mean as a snake and will gutshot you in an instant.

While Wren sprayed her next volley, I took a risky, stumbling dash, hoping my boots wouldn't crunch too loudly on the crumble. Fire nipped at my ankles and I dove into a jagged opening on the other side of the alley, just in time as shells nearly ripped off my heels. I edged my way up a ruined stair, my heart pumping blood, keeping my head down.

My breath came in ragged gasps. Some loss of blood. Enough to throw me off my game.

Klane was an idiot. You're running on borrowed time. What if they have more backup?

So you gun them down.

I squinted hard, thrust out the voices from my head and shook my reeling skull. *If Wren dies…*

She won't die. Keep moving.

Chapter 3

Through a broken window, I saw her, moving low, on the second floor of the building on the other side of the alley. Others'd be coming up the stairs after us now. A risky move, but I knew Froy's type. All risk and bravado and a sureness in himself that would make a leopard weep. He had to be juiced, on pure *invinco*—that would give a man enough courage—or a death wish—

Gunfire raked us from below, peppering the window where Wren had last hunkered down. Clouds of dust and plaster rose. Silence. No movement from within. I felt a sick dismay rising up from the pit of my stomach. I poked my head up to look out my window. A part of me sagged in despair. I forced myself to keep moving, telling myself she was still alive while dread haunted me with every step.

I shook my head in shame and mounted some more stairs and crept along an office of broken tables and water dispensers and whatnot when the *rat-a-tat* of fire nearly deafened me, ripping into the wall beside me. "Hold up! Weapon down." The harsh voice lashed out at me.

I slowly held up my gun, not daring to turn around. Think fast, Rusco. Stall them. It's the only hope.

"If it's me you're after, you've done it, Froy, let the girl go free."

"Turn around, slowly, Rusco. Kick the weapon away."

I did as Froy told me and saw he had his piece leveled point blank, his face a livid mask of contempt. Another rebel was fast booting up the stairs.

"Where is she?" the newcomer barked. "The bitch killed Brex."

Froy's white ferret eyes darted about the room. "How many more of you rats are hiding here?" he shouted at me.

"I think you killed the rest of them," I said.

"You'll wish you'd joined them, Rusco. Move!" He rapped me with his gun. "Now it'll go the worse for you. Those RPGs could have given my team cover and saved our asses."

"If you'd been using them now instead of chasing me, maybe you could have blown up some of your real enemies."

The distant roar of an enemy ship echoed above and Froy's head turned in a shiver of fear. I likened it to a squirrel that's got dogs on both sides of him.

The rebel gripped his weapon with instinctive reflex and twisted the barrel to the window. "Shut up."

He motioned to the others, three more mounting the stairs. "Take this bugger to base. I have special uses for him. The rest of you, ferret out the woman."

They nodded.

I made as if to stall.

"Move!" Froy rapped the butt end of his rifle into the back of my skull. Stars flashed in multicolor. I massaged the lump growing there. My only hope was that Wren and Blest had the sense to keep away and get to Noss and the ship. If she were still alive.

Despair gnawed at my gut.

Rusco, you're not thinking fast enough. I walked, as slowly as I could, with the gunman prodding me along. All your fancy footwork isn't going to amount to jack shit if you don't come up with something quickly! Look for an opportunity. Use your wits!

"If it's arms you want," I began, "I can get you as many as you want, Froy. Shitloads, discounted, no end to them. You name your price. Free, if you give me enough time."

"Too late for that, asshole," he spat. "This war's lost. Writing's on the wall. We're all dead."

"What the fuck are you on about?" cried his husky crony who guarded me. He turned on Froy. "You loco? I say we waste this bastard, close his gibbering mouth forever then use his girl and take those arms he brought and blow—"

Froy waved him off with a bitter snarl. "Quiet down, Garr. For Pete's sake. For months we've been fighting this dogged war. Mong's got black magic on his side—stealth wizardry and weaponry. Armor that doesn't crack, missiles that never miss, military intelligence beyond our scope. How else could his few ships have neutralized our entire air force? We only dodge like rats from one filthy hole to another."

Sense at last. I licked the blood off my lip. Froy must be coming down off his ride. The edge peeling off his belligerent hide. For the first time, I glimpsed the flicker of madness seep out of that haggard face.

"Some say he's the devil," jeered another of the gunmen, "an angel of fate."

"I say he's a rotten scumbag," said Garr, "one who desperately needs a bullet in his brain."

"Maybe so, but how long can we keep dodging him like weasels?" probed Froy. "We've been fighting this war with not one break yet. We'll all be martyrs. One of the few worlds that fight back—the rest of the pussies capitulate and become puppet regimes of Mong's feudal state—like lapdogs to a bull terrier. He's making an example of us. Look! Our beautiful city, once an oasis amongst the stars, is now pigs' swill!" He waved a fanatical arm, spitting fire at the wall, chewing it full of holes. "Palm trees ripped to shreds, fountains and gardens blown sky high! Public squares blasted, schools destroyed, women and children killed in cold blood in the streets, destroyed by that madman." He kicked fiercely at the plaster on the ground.

His comrades had no answer; Garr's tongue licked out to wipe at his dirty lip, followed by a sudden slap of hand on my face while the rage boiled in his leonine skull.

We were back in the alley under the weight of the looming buildings and their gutshot decay. No sign of Wren. A few men came loping up from the debris.

"Nothing," said one.

A darker rumble came from the sky. Eyes looked up. To a looming mass, turtle-green with a nose of mottled color. It was all menace, some fantastic monster as it tilted toward us. Before the first red flares came spearing from its port wing, I dove for cover. A bullet sheared through the thigh of the man next to me. I saw the flicker of pain register in his face and a barrel reaching from the second story window. I recognized the arm movement at once. Wren! So, she'd survived. Been playing possum. More fire laid in behind us. Blest came charging up the alley like a mad bull, all kamikaze, spreading fire in Froy's direction.

Mong's ship bore down on us, the pilot now recognizing the source of the blast back at the warehouse.

An odd thing happened, as if time warped. The ship slewed sideways, as if racked by gunfire from the side.

I strained my eyes upward. The ship pulsed green as a missile hit it broadside. For a few seconds it wavered as if it would drop out of the sky. But it didn't. The Warhawk turned and sent a red arc of fury toward the city in the direction of Froy's rebel base. A deafening boom rocked the air.

"Fools!" Froy croaked, clutching at his hair. "They need to launch triple RPGs at a single point to pierce those shields and armor—Aie!" His anguished voice rose above the roar of engines as some shrapnel caught his left leg in a cloud of fire. Black smoke mushroomed over the tops of the ruined buildings. I guessed the rebel base was no more. The massive army-grey bird of prey swung its nose toward us again.

In the cloud of dust, Garr lifted his R3 to plug me full of holes.

"Wait!" Froy choked on his own spit. He lay sprawled there amidst the chaos of men's screams, grimacing in pain, but lucid now, clutching his ruined leg. "Rusco, run while you can. Mong's taken enough sacrifices today. We don't need more. Get away from here, you stupid idiot!—before I change my mind."

I tipped my head. "Peace be with you, Froy. We'll see each other in hell." I half staggered from the shock concussions.

I limped off and heard Froy's savage groan as Garr and two of his last men dragged him to shelter. "Rusco!" he called back. "You see what war does to a man? Makes us no better than beasts! Killers and rapists. So far down the rabbit hole we go, we don't know who we are any more."

In a moment of lucidity, Froy had spoken truth. His last words evoked a sad memory in my brain. How far had I gone, with my morals twisted like pretzels and my long-running policy of turning a blind eye to the suffering of the universe? Hustling here, grubbing there, without a second thought of tomorrow or the consequences of my actions.

The gunmen dragged Froy off, cussing and screaming, his ruined leg beyond repair if he didn't get some regen soon.

Wren came stumbling up out of the building, her rifle cocked. She was ready to shoot anything that moved. Crouching, she moved in from pile to pile. Another deep rumble shook the sky. I turned. The Warhawk had edged in, banking sharply, its shields taking some of the damage of the RPG hit. But now another ebon shape rose over the crumbled buildings. It appeared out of the sky like a magic trick and for an instant a flicker of hope rose. Fire lashed out from its port guns and hammered the Warhawk in her rear flank, wresting wide its lethal fire, sending the grey streak smashing into the building next to us and crumbling it to ruin.

The building overhead exploded, sending a fresh spray down on us.

"Down!" I shrieked, covering my head pelted with bits of mortar and stone, my throat hoarse as the shockwaves rang through my bones.

Blest was panting beside me, his face nicked, his arms cut and a wild confused look in his eyes.

A whine of engines came out of nowhere. A hulking brown fuselage with an hourglass figure came swirling out of the dust to land in the square not fifty feet away. *Bantam*! Noss couldn't have been a more joyous sight. He must have heard my signal. Shoddy of me to have ever badmouthed him. Dust pooled at our feet and stung our eyes and lungs.

We coughed and stumbled out of the billowing cloud toward the giant black curve of the smoking hull where Bantam had taken fire. The cargo hatch slid open. We piled in and the engines gunned as the hatch slid back. We were thrown to the far side as the sudden g's accelerated us skyward. Noss was efficient; he'd gotten us this far. If there had been two of those bastard Warhawks though, we'd be goners now.

Return fire chipped against our starboard armor. I shuddered at the damage to our shields. I shook out the haze and stumbled down the companionway to the bridge. Wren was at my back. Soon she overtook me; Blest was still in shock, staggering somewhere in the hallway behind.

I took the helm and slapped Noss on the back. "Good man!" He gave me a curt acknowledgement and flung back his head of brown curls. He ceded the weapon's helm to Wren.

She worked the controls, lashing out at the Warhawk which was fast looming up on our viewport.

The holo grid showed black-green silent death stalking us. Auto-guided missiles blipped bright red on the most vulnerable areas of our hull; Wren fixed her own targets mid-wing near the power cells and the reactor on the bogey's weapon's port.

Torpedoes flew out of our wing cannons. They smashed harmlessly against the enemy craft's shields and heavy armor. I cursed, maxed out Bantam's impulse power, took us straight up toward the twin moons of this sorry world, away from our low wide arc that skimmed over the remains of Resus and the nearby sea.

We couldn't warp out in the planet's gravitational field. Not without risking structural overload.

Nerve-wracking seconds passed. Shields dimmed to 5%. The hull shuddered to surface blasts, then another. Shit, the next hit would finish us. Wren's lips parted in a gasp. The enemy missile launched, loomed on the viewport, coming up on our rear at gut-wrenching speed. A half second to impact. I felt that faint flutter of life flashing by before my eyes as we cleared planetary gravity. The Varwol light drive clicked in. Bantam's hull became a non-entity. Space-time collapsed—or whatever contradiction the physics people call it, for an object cannot be in two places at one time. In a half-light second we were thrown down the wormhole, unreachable by any Warhawk fire.

Through the slipstream of hyperdrive we passed like insignificant ants within an ethereal world. I saw Wren and Blest as they moved puppet-like on a screen out of a cartoon. As the nightmare slowly washed away from my mind, I thought of Froy and his doomed cause. Despite the man's madness, his unexpected turnaround had surprised me. It helped me better understand him and his people and others like him, terrorized by Mong and his military machine around the Veglos sector. The warmonger was a menace. He must be stopped.

But how? It looked as if no force in this universe could stop the man. Small time arms traders like me could hardly scratch a dent in his growing empire.

Chapter 4

My body ached from the bruises back on Resus. Staring at the silent controls and its maze of blinking lights, I marveled at the machinery that took us those light years and beyond, away from that dust-rubbled planet.

A hollow pang stuck at the back of my throat. The loss of Tager and Klane could not be brushed off. A sick feeling pressed at my insides, knowing the obscene thousands of yols I now owed my long-time seller, Gretch, from that failed arms' shipment. I'd promised him his share the first chance I got. Though he'd warned me of the risk of COD. Now he'd be breathing fire about the botched deferred payment and out for blood. Ready to set his enforcers on me.

We slid through the ethers like greased eels and I reflected on the wonder it was to be alive. The three of us had survived Froy's manic persecutions—though we all should have been dead. That said, I wouldn't be going anywhere near Uziles in Veglos nor Gretch for that matter.

A voice intruded on my bleak speculations.

"What now, Rusco?" came Wren's murmur. She turned, shook out her dusty hair and let out a long sigh. Studying the holo image of the vast star cluster of the Veglos sector, she looked a figure of enchantment. Noss stared at it too, gloomily, drumming his thin, pale fingers on the console, as if watching the stars with an air of fatality. Blest, beside him, oblivious to the others, picked at the mole on his left cheek.

I needed regen badly. I reached a shaky hand for the emergency kit in the forward bulkhead just as the orange light flickered on the transcall unit—I knew instinctively it must be a message from Gretch. I turned the unit off.

First things first. We needed to ease out of this stupor of battle fatigue so I held back on the regen, cracking out the Binny's Gin instead and the Black Dog Whiskey. I poured stiff rounds for all of us and pushed the shot glasses before our team of heroes gathered around the communal table on the bridge.

I poured Blest a double dose. Seems as if our bully boy needed it. All bleary-eyed and bruised and sullen, he looked like an alley cat come out of the rain after fending off a pack of wild dogs.

He lifted his glass, inclined his head at Noss, asked him why he'd come when he did.

Noss swallowed a mouthful of Black Dog. "I saw your beacon. More than far enough away from where you should have been. The Warhawk was taking crossfire from the warehouse. Figured it was the only chance to get you out alive."

"Lucky you did," I grunted.

"Took you long enough," Blest said. With a shake of head, he cursed under his breath.

"Get off it, Blest," I growled. "We all should be dead, you included." He shut up when both Wren and I glared at him.

"Klane was an idiot." Wren muttered. "Shot off his mouth after they tried to shortchange us. We'd maybe still be whole and with loot in our fingers if he hadn't gone south."

I gave a wincing grimace. So what was to be learned from this wasted exercise? The futility of war? The dumb luck of a crew of misfits? Considering my bad luck of the past, I'd been expecting disaster.

I sighed. We'd have to lay low for a while. The other bad news—Mong's bounty hunters would be after me. They wanted those pieces of alien tech bad. The little phaso disc I had on board, plus the larger, U-shaped amalgo I'd hid on Brisis 9 months ago. Both transporter devices sent animate and inanimate matter to other dimensions like a souped-up warp drive, so it seemed. Mong and his war ghouls had a reputation for persistence. They had placed an outrageous price on the return of such tech, inspiring certain desperate individuals to thrust an ice pick in my brain. Space hound Rusco was a marked man. I had a hunch, an almost certain one, Mong'd be tipped off after the Froy incident. If we could have wasted that Warhawk...but it didn't happen. Mong's goons would soon ferret out the rebels responsible for harboring fugitives. Then they'd interrogate Froy and his roughboys until they squawked like pigeons the name of Rusco, the details of our ship and the drop off, with all the willingness of vultures pecking at fresh roadkill. I winced at the bite of the gin sloshing down my throat. This caper was never supposed to end like this.

I applied regen paste on sensitive areas, the sticky stuff causing me to wince. Wren came to assist. She pulled up my leather pantleg and rubbed in a wad on the red, raised sore where the bullet had grazed my flesh. I could feel the skin stitching over. My supply of miracle glue was getting low, in need of replenishing. Another task on the to-do list. Once we got some money together, I'd get a whole box of the stuff.

I dipped my fingers in the jar to apply some salve to Wren's shoulder but she declined.

"I'll be okay." She waved my ministrations away then passed the jar to Blest.

"We need to go where the goods are," I said.

"Yeah, like really?" said Blest. "What goods would those be?—and where do you get the idea finding jobs is as easy as picking apples off a tree?"

"Stuff isn't going to come floating to us." My eyes stared at a faraway place in the endless panorama of stars that glowed in the viewport. "We need to go out and find them."

Blest sighed.

"We've got to keep moving," I reiterated. "We can't let a little setback stall us out."

"How about a little setback featuring two broken legs and a cracked back?"

"Hold on, that's not the kind of—"

"Tager and Klane dead and you want to flirt with more disaster?"

"No, to stay alive and keep our heads above water. Keep a cash flow going."

"It's madness," protested Blest.

"It's a mad world out there."

Wren touched the young man's arm. "We need to stay in the game."

Blest loosed a bitter laugh. "You too, Wren? I thought you had more sense than him." He glared at me. "I only listen to her. Not you. If she weren't here—"

I grinned. "What? You'd chicken-whip me, Blessie? Give me a big whooping? Good thing we have her."

Blest shrugged. The conversation was fast losing its conviviality.

"We lost big time on that last job," I said absently. "Paid a lot of money and got nothing back. Two dead. Damn it."

I let the words sink in. "So, needless to say, we have to amp up our game. We'll get stocked up—food, water, and maintenance at the next hub. O two hundred. I'll see what I can do to rig up some new angles on a gig. Always something out there, if we look hard enough, keep our eyes and wits about us."

Blest peered at me between his dark lids. "Seems you're always flying by the seat of your pants, Rusco."

"And so?"

"Just wondering when you're going to nosedive and get us all killed. I'd like to have some advance warning about my death."

"This isn't a ma and pa rig. If you want to go somewhere else, Blest, we'll let you off at the next hub. You can find your fortunes elsewhere."

The others looked at him with mouths set. A tense silence ensued.

Blest just growled and shrugged. "I'll stick around for a bit, Rusco."

"I thought you would."

I picked at my teeth. Blest wasn't a team player. Surprised he didn't get busted up back there. Klane was just plain foolish, a dumb fuck extraordinaire. We were close to nailing that deal and he had to go and foul up the nest and get himself killed. But then, that had been said too many times already, so maybe I should just drop it.

Chapter 5

On an inspiration, I searched through the free store—the spacefarer's planetary-wide network of information. I checked some ledgers and current events and set the course for Badinis Major. According to the register there, a space station orbited the rich world of Gistron, rich in Beryl and other minerals useful for drives and ship hulls. Gistron station had escaped the long arm of Mong's domination—thankfully. Apparently an auction was in the works on the station—for used and vintage star cruisers. Interesting. Likely it would draw a rich crowd that I could work some angle on. If not, vie for the ships themselves at least. I expected a mix of the usual space prospectors, entrepreneurs looking for easy pickings, the ubiquitous greaseballs, hangers on and con artists. My kind of crowd.

We turned in to our respective cabins and slept the sleep of the dead. We took turns to watch the helm. I instructed them to wake me in case of a contingency, no matter how minor. Not much could happen while we were in the slipstream cocoon of warp—or could it?

Bantam auto-kicked out of Varwol and I heard the tiny whir of engines. The thrum of power circuits booted up as they now returned us to the dimension of reality.

The space station loomed up in the viewport, a gigantic ring with docking berths on the inside of the ring. Gistron was one of the few places not ravaged by space thugs—her lattice of interconnected girders and spirals were a product of earlier generations, built in days of opulence. How old—a hundred, two-hundred years? Mong and his crew had not got to this part of the galaxy yet.

The planet Gistron Delta hung below, a small maroon disc, gleaming like a rheumy eye.

Wren studied me, as if trying to guess what went on behind that brow of mine. Good luck with that. Desert tanned, lithe as a country cat, she stood tall, back ramrod-straight, with a pride and toughness that had always been earned rather than role-played. She always gave me something else to admire about her. Younger than me, with good pizazz, knew how to handle herself in tough situations. Wish every one of my crew was like her. No hint of our bedroom antics in the workfield. On the job it was all business. A bonus on these long excursions—voyages to nowhere looking for paradise, or was it salvation?

She fiddled with the stock of her R4. "I don't even know why we're docking here, Rusco."

"There's always an angle to run at the auctions. You'll see."

We approached Gistron station with fake registration: Bantam registered to an asteroid mining speculator, entrepreneur, unmarried, one Jorry Rambo, a favorite pseudonym. I'd had the holo-disc with Rambo's registry doctored up to look pretty, with a clean bill of health, and a history of fake stops at various ports, times and stamps, courtesy of a man in Hzadn who owed me a favor.

I paged station control on a general hailing frequency. A young-old face with blue eyes appeared on the viewscreen.

"What'll it be?" the face said.

"Berth for one mid-range craft," I replied. "Crew, maintenance and cleanup."

"Premium berths are going at 400 yols."

"What, a week?"

"No, a day."

I gave a croak of disgust. "Highway robbery. You have anything cheaper?"

"Down the end, there are lower-end berthings, going for 180. For limited time. 12 hour max."

I grunted. "Okay, but it's still very high."

I saw his lip move in irritation. He gave me a distracted shrug.

"Busy today," I muttered. "It's like a circus fairground here. What's up?"

"Holse and Detran are hosting an auction. Starships galore. Wholesale."

"You don't say?" I looked on in feigned interest, my eyes traveling to the roster of sleek, grey silver hulls neatly arranged on the far side of the ring. "Nice vehicular lines. Those some of the ships up for sale?"

"Uh huh."

"I might want to bid on one myself."

He regarded us with a dubious grunt, then scratched his cheek. "If you get the proper clearance maybe. But I'll warn you it's a minimum 600 to enter a qualifying bid, refundable on purchase of a ship."

I whistled a low note. "That's a mighty steep entry point, chief. Still, if it fetches us a decent ship—"

"It discourages sharpers."

"How far will a man go to get a good starship?"

He shrugged, clearly not engaged. "You look like you're doing pretty good with your own craft, Rambo. Why buy another? You not pleased with what you got? What is it, an early Bantam?"

I nodded. "Big on the horsepower, lean on the energy."

"Go down to central to get your badge, though I warn you, if you want to bid, there'll be some serious players."

We berthed on the farther side of the docking ring amidst somewhat dodgier-looking vessels than those on display. The automatic air lock connected to our cargo port; we passed through, strode down the hall and passed customs, though I took a disguise kit with me and another two of those hide-saving explosives that could pass easily as coins. Needless to say, no weapons were allowed beyond the checkpoint. Rectangular artificial-grav units, regularly spaced around the station and emitting their characteristic low hum, kept us walking on our feet at expected Earth g levels.

A large open-air rotunda buzzed with activity. A milling crowd flushed with pre-auction excitement, jostled for position. As did we, in its main restaurant-bar, enlivened by the noisy rattle and hum of slot machines and video games set up to the sides. Glass ports overlooked the docking station where thirty some odd starships were moored. Wren and the others grabbed seats with me around the curved bar, complete with vid screens showing sports and news. A place to scout the scene, relax. I picked an area to the left and center of the bandstand, ideal for people-watching as it offered an unobstructed view of every movement. Banners and flags pinned on the high wall behind the bandstand and over the glass observatory fluttered in the air-circulator's draft.

We nursed our drinks; Noss, poor boy, ordered a cold glass of milk, on account of his ulcerated stomach due to stress. Blest chewed a mouthful of peanuts then shoveled a handful of crackers down his maw too before downing his two shotglasses of rum straight up. I looked at him in amusement, but couldn't see anything worth salvaging, or softening in that lackluster gaze of his. Eyes two pissholes in the snow. A rosy nose, like a drunk's. Comical with that mop of dirty blond hair, but a sullen stare like a teenage rebel. I knew he had more brains than what most credited him for. Not my usual recruit, but such are the woes of running a ship on a tight delivery schedule. Wren sat back in silence, her shiny vibrancy and health the epitome of cheer—at least next to Blest.

My brain gave critical scrutiny to the clientele. A mix of sorts, but somehow the partners, Detran and Holse, had attracted a stable breed of middle-incomers and well-off business-people searching for their next pleasure craft. Maybe one to upgrade their current vessel in need of an overhaul.

Loud talk, breezy smiles, energetic drinking—all marked a definite pleasure-cruise atmosphere. Men with women on their arms, pointing at this ship or that, the women cooing with delight at the sleek lines and chromium glitter, and the man lifting eyebrows at the luxury while secretly licking his lips at the cost.

A haven for hustlers too, from the two bit con with the shifty eyes and greasy smile and overused clichés, to the higher end player who will invent his own stories and likely instruct his assistants to bid against the competition, not unlike a ploy I imagined Detran had going for himself in an effort to inflate prices.

Where was my angle? Something was here. Just had to find it. Had to keep my crew busy too, keep their teeth chewing on something. The last run had nearly put us over the edge. Blest had become more of an annoyance than ever. May have to get rid of him. Though his heroics had surprised me back in the alley.

A big man with a loud voice came bragging about his luck at the space casino in Vega. A crew of cronies at a nearby table gathered about to listen. He was getting a little tight on the Black Dog, a few too many highballs light on the rocks.

"Boys," he said, just shy of slurring his words, "you stick around with me, and you'll go places. Give you shares in pickings that you won't find anyplace else."

The bald idler beside him, maybe his business partner, grinned ear to ear. "Now, Sal, don't you go shooting your mouth off."

Jolly boys, out for a romping time away from wifey and the kids and the haze of their humdrum lives. Living it up with big talk and big drink. Didn't doubt they had all the money in the world to buy one of those space yachts parked out there but not the brains to keep it. How hard would it be to lift one of those suckers off old Sal or one of his buddies?

"I'm going to take a little walk," I said at last, depressed by it all. "You folks settle in, mingle with the gentry."

I drifted over to the end of the rotunda, gazing at the mixed bag of folk and their garish dress, and the antiquated slot machines they played on to idle away the time, half listening in on random conversations with an amused grin. Out of the corner of my eye, I saw a big man dip into an exit. He looked important, wouldn't be surprised if it were Detran or Holse himself. On a whim, I followed him, down a wide stairwell to a service bay where some maintenance crew or what could have been the big boy organizers themselves and their lackeys were preparing a kind of pre-bidding lounge. A lower level, a mini version of upstairs with large picture windows granting a view of the vintage offerings on the docking ring.

Yep, Detran, all right. I caught the drop of the name 'Halley D'. At any rate, looked as if the two partners were setting up their wheel and deal spectacle to a few VIP customers in advance. I pushed a colored hair net over my head to make my purple streak more silver, then wiped skin cream on both cheeks to create a look paler than I really was.

Detran, even from a distance, I didn't like from the start. Swarthy, long-boned with sandy walrus mustache and big, fleshy lips, a match for his mouth and ego. Something off about him, his ophidian mannerisms, like when a certain song plays on the radio that makes your skin run cold, so did this man's strident tone offend me.

I did a subtle hop and skip and bounded in behind some crates of decorations and accessories being offloaded onto their starships. To make them look prettier? Every gimmick counted. I scootched in closer to listen in on what they were saying.

I heard Detran, who had been smiling all the time and murmuring to his crony with the grey-beard, blow air out of his cheeks. "Not bad for a day's work, Lew. Unlucky for those SOBs out in deep space who lost their ships." Detran gave a sour guffaw, one that had a mean and hollow ring to it. I caught some muffled words then of him bragging about how he had grabbed the ships out from under those about to be boarded after one of the Star Lord's blitzkrieg rampages. The corpses he had jettisoned into space. He turned to his two henchman, covered in grease. "Hurry up, you bums. What's taking you so long? These showboats aren't going to sell themselves. Remember, what we don't sell in the auction, we ship to the wrecking yards, piece by piece."

"What about these X2s?" one lackey inquired. "Sure you want to unload them, Hal? If we wait, we could get a better price on consignment at one of the local shops."

"Cost us too much." Detran's sneer widened. "We unload as much as we can. Plus, I have other reasons."

The hired hand seemed to grunt at that, but clearly disliked the decision. "As you like, Hal."

There came hurried footsteps. Someone approached, wheezing. "Hal, problem on pier 14. *The Lady Lou.* Some grifter trying to make off with the audio board."

He clicked his tongue. "What the flaming hell—Come! Holse, you too." He swept off to investigate with his entourage.

Wren hunched up beside me, apparently having overheard the latter part. I raised my brows, for I hadn't even heard her.

"Seems as if that lout Detran hardly deserves the fruits of his haul."

"No kidding." I gave the ships parked outside the glass a once-over then I got a sudden idea. Caution is not usually my greatest virtue, but when an idea sparks, I'm like a kid in a candy store. "Maybe this ticket is our next easy way to cheat penury."

"How? You thinking of conning an unsuspecting playboy out of a starship?"

"Why not?" I smiled. "Kinda like stealing from the rich and giving to the poor."

"Well, if it were my pick, Jet—I'd choose that newer, silver Starburst over there." She pointed to a stream-lined space yacht with smooth, seashell contours and high, curved bow.

I gave a slow nod. "On first glance it'd be my pick. But I have another in mind…"

Chapter 6

We returned to the bar and the subdued company of Blest and Noss. Blest stared, practically comatose. Noss, ever the ordinary man, flicked back his short brown hair, looked out from a bland face with pale blue eyes. The glare of the vid screens flashed lurid news in front of us. Thankfully the volume was lowered to allow some upbeat pop music to take precedence, but I could still read the subtext:

"The warlord from Hazzerot continues to exert his threat of terror over the free colonies. When will the madman stop? Here's live footage of the scene at Bajor's square."

The reporter's voice spoke quickly and somewhat garbled over the muted noise of battle. I saw shells dropping, towers toppling, kids fleeing with family members, the odd blood-streaked pet in tow. I gritted my teeth.

The camera went blank. There was a solemn pause, a flashing picture then static.

"That's all we've got, viewers. Our cameraman and news anchor, Jerle Tomas, are presumed dead on Bajor."

I reached to turn the set off.

"Hey," cried one of the jolly boys from the nearby table. "I was watching that."

"Tough break, chief," I said, changing the channel. "We don't need any more doom and gloom to cheer our little world. Let's watch some mindless soaps, or Dustin BeeJee yodeling along to a sing-a-long."

"You'd deny the threat of Mong?" the man rasped.

"Don't deny anything, chief. Just don't want to hear that bastard's name, is all." That was the truth. I grew ill at hearing the lunatic Mong's name, remembering well how he and Baer had blown off my hand from the wrist down. The warlord's captain, Baer, was a hole in the ground—I saw to it myself. The details came back to me in painful waves, how Wren had managed to get me out of that death hangar on Trellian with TK and get to a regen shop. Only by a hair. Then by hairs again, managing to get me this robot, mechanical right hand that was now my albatross and a killing machine.

The blowhard Sal came shambling up, rolling up his sleeves as if to make something of the news thing. Blest, with no love for bluster or Mong, stood up to face the drunk. "You, Mr. Fancypants, can go suck—"

Eyes turned in our direction.

I shouldered Blest aside, inserting myself between him and the flustered Sal. "Language, Blest, language," I hissed. "A respectful environment here, no need to draw any undue attention to ourselves."

"I hear you, Rambo. That lowlife Mong's ship almost killed us and made ghosts of us all."

"Let's not get into the eschatological points about this."

"Do you even know…" He looked at me sideways, lowered his voice, "Do you even know what that means?" He shook his head in disgust. Sal seemed to have shrunk at the sight of something crazy in Blest's eyes because he ducked back to his table.

So far my double-speak had kept Blest's brain busy. I liked it that way. I liked the boy's spunk, but he was a constant irritant. I cleared my throat. "Wren, what do you think about our prospects here?"

Her eyes made a casual sweep. "Good to fair."

"Yeah, why do you say that?"

"That mark over there, for example, he's carrying a wad of cash and low on luck. Get a few more in him, he'll be only too willing to lick salt from your palm."

I nodded. "Not bad. But what about baldy over there? He's looking mighty ripe."

"Yeah, but risky with the dead stare and the constant swiping of nose with a twitching hand. Might try something desperate. Don't like the turn of cheek either or the way he lifts his upper lip in a leer at the young woman behind. It's as if he's a lecher feeling plucky away from his wife."

Blest glared. "What the fuck are you two talking about?"

"Relax, Blest," I said. "Just a little game Wren and I play, not to worry. We talk shop when we're bored. How about we order some food and talk about cheerier things?"

"Yeah, with what money, Mr. Rambo?" quipped Blest. "The Sir Jorry compassion fund?"

"It's on me, kid."

Noss licked his lips and grinned. "Sure, steaks are fine, medium rare, please, with fries on the side."

Wren signaled the barman. Blest and she ordered barbecued *varamein*, apparently a big game delicacy on Gistron. Blest requested another rum.

"Rambo, you're not ordering," Wren said, cocking her head. She flashed me one of those wry looks with the dark lashes.

Lips parted, I let out a near silent belch. "Later, not feeling so good, Wrensy." I stood up to make for the restroom down the hall.

I felt one of those gut aches coming on. As quickly as possible, I hustled without looking like a complete clown. Sitting down on the can, I tried to void. Nothing. Only cramps. Too much stress. A frequent happening, ever since Mong and his cretins had blown off my hand. I settled down and felt the wires and machinery loosen inside then a sharp pain rip through my guts followed by a loud plunk in the water. I closed my eyes, let them glaze up in agony.

The door cricked open. Footsteps. A familiar voice. Detran?

"Sh—" A stern cough. "Don't be talking too loud."

Something caused me to lift myself off the seat, feet straddling the rim, even while half way through a dump. I felt a familiar tingle of the hustle in my bones and I held my breath. The new arrivals couldn't see my legs under the stall.

"Quiet down," I heard the other say then a shuffling of feet. "Nobody here, Lew, you know the deal." It was Detran's voice that hissed.

I smiled. Careless of those two to assume the stalls were empty without checking them. I'd seen it happen before.

"What about our little problem?" said Lew.

"What problem?" A pause. "Ain't no problem that I know of."

"Come on, you've skimped big this time round, Hal, now we've got eyes on us. When those fools find out you've rigged the ships to look good and they haven't got anything worth having, someone's going to blow. We'll get reported."

Detran laughed, an outright guffaw. "Report us to who? They'll never know. Little dumb tweety birds pecking around the dunghill for a bit of feed. These pigeons'll have no clue who they're running with, Lew, or what they're running—Myscol XR, Magoo's magical formula, toting it around the universe for us. Haha. It's in demand in practically every port. Tourists, laypeople, the odd wealthy middleman, take your pick."

I gave an unpleasant grin. So, scammer Detran was drug-running on the side. While ripping off the ignorant spacefarer, the man got his kicks and mega yols running Myscol to all ports of the galaxy. Nice scene.

Something didn't add up. I frowned, listened with perked ears, hoping my groaning guts would stay quiet.

"They'll take what I give them, Lew. Traders' rations, Squatters' rights, Governors' Law." Detran laughed. "Once an item's sold, it's sold. No law around here's gonna hold out to some fine print. We'll be long gone, rounding up more ships and more suckers to sell them too. Universe's full of suckers, Lew. Junkers, derelicts, impounded craft, especially with that warmonger Mongo or Bongo, whatever the hell his name is, on the loose."

"So, you didn't hear then? Maybe you aren't worried, Hal, but there's an RSA agent out there, posing as some bidder. Already checked out *The Alastar*. Targa spotted him. Remembered him from a job back on Jajaran."

Detran swore. "That fouls things up. Why the fuck didn't you tell me right off?"

"Thought Targa informed you."

"He didn't. You say this RSA person scouted *Alastar* already?"

"Targa says dogs were on board sniffing around shortly after the RSA left."

"Jesus, Lew! Lucky we didn't have any stash there. Somebody must have tipped somebody off."

"Still so sure of your little plan?"

"The only one of those ships worth anything is *Alastar*. It'll go for plenty. Vintage. Transfer the contraband off the other rigs to *Alastar*. *Mistress Luella, Flyboy*, the rest of them. Mr. RSA won't suspect at all. We'll stall out *Alastar's* sale, put her off the list if we have to, so the scam doesn't get out from under us."

"Security's locked down all the ships' ports—auction protocol."

Detran hissed. "So, go in the back door. Get it fixed."

"Hard to muck around when there's nosy patrols crawling around the station. They've got ear coms, networks galore, cameras."

"I don't care, just get it done." A pause. "Wait, Lew." I heard some beeps as somebody fumbled for something in his breast pocket. Maybe a mini-com or tablet as Detran pulled up some data. "Here's the code. 661XA. Override the main nav and unlock the control board on *Alastar*, loosen any hatches you need to stash stuff away. The code'll give you the nav."

Another patron came into the washroom. There were sounds of running water and the two conspirators coughed, shuffled their feet, cleared their throats and left without a further word.

I pieced it all together. So, Detran'd sell the ships to tourists and magnates as pleasure craft, hopping the worlds on vacation while his lackeys stashed the drugs on board. The tourists who'd get past borders and checkpoints, would be prime cash cows, being low suspects on the list for contraband. He'd get his boys somehow on the other end to sneak the stuff off their ships and sell it on the streets.

I waited some minutes before I finished my business. Been holding the rest in too long now. I strode out of the loo, pondering Detran's greasy scheme for more than a few minutes, half my brain taking in the auction ships on the nearby ring and the busy flush of activity at the lounge. It'd be hit and miss as some of Detran's unwitting stooges would not pay out. But when others did, the profits would make up for the losses. I rubbed my chin, pretending to take personal interest in a vintage cruiser with wide tail fins and beaklike prow, *The Starbird*. To ensure he got the right dupes at auction time, I guessed he'd probably bid them out with plants giving fake bids, if they weren't the types he was looking for. A slick scheme. I wouldn't have thought the oaf had the brains to put this together, but then again, it must have been his slimy partner behind it all, Lew, or whatever the fuck he called him.

If I could get *The Alastar* out from under them, I'd get two for one—a ship and a viable product. Sell the Myscol myself on the black market. Maybe even find the need to use some myself.

Chapter 7

I approached our part of the bar where Noss was trying to enliven Blest with a joke and failing.

"New plans," I whispered, "we're going after that old bird there, the one with tinsel color and queenly look."

Blest was all ears. "Oh, yeah, how? You suddenly got a quarter of million yols?"

Noss laughed.

"Better. What I want you to do is get cleaned up—in disguise to bid against any others and stall out the process. I need you and Noss on the floor."

"What are you planning to do?" Blest asked, squinting from Wren to me in suspicion.

"Give a little surprise to Mr. Halley Detran and his accomplice then jack his ride."

Noss's lips curled in amusement. Blest just shook his head.

"One missing piece." I frowned, snatching a glance down at the beady-eyed attendant by the cargo hatch to *Alastar*. "I don't want to be on the register, even with credentials as fake as Jorry Rambo. Ties me to the ship. Puts me on a list of suspects to crosscheck. So, that means going in incognito."

Blest scoffed. "You'll never do it."

"Never say never. What I need is that turnkey ring on Detran's belt. I've watched him, he punches little buttons and enters numbers into it. It's a kind of security register, I think, helps him keep tabs on his merchandise. If I have it, more credence when I try to con my way aboard *Alastar*. Prevents me having to strongarm any of his lackeys if things go sour."

"How are you going to get it?" said Blest. "He just going to give it to you?"

"What are you, Mr. Pessimist?" I jeered.

Wren winked. "Leave that to me."

I raised an eyebrow.

Wren lifted herself off her barstool with a suggestive movement of female magic. "I used to handle braggarts like Detran on Talyon," she explained. "Had lots of experience fending off mouth breathing cretins when I was younger. I know his type, plus I'm a better dissembler than you think."

"If you want to try, give it a shot." I shrugged. "I'd try my hand at some dissembling, but I don't want Hally Detran to have any reason to get a whiff of my ugly hide."

Wren grinned. "Wait here." I idled at a nearby table while she planned her approach.

One of the RSA people came bustling by Detran who was watchdogging *The Lady Lou*, and I saw him go red in the face. "You people couldn't have picked a worst damn time to come nosing around my ships," he rasped.

"Sorry, sir. Just a routine check."

"Routine check, my ass. It's called personal harassment."

"Step aside, sir."

Wren moved forward. At the last instant, she contrived to trip on the half steps leading up to the glass observatory and accidentally spilled her drink on Detran. She clasped him in a firm hug, making sure to give him a generous dose of her breasts. Meanwhile her hands worked like spiders around his back to get the key ring off him and slip it under her own belt.

"My mistake, omigod! My bad, sir, sorry, sorry!"

"You stupid cow!" he yelled. "What kind of a klutz are you?" When he got a better look at her, he licked his lips and stammered, "I mean—"

"No, it was my fault, sir, really. Here, let me wipe that gunk off your coat! Sorry. I really am. I feel terrible!" She lifted her head with grief-stricken eyes and peered up into his flustered face. Snatching a kerchief from her pocket, she scrubbed at his chest, all the while flashing doe-eyes at him and holding his wrist and touching his shoulder.

"Well, I guess it was an honest mistake," he grumbled at last.

"That's mighty kind of you, sir."

He frowned with a half nod. "These half steps are something of a liability anyways. Don't know why the idiot management positioned them here where decent folk can trip over them!" He paused, scrutinizing her with more interest. "Maybe you can make it up to me, doll. Stick around after the auction and we can both have a little nightcap, indulge in a drink or two at the bar, revel in how much money I made."

She winked at Detran. "That would suit me fine, mister. I love to hear how much money a handsome man like you can spend on a lonely girl like me."

That got him grinning. "It's a date then."

Wren disappeared into the crowd, did a round around the rotunda and hurried back to *Bantam* as I had instructed her. I followed a few minutes later and slouched at the *Bantam's* bridge's conference table.

"Clod," she muttered under her breath.

"No better kinds. Let's hope he doesn't get wise too soon. The others didn't come yet?"

She shook her head.

I rubbed my chin in speculation. "Gotta keep him and Blest out of trouble."

Noss and Blest arrived a quarter of an hour later, carrying a bag each of duty free water pipes and Black Dog whiskey.

I rooted around Bantam's utility bin and pulled out a strange hand-sized contraption with a magnetic stamp, feeder cable and small suction plugs. I called it the *spider*. "We just need the drive codes and this little baby can override the main nav system. Wonderful device. Works on the older models. Tricky part will be to con the guards."

"And how on Neptune are you going to get that eyesore through security?" complained Blest.

"Easy, an external pacemaker. Monitors blood. See." I hooked it up to my arm by a cable and a little red light beeped at a regular interval.

Blest shook his head and threw up his hands. "Rusco, one of these days your grand schemes are going to blow up in your face."

"Until then, let's celebrate." I poured drinks for them all.

* * *

I put on my best disguise, a blue uniform, black tie, greyed my hair, wrapped it up in a bun and hid it under a white maintenance inspector's cap. "How do I look?" I posed, did a ballerina's twirl.

"Hokey." Wren pursed her lips.

"Good. All the better. Won't take much to fool those sleepy sallys on watch. Like the one by *The Alastar*. He's practically sprawled out on the floor from boredom."

"Which might mean he'll take an active interest in you when he sees how dopey you look."

I laughed. "Nah. I fit right in with this crowd."

"You think?"

Blest drew me aside. "Why not get Noss or me to sneak aboard and fly that ship?"

"You're not up for that kind of theft, Blest. Plus, if security checks the roster, they'll see one of us missing and it'll give them cause for suspicion. Don't want any paper trails."

I pulled away from him and made my way back to the restaurant, passing easily through security. The attendant at the open cargo bay to *Alastar* just stared at me. Sure enough, he held out a hand blocking me with his R3. "Hold it."

"Inspection, sir," I said. "I'm with Gistron security, contracted by Secure-A1, LLU #4155, and we have to check the drive codes, for the usual stolen goods. Halley Detran gave me this chit." I held up the red tablet, the master passkey. "You can check it out with him if you want."

The monitor shrugged, grumbled and waved a hand. "Go on. Don't bother any potential buyers though in *The Alastar*. Tough enough as it is to sell a starship these days. Scares them away. People might think there's something wrong with our ships."

"Not to worry. I'll be discreet."

And discreet I'd be. I put on the deadpan look of a security inspector. "If everything checks, I'll be out in no time."

He turned away.

I entered *The Alastar's* cargo hatch and made my way into the inner service bay. A series of halls branched out to various areas of the ship. I took the main one toward *Alastar's* bridge. The ship was roomy enough and built with class. High-ceiling, pleasant grey and black panels. Not a lot of glitter on the bridge like a lot of the newer space yachts. Simple design. Simpler was better, in my opinion.

Did I have a backup plan if the monitor decided to call Detran? No. Bit of a risktaker there, Rusco. My crooked grin grew crookeder. Seems I didn't even need Myscol to work up the nerve for these scams anymore. The evolution of small time operator, Jet Rusco.

I made my way to the nav com, bent under the console that housed the main nav controls, with spider in hand. A couple of wires plugged into the right places and I'd be done. I shone a light under the cowling and saw the serial number lit in red underneath. Perfect. I punched the codes into the spider and let the magnetic strip latch itself to the cowling out of sight. I'd already entered 661XA, the secret passcode Detran had whispered back in the loo. The thing was smart enough to assume wireless control once it had the codes. A couple appeared, browsing the bridge, voicing their admiration for its roominess, its sleek lines and teal and enamel decor. I had to agree.

The guard had followed me in and was scrutinizing me with more than lively suspicion. "Find what you're looking for?"

I put on a frown. I pulled out a tablet from my breast pocket and punched in some codes into a fictitious fact checker, then nodded and raised my hand. "Checks out, mister. This here's an older model, manufactured at Orizon Enterprises on Falcion. Has had eleven maintenance checks, three owners over its lifetime. All legitimate sales of transactions. Looks like we're good to go." I gave him a clever smile and took a deep breath. Good thing I had Wren back on board radio me background info once I gave her the drive codes. I saluted and left.

With a grunt of relief, I made directly for the loo to chuck out this ridiculous disguise and wash the grease off my face. I unfurled my lovely hair, whisked it back with my fingers, sprayed it with more purple dye. There, back to Jorry Rambo again. Much better.

I came out a new man, but not too quickly. I headed back to Bantam for the final prep.

"All smooth," I said to Wren. Noss and Blest lounged nearby. "Now we work fast. In the next half hour the auction starts. When the buyers go in to bid, our Vega-6 star queen *Alastar* will suddenly come to life, start to lift of its own accord."

"Shouldn't we get the hell out of here first?" asked Blest. "Why stick around?"

"That's the safest thing to do, Blest, but it looks suspicious. Some too-obvious cons taking off before a heist. We'll wait a while here then we'll take our silent leave. I mean, what dope would be stupid enough to stick around as a suspect when he could have flown off in advance? Security'll go after all the ships that left before the heist."

"You're a sly bastard, Rusco," Wren murmured.

"Yeah, well we'll see how sly I am if they catch us. If they find the spider beforehand, we're in trouble. Let's hope that doesn't come to pass. That attendant'll squawk bloody murder and they'll backtrace it to me, or at least, Jorry Rambo."

I set to programming the wireless controller for the spider, setting *The Alastar's* course for Deneb, light years away. Next thing I did was reset the passcode to a new one, Mr_Rambunctious, in case Detran decided to get cute and alter the course, if he had remote access.

Blest didn't like his part in playing bidding stooge, but then again, he was always tending to be a little bitch. Noss was good to go and convinced skeptic Blest to go down to the floor with him and hodge the bids. "Let's get some more duty free liquor. Nothing's going to go wrong."

"Like the last time?" Blest quipped.

Chapter 8

The bidding had begun. A crowd of three hundred or more must have been herded into that hot, sweaty rotunda, milling about, most standing holding drinks, clutching bid cards, a few sitting at tables at the bar, murmuring the talk of big gamblers and bidders. Noss and Blest joined me near the back as the bidding started. Wren had stayed back on Bantam. She'd played her part and I didn't want her face anywhere near the action. I added Noss to the bid roster and paid the 600 squeeze fee—a worthwhile sacrifice, considering the possible payback—nudging him when I wanted him to raise his card. Blest was just there for dressing. Truthfully, I wanted to keep my eye on him. No better way to do that than to have him right at arm's length.

We pushed our way forward to about mid-central, looking through the glass at the line of merchandise. Detran had his arm around Lew's shoulder at the front on the dais, beaming like a new groom. Bids had started on some of the lower end junkers, and low indeed they were. 80k, 82k…A few people had raised their hands with tentative bids.

The auctioneer stood on the podium next to the CEOs, yammering auction talk through a black mic at a mile a minute,

"Anybody for a *Mars Mink*! Mars Mink going for 83, 83, yes, 83! Reserved to the gentleman in the pink tie, yes, 85 anyone? 85 anyone? Going for 85, who will bid 85? Yes, yes, you there with the busk hat and the bright smile. New, fun, relaxing, hip, gotta love a Mars Mink, she's ready to fly to your doorstep!…"

I grinned and studied the crowd. Flushed faces, speculative murmurs, backslapping, claps, mingled laughter with drunken murmurs. A bunch of kids excited at the prospect of gaining some new toys.

When the bidding skipped to the last of the eight junkers, a surprised murmur rang through the throng. "What of the other ships?" someone cried. I gave a sly grin. Probably Detran canned them because now that his drug scheme had fouled, he gained nothing by selling his ships. But the show must go on. I was curious to see how big wheeler Detran played it.

He approached the mic all apologetic and held up his hands. "Ladies and gentlemen, I regret to say the majority of ships are not for sale. Only two of the former line will be up for grabs today. Sorry, a technicality."

"What's this nonsense?" There came another fierce hum of disappointment and loud grumbles from the crowd.

Detran waved a conciliatory hand. "As a consolation, the vintage cruiser *Lady Lou* will be featured today, as our primary giveaway. Not a bad catch."

"Cheater, Detran. Shamster!" cried a red-faced bidder. "What kind of a cheap stunt you pulling here?"

"Now hold on," cried Detran. "I've never been called a shamster in all my twenty years of doing business."

"Well, there's always a first time."

I chuckled. Good little gambit, Detran. Too bad it's failing.

Detran roared, "Some security people have found a need to check certain of my papers—If you want to blame anyone, blame them. It's out of my control." He pulled at his cherry red nose and snuffled. Flourishing a fake document in a gesture of frustration and wearing that Jim-Bob-dandy flushed face and Aw shucks look, he boomed, "Be assured sales will resume on all other craft at 0400 sharp tomorrow!"

"Now the fun begins." I turned to Noss and silently engaged the spider's remote.

The Alastar broke free of her mooring. Her docking arms ripped away and with it the covered walkway leading up to her.

People's heads turned in surprise. The station's air locks closed in automatic response to avoid vacuum engulfing the main wing. For a second everybody froze. Then pandemonium broke out.

The Alastar floated on low impulse power like a big obedient butterfly ninety degrees to the radial axis of the station. I stifled a murmur as her wings and many dips and angles glinted in the station's artificial light. Noss and Blest blinked in unison.

Gistron's security cameras would show nothing. I'd remain out of sight. It'd remain a mystery to everyone how the starship had made her sudden exit.

I feigned my own gasp of innocence while a klaxon rang somewhere down the docking hall.

I turned to watch Detran's expression.

His face boiled in pure fury. "What the bloody hell—" He patted his side, felt for the missing passkey.

He clawed at grey-bearded Lew's arm. "The woman—" he rasped.

"Where is the she bitch?"

"There were a few dames on that last ride out," growled Lew. "Could have been on any of them."

"Go after them, for shit sakes!"

Detran scrambled to pull on the arm of one of his lackeys. Soon all were talking at once into coms.

I couldn't resist wading through the crowd to watch more of Detran's panicked antics. Fun being a fly on the wall.

"Stolen in broad daylight?" Detran blinked. "It makes no sense. Why aren't they going after my ship?" He turned and his big brown hound eyes bugged out of their sockets. "Damn RSA. They instigated this." He reached to his side and his face curled in a mean, prune-like grimace. "I'm sure that bitch must have been working in cahoots with those rotten RSA meddlers."

He turned to gaze in wild contempt at the dispersing crowd. Lew gripped his arm. "Wait, Hal. There's our so-called RSA agent there. He looks as surprised as the rest."

"Then who the fuck...?" Halley's perplexed moon face pinched and mouth pursed in a little 'o'. "Find the woman," he croaked.

"She'll be long gone now," Lew objected.

"Find her!" The big man waved a fist.

Lew stumbled off on a run.

Noss, Blest and I waited some minutes before the bedlam reached its peak then followed with a more leisurely gait after a few who made for the landing dock, perhaps gripped with the thought that their ships would do the same magic disappearing act. None of them looked as if they liked the way things were progressing. We headed up the padded carpetway down the boarding hall to the moored ships.

"Slow," I muttered at Noss. "Don't look so freaked out. You look like your granny drowned your hamster."

Noss murmured an apology while Blest looked at me in dogged wonder, itching to get to Bantam.

We approached the checkpoint and its wire mesh and I nodded at the officer at the turnkey on duty, decked out in his blue uniform. He packed a compact R3 at his hip. He gave me a stony inspection, then scanned us all with suspicion.

Something in the way we looked perhaps, the pasty face on Noss, gave us away. Or maybe it was Blest's challenging scowl.

The officer held up his firearm and blurted out a deep-throated order. "Hold it! Identification."

I blinked. "Is there a problem, officer?"

"Not yet, but you might have one. Pass me your ID, and don't try anything stupid."

"Why us?" blurted Blest. "Those people up there are going through." He pointed to the couple ahead of us.

"We're not running an equal opportunity checkout here, wiseass," the guard grumbled.

Turning to flash a reassuring smile at the officer, I felt the first beads of sweat running down my neck while warning bells went off in my brain. I glared at Blest. My hiss of warning did not reach him or Noss in time.

Noss made a move for something at his hip. The officer whipped out his weapon and tagged Noss in the wrist, shattering it. Noss squealed in anguish as a bright red smear appeared from knuckles to wrist joint.

"Down!" the officer roared. "On the ground, all of you!"

I knelt slowly, my hand reaching for the tiny disc I had smuggled in. I pressed the *arm* button and I made as if to put my hands to my head. I released the disc at the same time and it hit the hand railing and flared up. The guard, momentarily blinded by the bright orange ball, gave a howling cry. Blest charged him. They wrestled, each with their hands on the gun with Blest gnashing and cursing. The weapon boomed yet again, clipping the officer low under the chin. He slumped, gave a gurgle of anguish and fell to the floor as a bright blotch blossomed on his throat. A glazed look appeared in his eyes.

Blest grimaced in a daze. He threw the weapon down on the guard's chest.

I raised my hands to my hair and clutched at it. A moment of despair passed. I shook my head in resignation. "That'll do it, Blest. Drag the corpse behind the kiosk!" I hissed at him. "We've got exactly one minute to get the fuck out of here. This heist is going sour. It was all sewn up."

"Sewn up, Rusco? Not really."

We booted it to Bantam, wasting no time to scramble to the bridge and get the engines fired up. All the time klaxon bells shrilled at our ears. Nobody was supposed to get wasted.

Wren came running out of the corridor, blinking in perplexity. "What the fuck's going on?"

"All's not well, Wren." I fiddled with the nav thrusters. "Get us the hell out of here, Noss. Move! Program the Varwol! And for fuck's sake, Blest, don't do anything more to fuck up the day."

Noss moaned, holding his shattered wrist. Wren hopped to it while Blest glared at me.

I shook my head in sad acknowledgement. We pulled away from the berthing arms. Impulse power took us up from Gistron on to the stars.

I took Bantam on an opposite course to *Alastar*, our runaway yacht speeding to Deneb, my finger ready on the Varwol.

"Ignore the pain," I rasped at Noss. "Keep an eye on *Alastar's* progress. For Mary's sake, pitch *Alastar* into warp if shots come at her, or some SOB comes too close to tractoring her in. She'll lead Gistron's security bozos a merry chase." I hated to be hard on Noss, but the poor fuck need direction and these desperate times demanded desperate measures.

The first ship came roaring up on our tail. But it wasn't who I thought it would be. Wren pulled up the holo feed and zoomed in. A cigar-shaped fast-runner appeared, tapered on the ends, wider in the middle where the bridge lay. No security logo on her side. Odd.

The message came crackling over the com, on a general hailing frequency. "Jorry Rambo, Jorry Rambo, cut your engines! We've weapons locked on your hull. RSA and Gistron security are aboard with orders to kill, regarding the murder of a security agent."

I scowled. On a whim, I paused, my fingers fluttering over the Varwol slider. To find out what they knew could be expedient.

"Seems as if we have some uneasy people on our back," I murmured at Wren." I spoke into the com. "Don't know what you're talking about, captain. Must have the wrong guy."

A fat face appeared on the visual—Halley's—and his angry face spewing invective rattled the line. "Rambo! We've got your number and we know you're keeping a bimbo accomplice aboard. Turn her in. We might go easy on you."

"What bimbo? Are you mad?" Odd that Detran'd go after me instead of *Alastar*. The word 'bimbo' clued me into the fact that Detran and his cronies had no RSA or security team aboard. "Who am I talking to?" I croaked.

"Name's Halley Detran, you fucknut—organizer of the auction, a name you know well enough, unless you're the most clued out SOB in the universe! Turn that hunk of shit around—"

I killed the channel. "Rude bastard." I never took well to insults. I nodded at Wren. "Okay, let's make hay." I kicked in Bantam's hyperdrive while she engaged Alastar's Varwol. But Halley took a shot at us from behind. A deafening boom hit our hull. The shields held but I watched as the red light flickered on the structural overload gauge. The warp sequence failed.

"What kind of bombs is that fucker carrying?" I murmured. "You want to play, Hal? Okay." I swung Bantam about and grunted at Wren. "Fire at that bastard's ass."

Wren loosed a fareon beam. A jagged streak of ionized light flared from our port and shook Halley's craft till it was an ugly shade of dusky yellow.

"Rusco, get the hell out of here," Blest yelled.

As much as I hated to back down from a fight, he was right. I hit the Varwol control but nothing happened. I gaped again. The red light was stuck at the 'on' position at an eight out of ten intensity. "Now, we're fucked."

"Fix it, Noss!" I growled at him in utter helplessness. He grunted and rocked back and forth, holding his mangled wrist; sweat poured down his flushed cheeks.

I swore again, gunning the impulse thrusters. I took us in a tight loop starboard and aft to avoid Halley's continued fire. We played a game of dodge and dash for minutes until I saw our measly impulse thrust would lose us this game. From the direction of Gistron station came two security bogies, bearing down on us with wrath. Red flares issued from their port cannons. Directly at us. The jig was up.

Noss, bless his hide, started messing with the controls and gave a sharp cry as he diverted the auxiliary power to the Varwol drive. The overload warning light flickered off for a brief instant. I slammed the hyperdrive to engage. The high-pitched whir of light drive was music to my ears. Space and time suddenly flipped; we were gone from this sector.

Staring at one another in stunned silence.

"Any chance of them tracking us?" Blest panted.

"Not unless they have angels or psychics on their side," I mumbled.

They couldn't track us. Not at least with the gizmo cloakers I'd installed in the forward drive vents some weeks ago. More yols down the drain, but necessary ones to keep degenerates like Halley off our tail.

Blest drew a hissing breath through his teeth, "At least you avoided what was turning into be a lethal firefight, Rusco."

"For now. There's always tomorrow. That yacht *Alastar* and the booty aboard'll pay for our losses in Resus. We'll head to Deneb, cook up some schemes to get us back in the green."

"I'll believe it when I see it," Blest said.

I sighed. Noss gripped his hand and clenched his teeth to bite back the pain. "Good work, Noss," I congratulated him. "You saved our asses. Wren, get our friend some regen before his hand turns into a bird's claw beyond fixing." She reached for the extra stash in the hidden bulkhead—stuff I always kept in an emergency. There was enough there to deal with Noss's problem. At least I hoped.

Making enemies everywhere I went. Not a good modus operandi.

Chapter 9

Alastar was off to Deneb and we were out of radio contact until the starship came out of warp. Nothing we could do but sit tight and follow her light trails. My eyes kept scanning the overload gauge. The bright red light kept flickering on, then off, only to fade out for a few minutes then flicker back on again. Noss's efforts to keep a steady trickle of auxiliary power trained at the light drive seemed to be failing.

"Damn it, Noss, what's wrong with the blasted thing?"

Noss shrugged, wincing as the regen did its work on his wrist. "Could be anything. The last hit jarred something loose. Bad connection maybe, a corrupted stabilizer? Take your pick."

I grimaced. "Don't like the overload light coming on. We'll stop along the way, get it checked. Where's the nearest civilized world?" I looked to Wren.

The holo image showed a green gridded layout with nearby suns of various intensities as she consulted the star chart. "Baladar in Kepler's Reach."

"Baladar it is. Damn Hal and his bloody super ship. We'll keep regular shifts at the helm. Noss, you turn in, get that wrist healed. Blest, you and Wren fight over who gets the first watch." I turned to make my exit, moving down the hall to my cabin like a straw man, feeling the strain of the last few days building, a pressure under my temples.

I entered my berth, paused in front of the mirror before the sink, scrutinizing myself. The rugged ruffian look. Hollow pits under eyes too dark and purple to signify anything good. Nor did I like the crows-leg cracks forming around the edges plus the whiskers turning a visible shade of grey. The cynical awareness was still there, of a lone glimpse into the facts of life: after all the blood has been shed and the guns have gone off, only the lies we tell ourselves remain, about what heroes we'd been, and how lucky we were to have survived the day.

One Jet Rusco: a washed-up space hustler roving the stars, well past his prime, trying to strike some balance between having a stable life and making ends meet while risking others' skins in the process. Not the best way to play it. On the bright side, a man with some conscience, maybe scant little, but some backbone, and a shred of basic decency floating around there somewhere, but slim pickings lately. Not the best recipe for making friends, or keeping friends.

Perhaps it was this disquieting reminder of my own mediocrity that brought the greatest sadness, a life bereft of fulfillment, the hollow pit-in-the-stomach feeling while going through the motions of playing bandleader to other grifters on the path hunting for a paradise they'd never find.

A knock came at the door. Wren seemed to have won that fight for bridge leave. "Come in."

I looked her over, liking what I saw in her fresh black and grey leather and all her lioness cheekiness. "Well, this's a surprise."

"Is it, Rusco? You think I don't care for you?" She smirked. "What's the matter, not happy to see me?" She came up behind me and put long arms around my chest. In the mirror's reflection, I saw her eyes agleam, a wry twist to her sun-bronzed brow.

I turned and gave her a lingering kiss. I unlatched myself and led her to the cot then flopped down with a groan.

She came to lie beside me. "Rusco, you look haggard."

"You think? Wake me in two hours if I'm not up." I yawned, rolled over on my stomach and she pushed over to my side.

"What's wrong, Russy, out of sorts today?"

"Too many foul-ups, Wren."

"I can unwind some of those nerves," she coaxed. Running a warm hand over my shoulders, she pinched at some key places, which had me arching in response.

"Maybe you could." I turned and leveled her a meaningful glance. The briefest tigress's purr escaped her lips.

"How many problems can I help you forget?"

"A number maybe, but I'm just a dead weight right now, Wren, not much good for what you have in mind."

"You could be worse off, Rusco—think of Noss, poor bastard. Speaking of which, what do you think of our new recruits?"

"If I had my choice, I'd opt for more experienced people any day. Though I can't fault Noss or Blest for their bravery and coming through with the goods. Though Blest is a pain in the ass most of the time."

She nodded. "I think Blest is going to cause you some more serious problems one of these days."

"No doubt. I'll re-evaluate him and the situation once we get to Deneb.

Maybe give Blest his share of the spoils and send him on his way."

She snuffled out a laugh. "Good luck. Blest'll squawk like a rooster—he's such a hard-head and chronic whiner. It's for the better you send him packing."

She tickled an area below my belly that seemed overly sensitive and had me jumping up a few inches. "Hey, I'm supposed to be sleeping here, aren't I?" I turned to hold her.

"Sleep is for wimps, Rusco. You can sleep all you want when you're dead."

I laughed.

She rolled over. "How come you never tell me anything about your life?"

"You want me to turn into one of those jolly boy blowhards like down at the station bar?"

"Well, not that bad, I mean."

"I know what you mean." I sighed, rubbing my temples, trying to think of something. "Okay, picture it, me back in midtown Nepasi, on a nowhere world, the place where I started my security guard gig with a man called Trex. Trex—all fun and games. Boozing, whoring, gambling, you know, shows me the town, the hot spots, the low spots, the dives. Once while he was guarding a hock shop, he wanted me to cover for him while he picked up some stuff, and this wise guy comes up and wants to put the drop on me, thinking me a pigeon he can pump for information, maybe score an angle, seeing as I am new kid on the block. He doesn't know I was born on Jaunus 8, war shithole of every kid's bad dream, and that I grew up on the streets. So he asks me where's the best 'gauge'. Testing me out by dropping the word 'gauge'. Numbnut. Every greenhorn knows the new hip term for illegal tech and cop-channel decrypters and neuron stimulators and all that is gauge. 'Dunno, man,' I say, 'I've got like two hour's experience with the stuff.' So, he starts thinking twice about getting by me and taking me by surprise which is his real play, robbing the joint. He asks me if I'm interested in working for a guy named Makey, as in his boss. Me, twenty-three, a dumb fuck, knowing nothing about anything. I say, maybe, how much? 'Oh, a lot more than you're making at this dump.' And before I knew it, I was getting mixed up in a smuggling ring out of that backward planet. Mean fuckers. They'd drop your grandma for no more than the roll of a cigarette."

"Nice. How'd you get out?"

I paused, my lip working a little knot. "Not proud of it, Wren, but I wasted a couple of those assholes, deputies or zarks as they called them. I snuck out of there fast as a weasel, as in fresh off the planet."

She winced. "Rusco, always running from something."

"Yeah, well, sometimes it's just part of who you are and it's all you can do."

"Maybe."

I frowned. "Now your turn."

She gave her shoulder a small twitch.

"Aw, come on, Wren. When were you ever one to turn down a story swap?"

"Maybe because I don't have a story to tell right now." Her lips pursed, in a masked chuckle or a mock curl.

"I know that false smirk. What are you thinking of? Come on, I know you're recalling something."

"Just an old childhood memory." She let out a cooing sigh. "Never forget the time my little brother left the chicken coop open. A bunch of hens got out, so did two roosters. Then they scooted out of the yard and little Freedy, my youngest brother, went chasing them, thinking they'd get eaten by coyotes or something, and I got scared that he was going to get eaten by coyotes himself. We didn't get back for hours, wandering around the hills, all dusty and scratched by desert weeds and fire thistle. I was only eleven, Rusco. Oh, was my dad ever mad and he gave us a tanning for losing those egg-laying hens.

I grunted. "Very quaint, Wren. Glad you shared that story."

"Okay, Rusco, maybe not as invigorating as your shoot-em-up-and leave em in a body bag yarn, but I'm not up to blood and guts tales right now. Sure, got me some more to tell though."

"I'm sure you do, Wren, baby. Like those zombie creepsters you blew all to hell on Talyon."

She settled down, shook her head and laughed. "Sorry, I get a little defensive sometimes. Don't know why I thought of that dumb chicken story."

"The mind is a strange thing."

"Like shit it is, Rusco. You make this stuff up as you go along?" She pounced on me and nearly knocked the breath out of my tired lungs.

"Okay, I give up. Enough story telling for now."

"How about some quiet girl kisses then? I'm in the mood for looove..." She gazed at me with long, hungry eyes.

"Again? Didn't we—"

"Hours ago. Why, you not up for it?" Her kittenish arch of smile hit me with that level of challenge that stirs a man to bawdy deeds. Rusco, no matter how tired he is, can always rise to a challenge.

I rolled over to pull her to my bare chest. "After this deal is over, you and me have to go on some long vacation. Maybe Palm Monteray. Spas, beaches and warm rays. What do you think?"

"Sounds like fun. What are we going to do with Blest and his buddy?"

"Forget those two. Pack them off to Timbuktu with Winnie the Pooh. They've got each other."

She laughed. So the tired JR surrendered to the magical pump and grind of big, talented, desert girl with all the bells and trimmings to go, and the endless mysteries and unfettered openness that was Wren.

I must have dozed off to warm, bawdy memories of Wren, but then dreaming of shooting off down some wind tunnel like I was going to get blown to Arcturus. High winds were buffeting me every which way. Damn those archetypal dreams...

I was running through the bushes, breath huffing out a rasp. Gilm and his contingent of hoods were somewhere behind me, switchblades, billy clubs and bare fists on the ready. Reg, my buddy, had been robbed, beaten down. I was next. We were the only ones aware of the gang's doings on the east side of the river. They'd kill me. I'd only my wits about me. Precious little. I sucked in a wheezing breath, then another breath, willing myself not to make more noise. Up came a flash of pipe, for my throat. I blocked it, plunged a knife into the wanker's yielding belly.

Someone's hand jarred me awake. "Rusco, get up."

"Wha—"

"Signal came in from *Alastar.*" Noss stood over me, blinking like an owl. Wren was nowhere to be seen.

I shook my head as if registering for the first time what he was talking about and where I was.

Noss frowned at the slowness of my brain. "You left your door open. You weren't answering your com."

I let out a moan. "Alastar couldn't have gotten that far that fast."

Noss looked at me as if I were still jacked on Myscol. "You'd better come look."

"Aw, shit." I threw on my clothes and stumbled down the dim-lit hall.

Chapter 10

Wren and Blest were gathered at the bridge, Blest looking like some ragged, bleary-eyed raccoon.

"What's this about Alastar?" I growled.

"Beached somewhere in quadrant 3.21AZ." Blest stabbed a thumb at the holo star chart.

I blinked. "That's a fuckhole of a place to crap out in—"

"Right, she must have conked out somewhere at the edge of *The Dim Zone*. Her standard paging signal relayed through the world, Daerzoo. Must be regular transports flying in and out that carried the message through the warp tunnel."

"How far in is she?"

"A few light minutes from Daerzoo."

I sighed.

"You're talking dangerous territory," grumbled Blest. "Pirates, scum killers, freaks. Why don't we leave it, Rusco, try some easier fish?"

I scowled. "Wren and I went through a lot of pains to get that ship, my friend. We need to protect our investment."

"That ship may be worth nothing with the Varwol toast," Blest warned.

"But there's a half mil of Myscol out there," I argued. "If Detran was even half telling the truth, we've got to get it. We're already several thousand in the hole. We'd be stupid not to take a crack at salvaging her."

Blest puckered up his lips and shrugged. "Whatever. Do what you want. What do you think, Wren? Is it too risky?"

"I'm with Rusco."

Noss nodded his agreement.

"You guys!" Blest licked his lips, his red-face burning with annoyance. "I get pissed getting outvoted every time we're on this bridge."

The clock said 04:35 which meant that *Alastar* had been in warp for some three hours. My foggy brain tried to piece together the events. Facts: Encrypted messages are uploaded to servers and travel to other ships leapfrogging across the gulfs, until the messages finally make it to the receiver, the same way. Fact 2, the free store interstellar net shares information across the star systems. Fact 3—

Rusco. Focus. So that meant *Alastar* had dropped out of light drive at

02:00, and a few light minutes from Daerzoo put her something of an hour plus change away from us…Couldn't risk our own Varwol crapping out on us. Which meant—

"Where are we now?"

"Ten minutes from Baladar."

I nodded. "We get Bantam fixed up and immediately warp to *The Dim Zone*."

On the space dock orbiting Baladar, I rode Bantam in as fast as I dared. We made prompt dock and inquiries for maintenance. We were lucky to land a spot at Reyce's Gut Shop as today they were not inundated with service calls. The head mechanic, a slack-jawed man in blue coveralls, with grease on his chin and rag in his hands, listened to our story with grunts and nods, trying not to grin too hard at my fabrications. I saw it wasn't gaining us anything, so gave an expansive flourish.

"Okay, I'll cut the bullshit. Truth to tell, we were in a firefight in a world I shall not name. Bantam took a couple of hits that knocked something important loose. Can you fix it?"

He nodded and signaled his henchmen. I watched the man as he went to work.

We waited in the reception, pacing like tigers.

He came back wheezing and wiping his hands on a dirty white rag. "Good thing you got it looked at. Left stabilizer shot. Replacement 900 yols, labor 200. It'll get you through the next month. But there's more serious damage to the time-drive mechanism. My scanners picked up a hairline crack in the drive crystal. You're looking at minimum 5k repair job, and three days' work in the sweat shop."

"Aw, shit. Three days?" I groaned. "We don't have three days. More yols down the hole." I waved a weary hand. "Well, do the minimum."

The mechanic nodded and left to talk to his hired hands.

I had to dip into my reserve to pay for even that minimal fixup. Now I was riding on empty. More than ever did we need *Alastar* with its Myscol payout. If I had been a bolder man, I'd risk flying in without the repairs, but experience and wisdom of age told me to temper that impulsive plan. I didn't trust Bantam's warp drive not to leave us stranded out in no-man's land as it had *Alastar*.

We bundled up and set a course for Daerzoo. ETA 1 hour. I hoped the gamble was worth it. We'd be in time—for what?—to get the spoils, hoping no other parties had got there ahead of us?

I had Noss soon adjust our course to rendezvous with *Alastar*. If it weren't for her encrypted homing beacon, we'd have a tough time finding her, like the proverbial needle in a haystack. It was a risk. I just hoped others hadn't been listening in too long.

Alastar loomed up on the viewport against the faraway stars. A defiant old bird of a previous generation—her prow shaped like a hammerhead, her body that of a sleek mermaid with twin tail fins. Her robust Vega-6 drive was not so robust any more. I wonder what she thought of her new owners. I killed the homing signal that had alerted us to her position via the spider.

"Let's check her out and find that Myscol and transfer it to Bantam. How I'd like to get her to a safe port…then auction her off as quickly as possible for real this time."

"Won't they be looking for her?" Noss fumbled with the autopilot. "Crosschecking drive codes, insurance records, the like."

"They can't patrol every port in the galaxy, Noss. Places out this way could give two shits about some heist back on Gistron station."

Noss smiled. His wrist looked less puffy and bruised than earlier, though he wouldn't be doing any handstands too soon.

He murmured, "The ship looks okay. We can keep her on impulse drive to wherever she needs to go in the meantime."

"How long would it take us to get her to Daerzoo?" Blest asked.

"Two weeks," Wren answered. "Give or take a day or so."

"Two weeks we don't have," I mused. "This is *The Dim Zone*, remember?"

"Can't we go over and fix it?" Blest piped up.

"Yeah," I barked, "like the hyperdrive just needs a screwdriver and a bit of elbow grease."

"I dunno, just asking." Blest withdrew, flushed-faced.

"All the same, a few of us'll go over and see what's gotten into her."

Noss and Wren stayed aboard and I took Blest with me on the shuttle: a small oblong, eight-legged craft built for short distant hops from ship to ship. I flicked the spider's remote to engage and opened *Alastar's* starboard hatch. We maneuvered Lander to dock in the starboard port. The steel-grey door closed shut and we hung inside the landing bay while the pressure equalized. The little green light blinked and Blest and I hopped out, guns at the ready. I motioned him to cover me in case there were some unpleasant surprises we hadn't counted on.

We moved to the forward hall, weapons drawn, choosing not to err on the side of caution. The place was quiet as a tomb. Pilot emergency lights showed through a dim ambience. Eerie. A sixth sense alerted me to something indefinable.

We crept up the companionway then stalked the corridor leading to the bridge. I held up a hand to Blest to cool his heels. Something felt not quite right.

I saw that a small white plastic dish lay out on the conference table. A fresh vacuum pack of oat flakes sat beside it. Could have been maintenance crew. But why would they have been so careless when potential buyers were roaming about the ship? It seemed odd.

Blest was about to blurt out something, but I put a finger to my lips.

I heard a muffled sneeze. Also caught a glimpse of the console panel to the left of the nav displaced, as if someone had tried to put the cover hastily back on. So my suspicions were not unfounded. I cautioned Blest and crept over to the wall and kicked open the hatch.

A pale figure, some thirty-years old, sat hunched in the dimness, quivering like a jellyfish.

"Who are you?" I hauled him up. The pale-faced man held up his hands. I recognized him from Halley's crew. "Bloody hell." Blest's gun was in his face, the barrel practically shoved up his nose.

"My n-name's Krel Follee. Don't shoot! Lew told me to make sure Alastar was ready to fly on short notice. To unlock the nav system."

"So did you?" I demanded.

The stowaway shook his head, a pronounced quiver on his bottom lip. A momma's boy, some geek clever with tech, with a high pitched whine to his voice and a nervous tic on the left cheek.

He didn't answer right away and I wondered if his explanation were a cover. His logic made sense but now we had a problem on our hands. "Lucky we found you, otherwise you'd be a skeleton by the time anyone came looking for you."

"Lucky, how? I got your friend jamming a gun down my throat."

I croaked out a mirthless laugh, impressed despite myself at Follee's spunk. "Lower your weapon, Blest." Blest withdrew his R4. I gave an update to Noss and Wren over the com. "Found Halley's geek code cruncher hunched in the forward bulkhead. A Krel Frowlee. Seems our charmer, Detran, didn't check all his inventory before blast off." I chuckled. "One unlucky dabchick stowed away."

"That's *Follee* and I'm not a geek. I'd have fixed the drive eventually. Even if I had to rip every component out of the stupid panel and piece it back together."

Blest licked his lips and grinned. "So what do we do with this jitterbug?" He redirected his weapon at the stowaway.

"Maybe I have a use for him, Blest. Can you diagnose ships?" I barked at Follee. "Can you pull code, break into systems?"

"Sure, I suppose, all of the above."

"It's no 'suppose', Fowlee, you either can or you can't."

"I can," he growled.

"Then I give you a choice. You either work for us, or stay locked up in the brig on my ship."

"But you're thieves and pirates."

"Anything less than what your employer was?" I sneered. "You don't know the half of Detran's evil."

He struggled with the concept, working his lips in a frown and muttering. Then his eyes went wide and he gave a grave nod. "I suspected him. Never liked that puff weasel anyways. Where the blazes are we? Alastar dropped out of light drive in the middle of nowhere. I couldn't do anything with the controls. Hal's passwords were useless. I was lucky to even force open the food hatch as it was."

"That's because they're locked by my spider," I said proudly, holding up the black, square-faced remote.

"How did *you* get the code then?"

I fluttered my fingers and mimed a mysterious expression. "Little pirate magic."

"Yeah, right."

"Don't get so hot and bothered, Fowlee. I'm short on recruits. As I said, you may come in handy and your options are kinda limited. Where's the Myscol?"

"Myscol? What Myscol?"

"Like the stuff your blowhard employer uses to pad his ships with."

Follee blinked. "You mean the medicines? They're in the engine room, right behind the artificial grav generators."

Blest and I exchanged glances and raced for the hold, hustling our friend along with none too gentle hands.

"Medicines," I scoffed. "Where the fuck did you get such a bird-brained idea?"

"Hal said it was for research: a philanthropic move to fight cancer and other deadly diseases."

"Did he now?" I crooned. "Boy, you've got real dibs on the Gullible Gus award of the year. Your pals've been running drugs. That makes you an accessory."

"No way, I—" He gulped.

We reached the engine room. I heard the low hum of the Vega 6 impulse engines, electro-stroke, quasi-sol drives. Neat stacks and coils on her, running vertically up the wall to the silver-foiled ceiling. Follee pointed. "Over there, behind those black, square units."

I nodded and we crowded in close. Blest and I took the butt end of our guns to the fibrofane and we ripped off the paneling. I saw twin rows of clear plastic packs containing pink powder with elastic bands tied around them.

I shoved Follee's head down to take a look. "Does that look like cancer medicines to you?"

He gulped, licked his lips. "Hey, be careful. I'm not your punching bag here."

I ripped open a hand-sized pack and dipped a finger and ran my tongue over it. "Here, try some," I said to Follee with a grin. He recoiled, like a frightened baby. "Mmm good. Pure stuff. Blest, you should try some too."

"Here, you eat it." I had Blest hold Follee while I forced open his mouth and plugged my pink-snuffed fingers past his tongue. He spat and hissed like an angry cat.

"Consider it your inauguration to Myscol." I laughed. Follee struggled and I shrugged. "Won't do any good. Enters the bloodstream fast." Ah, Rusco, you're a real hoot.

Blest, wearing a lizard's grin, thrust the stowaway aside. I even got a rise out of Blest as he dipped his finger in the bag and took a generous dose.

Both our eyes glazed over a bit. I shook my head, enjoying the buzz. "Now, Fowlee, here's how it's going to fly. Your name, Fol, that's your name from now on. Mr. Fol."

"Naw, just Fol for short," said Blest.

I conceded to the name change.

Follee held up his hands. "So you got your stuff! What's in it for me?" His nervous gaze rested on Blest's itchy finger caressing his weapon.

"This is how it works. We look for opportunities. We split the profits down the middle. I take an extra cut, since it's my ship and I assume the risk. We share in the overhead. You try any fast ones, we blow your head off. Or at the very least, finger you as an accomplice for stealing this pleasure craft."

"Sure," he stammered, "but as long as I don't have to do anything illegal."

I took a deep breath and rolled my eyes.

Blest cast me an impatient glance. "Don't think I want to play nursemaid to baby brat here, Rusco. Though, may give me some amusement on a slow day on my shift." He reached over and rubbed his knuckles on Follee's scalp of thin sandy hair and Fol cried out, telling us to lay off him, not appreciating the threats and sarcasm.

We both laughed, feeling good on the Myscol.

We carted out half the product over to the Lander. Less than what I had thought. I guessed about 200 g's by the time we paid expenses and dropped the price down for a quick sale. Split four ways, that wasn't bad.

I hesitated with the other half of the shipment. Changed my mind. Left it aboard *Alastar*. Blest looked at me as if I had a few screws loose.

"Never put all your eggs in one basket, Blest—ever hear of that maxim?"

He shrugged and gave a muffled snort.

With Fol that made five in our merry band.

* * *

Wren met us in the landing bay, passed her eyes over the stash as Blest and I unloaded it into the utility bins. She gave Follee only a cursory inspection. He stared at her with nothing less than awe.

"Hi, Miss, my name is—"

She ignored his outstretched hand and shouldered her way over to me, all business-like. "We've had about 28 hours, Jet, and counting since the homing beacon was up. We should get the hell out of here."

Blest and I kept unpacking the rest of the bags of product as if we hadn't heard. I took Follee up to the bridge. Noss gave him a guarded greeting. Wren trailed, wearing a peeved look. "I'm talking to you, Rusco."

"Heard you, Wren. All in a day's work. You see how much stuff there is? You should be dancing for joy."

"I am, but this place gives me the creeps. Heard horror stories about *The Dim Zone*."

"Worse than your own shithole on Talyon?"

"Well, yes, worse."

I shrugged. "Could be all true, or maybe just wives' tales."

"Right, like mutants carving out brains and using victims' skulls as wine gourds."

I laughed. "That's a good one. Right up Mong's alley."

Follee looked and stared bug-eyed. "*Dim Zone?*" His eyes flicked back and forth. Thick glasses, clamped at the bridge of his nose, fat, meaty fingers, short, stocky frame coming up to about Noss's shoulders. At least he was keeping his mouth shut, unlike Blest.

"So?" Noss inquired.

"Noss, it's looking good, my man. You may be able to retire yet," I said with enthusiasm. Enthusiasm lit by Myscol.

"That's good." Noss grinned and beamed. His smile faded. "What about Alastar? Can't just leave the ship there to get picked clean by scavengers. You know the law of the jungle, Rusco, finders keepers."

"It's a problem, I know." I looked over at Wren, who seemed torn between ditching the craft and flying the hell out of here. Any moment our own warp could cut out even with the recent band aid.

Blest grunted. "Still say we lose her. Too much risk."

My lips curled in a grimace. "Still could get some appreciable salvage for her. I hate leaving a starship behind."

"Who doesn't, Rusco, but—"

"Look, we have to act fast," interrupted Wren. "Raiders could be out there sniffing down our trail right now."

"She's right," said Blest.

"Any other place we can hide her at?" asked Noss out loud.

Blest snorted. "What, at the edge of *The Dim Zone?*"

"Wren, check it out," I urged.

She pulled up the holo register and began zooming in on nearby worlds. "What am I looking for?"

"Asteroids, space stations, moons, planets, mining operations, any space junk that could create a smoke screen for us until I figure out a better plan."

She shook her head. "Nada, Rusco. Wait! There's an abandoned station."

"What? Where?" I leaned over her shoulder.

"Dunno. Some decommissioned space station. No… Too big for that. Look. Holy, Christ, it's a fortress."

"How far?"

"A couple hours away on impulse thrust."

I chewed my lip. "We could warp in, check it out. If it looks promising…" I saw the overload warning gauge flicker. "What the—" I whuffled out a breath. "Those bastards. Mechanics promised me it—"

"He warned you it could go at any time," grumbled Noss.

"Said we'd get a month," I groused. "Hairline crack must be getting wider."

Blest waved a restless hand. "That station could be a magnet for trouble."

"Few other options are knocking on our door. The long and short of it, our light drive's buggered again."

Blest threw up his hands. "That's just fucking great."

I shrugged. "Well, not much we can do about it. We'll have to risk it."

We headed out on max impulse to the station. I tossed the spider remote over to Noss, who used it as a guide to get *Alastar* trailing on our heels.

Chapter 11

The last leg was the longest and glummest ride I could remember. We were trucking along on impulse with both Noss and I trying unsuccessfully to get the warp drive up again when we came across a blip on the sensors.

"Visual," I hissed.

"There." Noss pointed.

The station loomed out of the darkness. An obtrusive cube with circular pods at either end. But much more than that, a complex wonder of science and technological engineering. Lights glowed on the superstructure. It wasn't completely dark there and that worried me. Automatic lights? Still operating under some weak solar power from Daerzoo's sun? It seemed a stretch.

"Wren, give me more info on this place." The monstrous station had a look of promise—and menace. It looked too new for the age that Wren had quoted earlier.

"It's four hundred years old. "

"No way!"

"Yes way. Name changed from Cyber Corp to Cygon, somewhere in the last few years of its life."

"What else does the omniscient computer have to say?"

"Supposed to be haunted. A ghost station, actually."

"Yeah, haunted my ass," I scoffed.

"Why out here?"

"Some space laboratory. Experiments, controversial research, close to their base of operations, somewhere in *The Dim Zone*. It is said the firm's senior scientist, Dezmin Yadley, assumed control of the company after the CEO, someone named Mathias, went mysteriously missing. The company dissolved, after repeated disasters rained on its labs."

"Give me the visual on the schematics."

Wren pulled up a complicated diagram on the holo display showing several bays, a series of side wings and work areas across four levels, fanning out radially from a massive warehouse several stories high and breasting out on the hangar.

"Last known to have been searching for alien life out on the remote planets, mostly *The Dim Zone*."

"Makes no sense. Why *The Dim Zone*? Why would a cybernetics company be messing around with alien life?"

"Who the fuck knows, Rusco, or cares," said Blest, "we've got ourselves a serious problem here—"

"Yeah, I know, and we're trying to solve it without you naysaying my every word."

Wren squinted and read on. "The firm is shrouded in mystery and scandal. Known for employing unconventional means—escaping government jurisdictions and facing multiple infractions in both ethics and tax evasion."

"Sounds just like our kind of guys." I laughed. "Dead guys I bet now, unless they built some longevity serum."

"No, afraid not. Afraid the company hasn't been active for centuries."

At one time, it had been formidable, now its defensive cannons had been blown to bits or ripped off by scavengers. A gaping hole loomed in its side, allowing a shadowy glimpse into the docking hangar. I motioned Noss to steer us in closer, my eyes peeled for anything untoward.

I guessed Cyber Corp maintained an extensive empire at one time, perched at the edge of *The Dim Zone*. Maybe their fingers had dug too deep in the pie? Found something they wished they hadn't? What had they been fucking with?

Once inside the hangar hole, I trained Bantam's floodlamps down to see what we were dealing with. Noss guided the ship through the darkness. *Alastar* followed behind. We saw a brood of lurking spaceships. Ancient models—Phasons, KV-Levlars with odd, sleek, tapered outerbodies like the V-Ugons of old. Odd that nobody's taken them, I thought. Vintage. Fly on, Rusco. Maybe the station's unsavory reputation would detract any avid raiders from taking a crack at us. But why go after small fry when you could have a whole squad of ships? There were lots here. Though some had drifted from their landing berths, chipped and battered, looking not so lucky in their fight against the ravages of time.

"Those ships aren't chained down," said Noss. "Artificial grav generators still functioning. A miracle after all this time."

"Yeah, fancy that."

The hangar loomed in all its glory. I was impressed by the sheer size of it. Could fit a mountain in here. We traveled through the warehouse of the station and landed at the end of a line of ancient craft that looked like antediluvian freighters. Carrying what?

Wren punched some keys and a green, wireframe grid appeared. It rotated on the holo display to show more bays and hidden alcoves.

"Turns out this station has been a hazard for salvagers and scavengers for centuries."

"Great, a motherload of bad karma." I chewed on my lip. "But maybe it's just the type of place we need—"

Two Skurgian vessels came streaking in from the entrance. The first ship's fire hit us broadside.

"Motherfuckers," rasped Blest. His fist clenched his rifle.

They'd been hiding on the outside of the station's superstructure, stuck there like leeches, blending in like grey-green lichen on a tree's trunk. If we'd been able to warp in here earlier, we could at least have saved *Alastar* and maybe our own skins.

"We can't warp out," said Noss. "Trapped in this goddamn creepy hangar."

"How to evade these asslicking fuckwads?" I mused.

"Fight our way out. What else?" Blest howled.

"No, too many of them. They'll blow us to shit." I saw two more come in to join their pals as more fire splatter licked out at us. "We've got two ships running on impulse power. Useless. We take them out there, they'll pepper us with bombs. We have to do the unexpected."

"Like what?"

"Dump Bantam and take our guns and go in on foot. We can hole up and ambush them in some cubbyhole in the station."

Blest stared at me as if I were loony. "What? Take on a small army of Skugs?"

"They'll never find us in this maze. At least easily. Even if they do, we'll gun them down—and it'll be better odds for us."

"Great," said Noss. "We go in there, get blown up and charcoaled by laser trip beams."

Blest gave his head a laughing shake. "It's just crazy enough to work."

I got them rushing down to the cargo bay while I stayed behind to reach in the utility bulkhead and grab the silver phaso I stashed there. That slim little silver disc had saved my ass before, the same device 'friend' Mong and his goats had been after since the beginning. Why the freak wanted it, I wasn't so sure. A powerful artifact of ancient alien technology: it could transport an unwary being to hell and back, or if one was lucky, to some other alien dimension. No easy way of getting back from there unless the disc was clutched with fierce force in one's hand, not so easy. I'd been there once and did not care to return. I was damned if I'd leave it for the Skugs to find.

I caught up with them in the hall leading to the hold. Follee tugged at my arm. "But won't they take the ship?" he stammered.

"They might, Fol, but there's a chance they won't. I'll rig some explosives on the hatch, that or give them a mother of an electric shock if they touch it plus something extra for Sunday brunch."

"What if they blow the hatch—?"

"For Christ sakes, Blest, get your ass moving and shut the fuck up for once. These scavengers don't seem to be after ships. Didn't you see the row of them all sitting here?"

"That's because they're dead."

"Could've scavenged them for parts though. Why didn't they?"

"It's a bad idea, Rusco." Blest shook his head.

"You got a better idea?"

Wren waved a hand. "Let's just hurry up for fuck's sake! We're wasting time."

Blest grunted in resignation.

"Suit up!" I growled.

We grabbed the reserve pressure suits off the wall, snugged in and checked each other's helms and air supplies. Follee's face was green with apprehension in the dim lights, reluctant to move toward the cargo hatch. "I don't want to go, Rusco," he pleaded through his mask.

"You want to stay back here, Fol, and get mauled by mutants? Or blown to shit?"

Fire hit our port stern but our shields held. Follee cringed at the idea, shrinking like a bug. "Since you put it that way—"

"Get going." Blest pushed him along. I stuck an R3 in Follee's gloved hands. "Use this. Here, safety on. Safety off. Get it? You point it at bad guys and shoot if some come trying to blow your head off."

Follee gave a vigorous nod.

Wren looked at me, a flushed look of uncertainty there—Are you sure you want this guy along?

No, I wasn't sure, Wren, I answered her voiceless expression but I didn't see too many options here other than signing the poor guy's death warrant leaving him behind.

Noss powered down the ship, save for shields. We rushed to the cargo exit pad, so it left no easily traceable signature. I booby trapped the hatch with my regular batch of tricks—explosives and high voltage. If Skugs managed to penetrate it, we'd be stranded here—an unwholesome thought. *Alastar,* I could do nothing for now. I'd spidered her to a safe landing place a few hundred yards away, couched in thick, gummy shadows.

My breath hissed out a ragged whisper through my mask. We hurried out onto the docking pavilion, keeping to the wall. Blest and Noss gave covering fire while Wren sprinted ahead in a crouching trot to get the air lock to the station open, even as the Skug vessels, beetle-like shapes, swarmed closer. I could tell they were Skug by the lady-bug shape of their hulls, and the crude symbology writ on their sides: a long spiked anvil with a red slash through it. What significance it had, I'd never known. Something to do with some industrial accident that had maimed them.

The air lock, about a hundred yards away, was intact, another thing that puzzled me.

Blest cursed as I hustled Follee along, a slow bastard by anyone's standards. Barked into the com to get his ass down and lie flat on his stomach while fire ripped around us. Wren had the air lock mechanism figured out; *tada*, the doors suddenly jerked open to the square chamber beyond. We would have blasted it to shit if it were too stubborn to open. We dragged our hides in before the Skug blasters could rifle us with holes. They'd be landing and assembling their own teams. Whether they went after us on foot, or went for our ships, remained to be seen.

The chamber pressurized, then the inner lock opened automatically. We spilled out into a hall.

Surprisingly, the air lock wasn't seized. Blasting it as a last resort would flood the whole station in vacuum, but I was guessing the station had backup systems for that.

"The air is breathable," said Wren, "according to our suit sensors."

I motioned them down the dusky corridor to the right, Follee making googly eyes at the state-of-the-art tech. The lumo shields draping the walls, the fibrofane shock and sound bafflers, the intricate myriads of sensors and scanners for contagion, contraband and weaponry, luckily manned by no one in these brave new times. There were even a dozen emergency suits hanging behind glass showcases.

Not far down the hall we peered through more massive glass windows into broken laboratories, shattered tables and lab equipment, benches askew. Bins of chemicals lay strewn on the metal-plated floor; sealants, robot parts, component boards scattered everywhere. It looked as if the place hadn't been walked through in an eon though. A weird, ambient violet, self-perpetuating glow permeated the surroundings, as if some ancient power still lived here and was still in operation. How, I couldn't guess. Maybe solar power still up and running, as I'd speculated earlier? I eyed the grey crystal fibrofane panels on the wall. Dead camera eyes watched us like insects. Noss opened his mouth to speak, but I signaled him to silence.

We hustled down a wide stairwell, another corridor to a lower level that opened into what looked like a giant depot. The space was enormous. The domed ceiling rose unfathomably high. Monstrous shapes, mechanical things, loomed out of the artificial gloom, like ill-conceived ghosts. Wren's jaw dropped, as did Blest's who had curbed his wise-guy tongue for once. We all walked smitten to silence.

I listened for the expected flurry of enemy fire and feet. Nothing. Only a faint, faraway echo of boots on metal—wary and hesitant. Then another, louder, duller thud of metal—like a ship's landing pads touching down. "If we're lucky, we can lose those gooks," I whispered. "They'll go looking somewhere else." Somehow my own words sounded comical and naive in this ancient murk. I didn't believe my own vain hope for a second.

I recalled typical Skug physiology. A cross between a mutant warrior and a walking mummy. Once human, these mutants were victims of some plague or chemical spill disaster. Freaks, albino genetic rejects forced to wear headgear in the form of blue-grey fabric scarfs wrapped around their misshapen skulls. Reputed to have dull white horns peeking up on their oversized heads and tusks protruding from cheeks with black nozzles affixed to noses with wire mesh where mouths should be. If such mutations were accurate, I assumed the nozzles facilitated breathing. Maybe they siphoned drugged up gas there? I didn't want to meet one of the mutants face to face, or for that matter, ever.

Even through the filtered ages of decades, I tasted the faint waft of death here. Ancient death. Old corpses lay strewn about the feet of the mechanical monsters on the steel paneled floor, victims struck down from the look of their eyeless sockets, by some mysterious, brutal force.

My mind traveled back to a distant memory, a time when my father took me to some natural caves outside our home town on Jaunus. Strange how memory is jogged by the weirdest of triggers. I was scared shitless of bats and snakes and anything fluttery and crawly, but my father took me down there anyway, where the drip-drip of water from stalactites and the cloying darkness had my knees knocking. Despite the dank air chilling my bones, he wanted me to get an appreciation for 'nature', its majesty and terror. "All is not as it seems, Jet. Nature comes in all shapes and sizes. Never all just sun and bright sky and fresh air. Mother Nature has secrets that no one will ever know. Observe and find out, if she wishes to show you. You may learn something." And I lurched back as a snake slithered out of the shadows and lashed its wedge-shaped head at me.

My feeling now was not much different.

We took stealthy steps through deep gloom, keeping our eyes off the ancient corpses. Blest kicked at some moldered bones. "Are these for real?" A clattering echo rebounded through the dimness. I waved him to silence. We threaded our way among the hulking shapes of the weird mechnobots, robots of some savage origin, some as high as a second story apartment with pincers for arms and strange metallic outerbodies and turret-like heads. Others materialized in the gloom, as short as midgets only knee high, human, animal, a mixture of the two. The cavernous ceiling rose more stories above than I cared to guess and seemed to exude a maroon-purplish glow from somewhere high above, almost phosphorescent. Whatever these hulking shapes were, they constituted an intimidating rack of armory, scaring the crap out of us all in the eerie light that filtered through the opaque dome.

Chapter 12

I felt a shudder pass along my spine as I threaded by those inert goliaths looming in the eerie darkness. They'd been spawned in a day when technology far outmatched our current science. Now only shadowy hints lingered of the dark age humankind had lapsed into since the last alien war centuries ago. I swallowed the lump in my throat, wondering about that violent, bio-mechanical heritage we'd evolved out of, and of which we remembered little.

Cyber Corp had been messing with robotic experiments, prototypes of weird and wonderful kinds. Aggressive ones, judging from the weapons and guns, the flamethrowers and ray sprayers mounted on the turrets, also the size of those dinosaur shapes and the quality of their armor.

So many mysteries and relics of the forgotten past...The only common thread, invariably, was war and its cruel aftermath—the glue holding it all together.

Here a garden sprawled, as if a horticulture or greenhouse experiment of loose soil and potted plants, there a shattered glass bin of shriveled ferns, long browned with striped leaves and stigmas of curled proboscises. I couldn't help but shiver, almost forgetting our Skug menace.

I tapped on the glass of a certain rectangular glass lab cage, eighteen feet long. Inside was what looked like withered ferns clinging to chunks of dry soil. It appeared as if the vessel had been hurled from a distance; from one of the labs spread along the side walls. Uncannily, the tempered-glass had not shattered.

I tapped on the glass again. Nothing…And yet, I detected a small flutter of movement within.

I gave a hollow laugh. Impossible, Rusco, you're a lunatic. I breathed through my mask. I chuckled, attributing my imagination to the Myscol I'd tongued.

Yet that primitive awareness that lurks at the back the mind and knows something is watching it, tingled my spine. I knew it was something not quite arguably human. So did the others. We all watched in a kind of glazed horror as a monstrous hulk, some twenty-foot-high half-armored ape and scorpion, came to sudden life, a bluish-grey pilot light beaming from its turret-like head. Ridiculous, of course. Not even possible to hallucinate such a thing, but we were the fools striding through a forsaken, molder-ridden mausoleum of the haunted past, and evidently a living vessel for things that should have been left alone.

No time to ponder the chilling horrors of the past. The first gunfire came at us in green energy beams from the wings where we had come. I hissed out a curse and beckoned Follee forward who hunched behind a shoulder-high, four-legged mechnobot with a hideous oversized head and downturned sloping back.

We slunk like panthers to a place where three giant mechnos stood poised on human-like legs, poised in the violet gloom like grim guardians of a tortured past. We hunkered down behind them, taking up ambush positions.

Figures moved in the murk. They came upon us like wildfire, flanking us in a wide semicircle. A small army of horned heads, mummy-wrapped figures with tusked noses came lumbering like stalkers out of screaming nightmare. So, the tales of Skugs were true.

Their sawed off R6s spat blue fire at us.

Fire flare was all around, shredding glass cases, sending bright streaks off the tough armor of the standing mechnobots.

The Skugs grunted through their nosepieces like wild hogs. I saw bits of plant and earth flying up as their fire flares shredded the aquarium next to me. Were those plants moving, or hissing? No, a stupid trick of the mind, amid the sudden carnage and chaos.

I dove for deeper cover, missing a spray that would have ended me.

I gained my feet and stood back to back with Wren emptying fire into moving shapes. Noss and Blest worked in a similar manner. I didn't know where the fuck Follee had gone. Had he fled? Was he dead?

These mutants were going to flank us and take us down in minutes. My head struggled to make sense of it. A flurry of thoughts coursed through my mind. Primitive cannibals these headhunting Skugs, relatives of the Skurgs, drinking blood from carved goblets of skulls. Up to this point, I'd assumed these freaks were just raiders seeking plunder, not the bloodthirsty savages of local legends passed down through the ages.

That illusion was shattered with the rush of a seven-foot giant from my right. He bowled me over, snorting like a bison, and reached out a deformed paw to hurl me against the mechnobot to my left. I let out a wild grunt. My gun slipped from my grasp as I slid down on my haunches. I shook the daze from my skull, rolling and reaching for my weapon. Fingers gripped the stock. Brain hoped he didn't grab and toss me again. I brought the butt end up, whistling steel for a Skug crown. He reached out to catch it in his tatter-wrapped fingers, but the barrel snapped past and clipped him in the skull. For a second he teetered. I caught the whiff of meaty breath and almost gagged. Bloody teeth showed through an oxygen mask. The creature staggered back and shook out the daze, grunting obscenities. I plugged his rat-bastard ass full of holes and he fell face first in a pool of blood.

I looked to the others. Wren and Blest fought tooth and nail to repel a swarm of the mutants. In the flash bursts, I caught glimpses of blood and guts flying. Amid animal roars and the *rat-a-tat* action of multiple fire, I plugged death into the backs of two freaks trying to take down Wren. They fell, hands reaching high over their shoulders.

Blest turned, looking like a wounded, feral animal in the dimness. Noss was hunched behind him, making use of the cover of an arching mechnobot. His hands were too shaky to aim and his gunfire sprayed uselessly in the fray. They'd die soon. As would we all, if we didn't—

A sudden thought intruded on my mind. The thing had tried to catch me, not kill me—so, capture was their game—They were preparing to gather us for their stew pots or some deeper evil which chilled me even more.

The mechanical monster that had come to life flashed fire from its twin guns sticking from its mouth. The thing scorched a mob of running figures. They disintegrated in a burst of legs, twirling arms and shredded masses of flesh. Into the carnage the mechno moved on its armored legs. It killed, trampled and sprayed fire. For whatever reasons I could not fathom. Powered by some mysterious force? My jaw hung on its hinges. Was the thing killing our enemies because it liked us? No. Perhaps it was an automated angel of mercy?

One of the Skugs went racing back to the hangar. Others followed. A surcease?

A group came loping back, how long later I don't know, carrying long, tube-like weapons: RPGs? Barrel-blasters?

A blast from one of the weapons rocked the mechnobot from the side. The metal thing toppled backward and smashed into another of the glass aquariums housing more of those eerie plants. My hope died.

I gaped in wonder. Some bug-like creature emerged from the shattered ruin of the turret, spreading iridescent wings. A majestic creature, with at least a foot-long wingspan. It was some wondrous dragonfly, or moth, boasting wings of all colors of the spectrum. Had it been hiding in the armored shell all along? Perhaps it had been commanding the armored shell? That was impossible. It sprang aloft, made tentative motions of flight, as if disturbed from its ancient slumber.

Without warning, another new, weird creature emerged from the ruin of the glass aquarium. Part dragon, or flying snake. An eelish lizard was as close as I could peg it. It took to the air with wings of its own—alien, freakish, of a design a stroke of majesty. The creature was much larger than the dragonfly.

The dragonfly and eel seemed to be allies, if such a word could be applied. Within hairs' breadths they flew past each other, crisscrossing without causing each other injury.

I marveled at the aerodynamics, but gazed in horror as the eel-thing swooped over our company. It settled nearby, wrapped its swordfish-like body around a skulking Skug and twisted its head off. The flower-shaped, petal-ringed mouth snatched at the mutant's spinning head and gulped it down in midair, as if such were a juicy snack. The serpentish body convulsed. The lump moved like a blob under the iridescent skin as did a python digest fresh meat. Yet the greedy, fanged-toothed mouth ignored the rest of the carcass.

Something, in the meantime, had affixed itself to Blest's left leg. He shrieked. One of those narrow, striped, petal-like leaves from the nearby glass case. It had ripped through his suit. Cursing and moaning, Blest tried to pull it off with his fingers, but the effort only made it worse.

"Agh!" he howled in anguish. "Get it off!"

Follee and I tried, but we shied back at Blest's next gruesome howl. Wren watched in horror as it curled tighter around Blest's shin. The harder he tugged, the more it clutched, to the point that he grimaced in agony.

"Don't try to rip it off," I cried.

"Easier for you to say, Rusco," Blest moaned. "It's not suctioned to your leg!"

"What the fuck is it?" Wren hissed.

"Don't know." I scuttled away. Something similar tried to latch onto my own leg. I squinted in the gloom, as quivering plants stood on root ends and leaped to attack as do aggressive leeches spring from trees in monsoon season. Something warned me not to vaporize the plants as the Skugs had done. The poor bastards were now getting slaughtered in numbers! "Quick, get away from them!"

Wren shuttled Blest hobbling along to safety, toward the smoking mechnobots.

The dragonfly swooped and slashed at the Skugs with its razor-edged wings. Skug gunfire blasted up at it, but the rays seemed to glance off its wings or be absorbed by its body as a lightning rod channels electricity.

I could not in any way figure out this scene. Perhaps nothing more terrifying than watching a primitive force unfold before your eyes. Magic and terror of the unknown rolled up in one—an alien species flying with prehistoric fervor feet above your head, doing the imaginable.

Wren was uttering a warrior's cry. She aimed a spray of death at a gang of Skugs creeping up on us from behind. I climbed the back of one of the intact mechnobots and dove into the broken window of the cabin, using it as a shelter to peg off raiders.

The bullet-proof armor saved me from becoming a charred crust. Hero Rusco to the rescue. All the while the crazy dragonfly veered around us like some colorful kite out of a nightmare. The creature slashed down on the Skugs again with its razor wings, spraying blood and guts everywhere. A trail of carnage painted the ground in a way that would make a war vet weep. Nothing could kill the insect. It wheeled around, regrouped, slaughtering Skugs right, left, and center. What did the Skugs want with us? A sick feeling came over my gut, as a grisly thought surfaced again. Suddenly it all began to make sense. I gritted my teeth.

"Die, you fucking mutants!" I peppered the approaching raiders with R4 fire, watching a bunch of them drop, their heads exploding in clouds of crimson. I kept them away from Wren and the others—for now.

Whatever it was, the dragonfly didn't like its habitat disturbed. But how had it survived? The place had floated derelict for centuries. No one had disturbed it. Why?

I watched spellbound, aghast as the dragonfly creature tucked in its wings, plunged through the throat of a Skug and emerged out his back, somewhere at the same level as the kidney. The mutant split into two pieces in a glistening spray of guts. That Skug had been skulking up the feet of my perch to get at me.

That butterfly, moth, bat, dragonfly—what the hell was it? I could only guess that whatever CEO Dezmin had done, he had delved too deep and the creatures had nuked this operation, turning it into a ghost station which nobody would touch for eons. Except maybe some desperate travelers like stupid old us. Question was, how could an obscure alien life live that long? I mean, this was some centuries ago, right? Like what were the chances? Had the plants spawned that dragonfly thing an age ago and it had gestated to life just now? Unlikely. A better question was, how had it powered that mechno?

Or even better: what had it eaten during all those years? The hapless flesh of raiders? I shuddered. Maybe it didn't need to eat? Maybe it could get its nourishment from anything? Even darkness.

I shook my head. Conjectures like this meant jack shit now. Jet Rusco had stumbled onto one of the mysteries of the universe, an archaeological goldmine, and here he was blasting everything to shit.

One of the Skugs had the sense to launch a flash bomb at the titanium base of my mechno tower. The metal hulk shook and shimmered with heat then began to topple. Red fire rose around me in the turret. "Shit!" I loosed a long wail of agony as the tower came crashing to the ground. Whump! The impact reverberated through every bone in my body, cracking my helmet, whooshing the wind out of my lungs. I crawled out of my hole, gasping, choking on the dry, tomb-like air. But it was at least breathable. Young Noss or somebody ran out, dragged me to safety behind the other mechnos. I wheezed out another gasp, looked up into a masked face with black hair behind the faceplate. "Not time to die yet," the figure croaked.

"Getting too old for this shit, Wren." The com was staticky, but still legible.

I felt myself slipping, my mind tumbling as I danced with a tribe of Skugs around an ancient fire... The Skugs who were once human. Skugs come to kill us now, saw off our heads and drink blood from our skulls.

I snapped out of my daze. I punched through my faceplate and pulled away the glass fragments. The two alien creatures buzzed about the chamber, twin horrors from another dimension. The Skugs peppered them with fire: blaster burls, ion-fire, heat sinks. This time a flare caught the eel-lizard's wing and ignited it. The creature gave a mournful hiss then tumbled out of the air like a crippled bomber, skidding to the metal grates. It flapped around like some demented squid out of water.

I winced as a bunch of white-grey effluvia gushed from its side, along with a half dozen, strange, fist-sized bulbs, as if the thing were giving birth to a premature spawn, like a phoenix reverse birthing from a worm. I almost heaved. The dragonfly seemed to go berserk at the fall of its comrade. The winged horror dove over to the mangled, sizzling husk and careened into the killer Skugs with fury. A whistling shriek issued from its nostrils and it chopped and slayed with its razor-sharp wings.

A hunched figure stepped out to study the unusual ruin. The figure ran curious eyes over the twitching carcass and the otherworldly bulbs. Follee? Was this for real? The man wasn't dead. He'd been hiding somewhere; hadn't even fired his weapon. In a trance Follee stooped to poke at the eel-like body.

What was with the sod? The fool must be in shock. "Get the hell out of there!" I called.

I saw Follee's hand flick to his suit's belt. Why? I had more important things to do than babysit the fuck. I hustled Blest along who was in a bad way with that thing wrapped around his leg. Follee lumbered after us with a crazy grin carved on his face, as if to touch a dead alien was some novelty. Loony, dumb, loser idiot.

"This place is a robotic glass menagerie of death," Wren rasped at me. "We're better off taking our chances in the ships."

I gave a grimace of defeat, seeing the chaos around us.

Follee croaked, "What about you and Blest? You can't go out there in vacuum with screwed-up suits."

"We'll use the extra ones back at the airlock."

"Think they'll be any good after all this time?"

"They'd better be." I turned to Blest and wheezed out an apology. "You were right, Blest. Bad idea coming in here."

"Thanks a fuck of a lot. Now I've got Mr. Friendly clinging to my leg."

"Could be worse. You could have Mr. Follee pawing at it. We'll get it off," I grunted at him.

"Yeah, with what, Rusco? Your handy-dandy crowbar back on Bantam that has no warp drive?"

"Shut up! Move." I shouldered him ahead with a rough hand and he gave a howl of pain as the thing gripped his leg tighter. I shoved Follee along also who'd caught up with us.

We hustled our way back through the corridors to that airlock adjoining the hangar. I smashed the glass housing the spare suits. We pulled down two black, durable sets of space gear at random and tested the breathing apparatus. The flow of cool air on my skin indicated they were operational. I gave a sigh of relief. Blest and I struggled into the sleek coveralls while Wren and Follee helped Blest into his, taking care not to get near the plant thing which seemed to ever tighten around his leg. We entered the airlock, crouched by the exit door with our guns on the ready, not knowing what to expect.

We came charging out, blasting full out. Two Skug guards went down in bloody heaps, caught by surprise. Wren and Noss ran ahead to Bantam.

I gaped at the hopelessness of it all. Another Skug vessel moved on us, its weapons trained.

"Wren, Noss! Get back."

I turned my head away as Bantam went up in a ball of flames. Wren and Noss were knocked backward, sliding down the metal runway. They picked themselves up.

Shock hit me in a blind fury. Half a shipment of Myscol and a half mil credits of ship up in smoke.

I saw Noss grab up Wren and they hurried to Alastar.

I turned to fire at the ship in the air. Blest tugged at my arm. My mouth dropped when I saw steam coming from the rear thrusters of a Warhawk parked nearby. The ship was stationed beside a Skug craft. My suspicions confirmed.

"How in the name of Jesus—"

"I'd recognize those Warhawks anywhere," said Blest. "See the eagle insignia on the left side?"

"Must have been our friends, the Skugs. Can always count on them. Mong must have put the word out to even the raiders to keep an eye out for us."

Blest groaned. "Either way, we're fucked."

A rustle came to my left. Not Skug but human. A swarthy, slant-eyed, bushy-browed face of a muscled ball-breaker peering at me. "Weapon down. We've got you tagged, Rusco. We don't want to kill you but..."

I gaped. The three black kevlar-vested figures had 'bounty hunter' written all over them. I went kamikaze, spraying fire in their midst, roaring as they ducked back under the struts of the Warhawk. I grabbed Blest, pushed Follee behind the nearest vessel, the beetle-shaped Skug craft.

Blest gave back fire at the enemy, cursing aloud, hobbling on his fucked-up leg.

Looked as if I'd underestimated Mong's obsession with getting his hands on my phaso.

"The phaso, Rusco!" one of Mong's men called out in a raspy voice from the curling smoke. "It's all we want."

I looked left and right. No options.

"You want the phaso, you fuckbitch?" I called. "Catch." I snatched at a kerchief and pulled the disc out of my pocket, careful not to let my fingers touch it while chucking it at the foremost attacker. He went to slap it away from his face. But in that split second his body mushroomed into a shimmering halo of heat and flame. The man fizzled out to nothing, as if sucked into a black hole. The phaso had done its dirty work and fell ringing to the ground. All this after shuttling its victim to a far off, dark and deadly universe or some unimaginable dimension. The nearest thug gaped, licking his lips. A section of the hangar roof caved in and fell on his head, crushing him along with the phaso.

The bounty ranger-captain crouched behind the tail of his ship and stared bug-eyed. "You're dead, Rusco! Mong will skin you alive for destroying that most precious artifact of his!"

"Tough luck," I yelled at him. "Give Mong a personal message from me that he can go fuck—"

Fire bit back at us, nicking off the metal struts of the Skug's landing gear. I cursed, ducked back under deeper cover.

We would have gotten away. All of us would have, if not for ill-fated luck.

To my left came a clink and a roar. I dropped to my knees, tagged a grotesque shape with a full head of horns. The thing sagged, snuffled like a bison then fell in a sloppy heap. I ran and kicked the energy gun from the twitching hand.

Skugs, I hated them all, hated the look of them. This mutant was no exception and still alive.

I peered ahead, seeing gunfire lancing from all angles. A regular midnight fireworks show. Follee breathed like an animated doll, still clutching his unfired R3. Blest stared in shock at our unlikely prospects. Wren and Noss scrambled to reach *Alastar* before she was blown up.

They were fast on their feet, disappearing into *Alastar's* airlock, but we were pinned down. Skugs held down the hangar. No way of reaching

Alastar without getting shredded by crossfire. Despair crept over me.

I flicked on my com, rasping, "Wren, listen to me."

"Rusco, there're too many of them. Alastar's warp is screwed—"

"Shut up and listen. Take Alastar and get the fuck out of here. Use whatever drive you have. Forget the shipment. Forget I ever got you into this mess. Sorry Wren. Get Noss to fix the problem, if he can."

"But you'll—"

"I'll make my own getaway on another ship. We'll rendezvous—somewhere—the usual place. I'll draw them away." I cut communication and dragged the fast-dying Skug before the cargo bay. Blest helped me. Maybe we'd need him to fly this thing. I didn't know what condition the mutant'd be in, in the next five minutes. "Into the ship!" I croaked. I dug through his suit pouches and snatched up a grey-red keyring, looking like a wireless hatch control.

"A Skug vessel?" Follee whined.

"Move!" I swatted him with my gun. I'd wasted one Skug. I hoped there weren't others aboard.

"Get in," I commanded the two of them. Pushing buttons on the keyring remote, I got the airlock opening. Follee scurried in to the small pressure chamber beyond. Dumb fucker. If he hadn't stopped to play peekaboo with that stupid eel, maybe we'd have had that extra minute to get to Bantam. Yeah, and maybe be blown up in the meantime. All real useful conjecture, Rusco.

I darted into the mutant craft's airlock after Blest, dragging the Skug last. He didn't look good, his tusked face a pasty white and drenched in sweat. We sealed the door and re-pressurized the chamber. Then we scrambled out the back into the cargo bay. Blest combed the periphery, hobbling on his one good leg. Nobody seemed to be around. The other Skugs who'd manned this vessel must have gotten baked back in the station.

According to the suit sensors, the air seemed breathable so we took off our helms. We shuffled to the bridge, Follee helping me drag the Skug down the hall. A bloody slime pool trailed from his bleeding wound. His breath came as a tortured rasp.

"You can fly this shitbox?" I barked at Follee.

"Y-yeah, I think so. Not so different than an A2X."

"Do it! What are you standing around waiting for?"

He scrambled to attention, flicking controls on the console while mumbling under his breath.

"We can force this mutant to show us how to run this thing," I said, "if I have to wake him from the dead and shove his teeth into the nav panel myself." I looked down at the control panel in growing disgust. Lots of green and red lights flashing amid myriad dials, more intricate than Bantam's console, packed with symbols and script incomprehensible to my eyes.

Follee got the craft moving out of the hangar. Some of the Skugs had tuned into our escape. Their ships lifted off after us.

I grimaced, uttering nasty words. Wren and Noss had *Alastar* up and running, limping along at impulse speed. Christ, their warp was still inactive. What could they do? Skugs took pursuit, three of them, and now one of Mong's Warhawks lifted into the fray. My heart dropped. I looked out onto a dead hope as the station slipped behind us, a massive grey cube with broken antennae and cannons fading in the rear viewport.

The logical course was to engage the Skug light drive and warp out of here, drive away the memories with a lot of drink and Myscol. But the memories of Wren played in my mind, and how they would haunt me to the end of time. The times she'd saved my ass and aroused my passion and caressed my body. As much as *Alastar* was doomed without light drive, I couldn't leave Wren or Noss to die.

With a roaring oath, I smashed my fist on the console aside Follee and ordered him to speed after *Alastar*. He blinked in confusion. To avoid my wrath, he set the craft chasing after her. I manned the warp if things got dicey. I shot beams of fire at whatever came out of the hangar.

An echoing boom struck our hull, high and aft. Echoing hits raked our hull. My eyes squinted at the grey panels above. Blest licked his lips, clutched the table with a white-fisted hand.

"Dodge them!" I bawled. "Follee, keep them away from Wren and Noss!"

Follee was no fighter pilot. Our shields were getting hammered. But he maneuvered with confident hands clicking the toggles and pushing sliders, guiding the Skug beetle on a tortuous course after the beleaguered Vega 6. Blest watched in white-faced horror.

Although we were *Alastar's* rearguard shield, I saw she was getting hit hard by fiery blasts. Follee hailed her on general frequency. "Noss!" He blurted out in a hoarse voice. "Do you read me? Noss!"

Noss's voice came fluting over the com, a faint-edged staticky rasp.

"About the warp...reboot the time relapse circuit. I know that ship! It must have flaked out while on course to *The Dim Zone*. The reboot will recalibrate the light drive..."

Despite Noss's maneuvering and Wren's fire, *Alastar* was taking too much damage. We looped inside each other's paths. Suddenly there was a wild swarm of enemy ships all around us. Skugs, Warhawks, green, red, yellow, blue beams flaring in all directions.

Fareon fire flashed in wild torrents. A complete soup bowl of chaos. I saw a Skug ship explode in front of our starboard viewport. Then it took out another of its kind, rolling, burning, flipping end over end to splatter shrapnel against our hull. The junk clattered like hail stones. Our heat sensors beeped out warnings as temperatures rose. A thin, robotic voice called out in some guttural tongue, which I guessed was something like, "Danger, Will Robinson, danger. Hull integrity at 30%!"

I targeted anything that moved. Another Skug vessel caught fire and exploded in a blazing ball.

Sudden triumph dawned as the light-drive trails on *Alastar* gleamed from her stern. A rainbow color blazed from her like a light highway turned to infinity. She stretched to a pancake, then was gone.

I howled in glee. "Follee, get us away—"

But my voice faltered as the cabin lights dimmed and the bridge went dark. The ship lurched. A hell of a whump hit our starboard side, knocking us tumbling end over end.

I picked up my feet, scratching my head where it had struck the console weapons' board.

Mong's warship loomed in our viewport. We yawed and rolled. I caught flares coming from the fuselage just aft of his wings. The reserve power came on—an eerie maroon light. Follee gave a hoarse shriek. Blest looked up from the place where he was sprawled.

My eyes flicked to the display. All too well did I know the spider-gripping force of the tractor beam that now drew us toward Mong's much larger vessel.

Chapter 13

I watched Follee in the pilot's chair clutching at something at his side—it's as if he had a monster itch or some nervous tic on his gonads. "You okay over there, chief?" I groaned. "You picked a hell of a time to choke your chicken."

Follee's face paled as our power drained from the main thrusters. They petered out. I felt the sudden g's of deceleration and I teetered in dismay as our ship was pulled toward the larger craft. Its big quad fareon cannon loomed, enough to blow a hole in a small planet. It'd make mincemeat of our shields. Stars slipped sideways past the glass viewport, then a massive cargo door slapped shut behind us.

We were trapped like mice in the enemy's ship.

I heard the clinking and cutting of tools at the hull's hatch. My blood turned to ice as I stared at Blest. "Christ, can't you do anything, Follee? Anything at all?"

"I don't know how to work these shitty Skug weapon controls!" he brayed.

I looked around. Panic swept over me like a bad rash. The electro shock. The explosives. Where were my usual bags of tricks?

I stumbled over to the weapons console, slamming my fist down on the panel before Follee. "Can't we blast our way out of this situation? Take over their ship?"

He stared at me as if I were a lunatic.

"Direct the shield power to the outer hull. Quick!"

Follee nodded. Nearly wagging his head off, he fumbled with the touchpads while Blest stared, green-faced, fists clenched in agony as another wave of pain rippled through his leg gripped by the alien plant. The door to the bridge door burst open in a blaze of blue fire.

I dropped to my knees, bringing my R4 up in one continuous motion. Shots emptied from the barrel. Blest choked out a gasp. He leveled death into the area behind us.

A hulking figure loomed at the doorway, weirdly immune to our fire. He held himself erect, fearlessly confident. Long leather wine-colored trenchcoat trailing with golden eagles on the sides. Wolf furs draped around his shoulders. Hair thick and black as buffalo fur trailing past the middle of his back. The man was enormous. He filled the doorway, must have been seven feet tall. I recognized him at once.

Silent despair crawled over me. A tidal wave of fear and loathing all at the same time, like no other.

The Star Lord.

I fired back at him but he ducked, seemed to flick out his hand and deflect impossibly that burst of fire and absorb it back into his body. What the hell did he have under that leather of his, hyper-kevlar? Plate armor? He wore a sick grin on his wide, sideburned face, eyes windows into nowhere. He jerked his other hand. The weapon sailed out of my grip to slap against the wall. "What the fuck?" I cried.

Staring at my empty palm, I felt a stupor enveloping me as I rolled for cover.

Blest lifted his weapon to loose hell and blast the shit out·of the intruders, for there was another figure coming up behind. Blest's fire went wide and ate into the wall, shredding it to pieces. But it was too late. Mong's techno-psi power was in motion; with a twist of a wrist, Blest's weapon seemed to wither in his hand. He gave a mournful cry. The R4 clattered to his feet. Blest blinked, shaking his head, staggering and reaching to grab it. But Mong was a step ahead, kicking it out of his grasp.

Follee was too stunned for action. He just sat there, staring like a zombie. Mong turned to him, a fatherly expression on his face, ignoring me while Blest writhed for cover on the debris-ridden floor.

Two gunman came in behind to waste Follee and the rest of us if we dared to breath too loudly.

Mong grabbed the nearest gunman's barrel and shoved it down. "Wait! I want these people alive."

Follee jerked in a weird way. Maybe it was just panic or madness taking him over. Lurching off his chair, he clutched a dark lump in his palm, the same pod he'd been fumbling with earlier. One of those damned bulbs from the space station. The thing in his hand had been birthed from the dying eel-lizard, pulsing now and shimmering with an eerie expectancy.

Follee gave a harsh laugh. "Stop, or I'll chuck this at you. I've seen what these things can do."

Mong hesitated. His lips parted and his large brown eyes stayed trained on the bulb.

The other two gunman circled us. Raising the bulb in a trembling hand,

Follee gripped his firearm in the other, as if he'd never shot a gun before.

Mong motioned. "Who is this momma's boy?"

His nearest henchman shrugged.

I lay on the floor by the debris of the destroyed door, praying for a miracle.

"Come on, boy," the dark figure said to Follee, "you don't have the nerve to shoot me, a Star Lord, do you?" His deep-throated voice echoed through the seashell-shaped bridge.

Follee faltered. The tech man was cracking. Why didn't he shoot? It was unthinkable to just stand there and threaten Mong with that bulb...and yet, Mong did not advance.

Follee hoped to bluff his way through this. Like as if something was going to hatch and attack on his command—even if it did, so what? I remembered the Myscol I'd force-fed him and I did a face palm—a fool gag to play. One that could get us all killed now.

Mong continued to stare down Follee with that avuncular look. It was a look of grave concern, one I remember all too well back on Trellian when he blew my hand off and plugged acid in the stump for kicks. The memory, burned indelibly in my brain, was one I wished to erase. Follee seemed to freeze, as if hypnotized by Mong's mesmeric stare—caught like a deer in the headlights.

"Shoot him, you idiot!" I croaked.

Follee gave his head a vigorous shake then his hand twitched as if to make a move with the bulb.

"Don't—" Mong's warning came too late.

The nearest gunman pegged Follee's nasty little bedroom surprise, blowing off some of Follee's flesh, maybe a finger or two. He sagged with a thin-mouthed squeal. The shifty-eyed gunman whipped up his gun, firing more warning shorts. He leveled blasts at me and Blest when we started to inch forward.

The shattered bulb clattered to the floor like a Humpty Dumpty egg.

I watched spellbound. It hissed, imploded, suddenly sagged inward and rippled, as if bubbling with hot lava. For Christ sakes. It then burst in a splatter of red and green pap, spraying the nearest gunmen with acid, sizzling his leathers and flesh. "What the fuck—?" cried one.

A winged cricket, or some other unnameable horror, burst out of the mash and flew around the room, buzzing and hissing above the gunmen's heads. They ducked, cursing in bewilderment. They swatted and fired at it, but it evaded their shots, hissing like an angry serpent. Without warning, it dive-bombed, burying itself in the face of the first gunman who'd fired at it. He gave a wild shriek and clawed at his face, beating at his nose until it was a pulp of blood and gore in what was left of his disintegrating face. The thing burrowed deeper into his mouth and nose like a termite.

The other gunman gave a cursing yell and rained fire into his comrade, frying both man and winged thing.

"Bloody hell," moaned Follee, staring at the crimson ruin of his palm. He stared around him from one horror to the next, then back to his maimed hand. Fumbling for his R3 which he'd dropped and lifted it to pepper Mong and crew, he gasped, but Mong uttered a hypnotic word and Follee seemed to suddenly freeze, as if beguiled by the Star Lord's impending powers.

"Shoot! What are you waiting for, you dumb fuck?" I cried.

"Try." Mong mouthed the word as if blowing a bubble to a baby. I could see the snicker of triumph curl the lip on his swarthy face. The sightless eyes penetrated into a person's soul. The man's presence was what awed one most. Terrible, unwielding, irresistible. He flicked out a hand in an almost negligent gesture. Follee suddenly flew across the room as if propelled by an invisible force. I heard a snap, then a neck bone break as Follee's back thudded hard against the panels. He slid to the floor, a straw puppet, gazing up in dumb fascination, his spinal cord snapped in two.

I closed my eyes. Now I shook my head in despair and mumbled a prayer, something I hadn't done since my youth.

The other bulb at Follee's side hadn't hatched. Though maybe such a horror could have saved our asses—if only Follee's desperate plan had worked.

Maybe we all should have died back in that Skug tomb of the space station...

Mong turned his feral gaze to me huddled under the nav console; his gunmen's wide-barreled R6s trained at me and Blest.

"I knew," Mong spoke in a sudden raspy voice, "you'd poke your meddling nose forth sooner or later, Rusco. So here we are, each with our unique purposes, though they be vastly different."

"So what's your plan, Mong? Your grand vision?"

"To conquer the habitable worlds, what else?"

"And then?"

"I'll conquer more. To achieve what no other visionary has done in the history of time. Outdo all the warlord chiefs. Even Julius Caesar, Alexander the Great, and Genghis Khan."

"I've heard of those dumb bozos. Good luck. Seems as if you didn't study your history. Look at where it got them, holes in the ground."

"You're a funny man, Rusco. But a keen sense of humor won't save your skin, especially in so disparaging a position. I should keep you around—sharpen my wits, trading jokes with you. But I feel the gods have punished you in a far crueler way." He stared off into space, as if in some trance or other. "Yes, I believe the gods have chosen a much more grievous fate."

He licked his lips and made a loud smacking sound with his mouth. Blest tried to get up and charge the nearest gunman while Mong was occupied with me. It was a brave but foolish mistake. The gunman twisted and smacked his gun barrel into Blest's head and sent him flying into the rubble.

Mong trudged over and clicked his tongue at him. "Poor fool." He shook his head in sad reflection.

Blest moaned in a sprawled heap. Clenching a fist, he shuddered as delirium took him. His eyes rolled back in their sockets.

Mong studied the flap of plant material curled up high on Blest's leg with new interest. "This creature appears to be an epiphyte of some sort, perhaps a symbiotic lifeform forming a strange and rare bond with its host." A frown graced his leonine face. "I doubt if Mr. Rusco's colleague is getting much benefit."

"It's a fucking parasite," sputtered Blest. "Get it off." He had for a moment drifted out of his delirium.

"Oh, no," chided Mong, "we mustn't interfere with Mother Nature. Such singular phenomenon are examples of a reaction to a super-charged environment."

"You fucks are a real scream," croaked Blest.

I cautioned Blest, shaking my head. "Watch it, Blest."

The gunman who'd fired on his comrade made as if to cut off the tapered leaf wrapped around Blest's shin with his knife, but Mong held him back. "Don't touch it, you fool. The thing'll likely attack you. Watch." He stepped forward, reaching in his leather pouch to bring out a silver vial. He flung a pinch of acid on the curled leaf.

The alien plasma immediately sizzled and a round blotch, like something of a dark eye, widened and glared at the two curious gunmen. Mong nodded. "We will take Mr. Blest back with us to Othwan. He'll keep Mr. Rusco company." He sighed. "An interesting creature," he mused, "but of little utility at this moment."

He sucked in an expansive breath through his nostrils and studied the charred remains of his colleague now slumped in ignominious death with some charred cricket creature half burrowed in his nostrils. "Take its comrade, Balt—the one intact in the form of a bulb beside that other corpse." He gazed at Follee and the now lifeless Skug we'd dragged in sprawled at his side. "Be vigilant in its handling. It may decide to eat you for breakfast."

Balt recoiled. "Sir?"

"The thing exhibits a rare, predatory trait. A hunter that is well worth studying. The thing demonstrates remarkable propensity to protect its habitat, like a she-wolf defending her pups."

"Are you sure?" Balt lifted his weapon.

"I'm a man of research, Balt, you know that. I study the wilderness and all its mysterious creatures, priding myself on my knowledge of predators. Only on the most evolved of creatures do I model myself."

Balt nodded, wincing. With a nervous motion, he signaled another minion who had arrived at the scene. The man fetched a glass case and scooped up the intact bulb.

Mong turned blazing eyes back to me. "A waste, Mr. Rusco." He kicked at the lifeless body of Follee. "I hear you recently disposed of my phaso in most careless a fashion. Alas, a costly error."

I struggled to bring my hoarse voice to life. "Maybe your Skug friends shouldn't have blasted my ship and brought the ceiling raining down on our heads."

"The Skugs, a foolhardy people, will be punished. But there is still the matter of my amalgo—which Captain Baer, sadly, failed to deliver. I fear he is a 'hole in the ground', to use your expression."

"Maybe, how would I know? Should I care? What are these alien gizmos to you, Mong? You're obsessed with the mere sight of them."

The Star Lord's expression grew grave. "To live and breathe air—life is an obsession, Mr. Rusco. Tell me where my amalgo is."

"It's not here," I growled at him. I needed to think, stall for time.

"That is likely true. But it does not answer my question."

I firmed my lip.

Mong gave a weary sigh. "As you wish, Mr. Rusco, we will settle this the long, hard way."

Chapter 14

After a time, Mong turned to Balt. "Give the Skugs back their ship. They can clean up this horrid mess." He gave a negligent flourish. "Tell Lord Raspin of Zuut he will get his 50k yols, minus a 30k damage fee, of course, for his stupid pyrotechnics that destroyed my phaso."

Balt stirred. "Raspin will be pissed. He delivered up Rusco. How many mutants did he lose down there? A hundred? Two?"

Mong shrugged. "Means nothing to me, Balt. Mutant flesh, what's it worth?"

"Unwise, lord—to anger such a primitive warlord—we could face a full blown rebellion against us."

"And what do I care of rebellions? I'll raise a thousand more recruits this year. These fools destroyed my phaso!" The whites of his eyes flashed red. "If Raspin decides to raise his hand against me, I'll bomb the shit out of his little hideaways like I do all dissenters. Every Skug rathole will feed the fires of my wrath. He'll learn to fear the name of *Mong* to his grave."

Balt gave a brief nod. "Very well, sir."

Mong beckoned Balt with a curled finger and strode off the bridge, his furs flapping behind him. He ducked his head under the smoking lintel. Balt grunted and motioned for the other gunmen to haul Blest and me up.

In Mong's wake, the gunmen dragged us down the hall through the melted hatch whose metal hung in shreds. We marched through the impossibly massive cargo bay then past other men garbed in armor and leather, R6 blasters strapped snug at their side. Steel chains hung from the ceiling from which I saw other ships suspended: captured vessels with similar holes in their sides. Mong stared and strode on; the man seemed to make a habit of trapping ships like flies.

We weaved our way around the impossible maze of ships, out of the cargo bay and down some more halls, with barbaric symbols and panoramas carved on the walls—3D murals of famous ship wars, epic battles, faces of Mong and his lieutenants, warriors of feral disposition in poses of combat. These were a crew of badasses, proud of their achievements. I looked over at Blest. The poor bastard wasn't responding. His head hung slack in the guard's arms. Occasionally he'd mumble an incoherent phrase, probably suffering from a concussion.

We passed a glass viewport and I caught glimpses of faraway stars, and the doomed station, a far point dwindling to nothing. My mind whirled in panic, searching for a way out of this mess. There appeared none. We were weaponless, powerless in a warlord's invincible flagship. I recalled the fareon cannon on its side that could blow holes in planets. The fiercest warlord in the galaxy strode a few feet away in front of us. Impossibly strong. Armed with weird powers. Leader of an invincible fleet of warships hell bent on dominion of all human worlds.

We passed more guards, two now on either side of a U-shaped door. Mong ordered us thrust into an interrogation room, one that looked disturbingly similar to that of stark, grimy quality back on Trellian where I'd lost my hand.

A plain table sat with three chairs to one side. One of those chairs had leather straps on the arm rests. Didn't surprise me.

They tossed Blest like a sack of potatoes on the floor where he lay dazed and groaning. I looked over at Mong with sullen contempt.

He stood facing the wall where a star map glowed with a simple console and buttons fitted below. His back was to me and gnarled, massive hands knotted behind his rippling back. "Now, Rusco, about that amalgo."

I sucked in a breath, ignoring the question.

Mong signaled and Balt struck me in the kidney, causing me to buckle over with a gasp. I lashed out with my machine hand, clipping Balt on the hip, prompting a startled yelp. He smacked me again as his cohorts pinned my arms behind my back.

"The thing was on the *Bantam*," I gasped. "Your bungling Skugs blew it to shit. You saw it yourself."

Mong motioned again to his man, Balt. They had an ingenious way of getting a hostile and unwilling participant to talk. One clamp on the left hand, another on the right foot. One man to apply a squeezing force. Balt clicked a remote which opened a drawer in the wall, withdrawing two black squarish devices as ancillary props with prongs and vises and a base not much bigger than my spider. The fastened those devices to both limbs and kicked Blest in the gut as they walked by. They forced me down into that chair. With the screws tightened, those clamps would have a regular GI Joe confessing to stealing money from his momma's purse or pranks like snitching on a big sis's sexual theatrics with Jocko the Stud while parents were away.

I babbled more, blurting out nonsense, but pretended as if I were jacked on Myscol. They weren't buying it.

"An easier question, Mr. Rusco," said Mong. "Why were you and your crew in *The Dim Zone* at that abandoned station? Seems a long way to venture out on a pleasure jaunt?"

"We were collecting my ship, Alastar. The Varwol cut out."

Mong frowned. "That seems improbable."

"Well, sorry then, for the truth. Maybe I always wanted to tour *The Dim Zone*."

Mong nodded, a sigh of amusement on his lips. "I think conventional means would be better, eh Balt?" He gestured and Balt removed the clamps and hooked his thumb around my baby finger.

Snap. My baby finger hung askew, nearly twisted off.

"Aw, fuck you," I roared. "You fucking ape, baboon, dipshit, fuckbitch bastard—"

"Hush, Mr. Rusco," chided Mong, shaking his head. "Back to my amalgo. Where? You still have to tell me."

I shook my head, uttering profanities, spitting insults.

Balt snapped another finger and I howled in pure agony.

"The amalgo!"

Mong sighed. "We will continue to break every bone in your miserable body, Mr. Rusco, until you tell us where that alien tech is. You're off to a bad start here. Remember, you're of no value to me without giving information." He inclined his head to Balt, who grabbed thumb and forefinger for another twist.

"Wait! Hoath," I yelled. "Go to Hoath."

Better to get it over with quick. I wasn't so good at enduring torture—ever since he'd blown off my hand. It kind of sticks in the memory. Cellular memory and all that.

"What about Hoath?"

"That's where you'll find your stupid toy."

The Star Lord's face twisted in interest. He rubbed his chin. "Hoath...So, it was always there, and you tricked us into believing it was elsewhere." He breathed. "I might have known. Amazing how a few broken fingers will open a mouth."

"Set the course for the Tiga system," he ordered. "And Rusco, you better not be playing games with me, unless you wish to become a paraplegic sipping pablum out of a straw."

We took a ride to Hoath on Brisis 9. Vowed I'd never visit that shithole city again—at least of my own choice. A walk down memory lane, those shabby warehouses out on the north end of town, wrapped in barbed wire, squalor and neglect. The smelly, scummy, sallow-skied excuse of a planet. The local cops, nothing more than crooked mercs, who gave our five Warhawk team a wide berth. Probably savvy of what Mong was capable of. It didn't take much to follow the holo-screen broadcasts and see what such a psycho did to uncooperative worlds that resisted his tyranny.

We transferred to one of his smaller Warhawks by shuttle while the other four escorts stayed not far out of range.

"Where exactly?" Mong demanded.

"Some old warehouse near Baer's." I grimaced, nursing my mutilated hand.

"Which one? There are many."

"Some old moldy place, maybe a mile from Baer's crib." I shrugged. "I dumped the tech in haste. Memory's a bit dim."

"No doubt. Let's sharpen it up. Tell you what, we'll visit every rusty warehouse in this section until we find it, or something jogs your memory."

"I don't know why you have such a hard on for that crap device—Ever try getting your kicks over a woman?"

Mong nodded and Balt, catching the look, biffed me in the face, sending a stream of blood down my nose. Bloody fuck!

"The amalgos are sacred, Rusco, and I'll tolerate no disrespect for them."

There was no point in antagonizing that big lout further. He was going to get his transporter anyway and he knew it. He'd tear apart this universe, killing everyone in it to get it. I was already a dead man. Soon as I gave him the location, bye-bye Rusco.

The ship circled low over a jumble of rusted factories and boarded up warehouses visible through the viewport. A swollen river flowed behind the line of industrial buildings from an era of the past.

It seemed like eons ago when Marty and I had scouted this terrain, planned that fateful heist on Baer's turf. I remembered that scumbucket warehouse, the long, rectangular shithouse with a broken, blackened brick smokestack at the one end. Couldn't miss it. Then there was the other one where I'd hidden the amalgo—a lower structure but with two smokestacks piking up instead of one. There it was. I debated not saying peep to Mong, just stalling him out in this charade, but I could see black death coming my way. When they had to circle back to the same row of warehouses and I squawked out the exact location, torrents of pain would follow.

I lifted an aching hand. "That's it."

Mong nodded. He instructed the pilot to bank.

We docked the ship in an equipment yard behind the warehouse. We stepped out onto the weed-eaten hardtop with Mong's gunmen crouched low, guns trained on the open ground, casing the joint on the odd chance there was anyone about. No one was about. I caught a faint, acrid whiff of Brisis's scummy air. My ears perked up at the purl of the river flowing alongside the service road over the sound of a gentle wind.

Brisis was as I remembered. A brittle coal-sulfur smell lingering in the air, random wreckage and rusty forklifts left to disintegrate, the sullen quiet of a violent past of rage. One of the original slum worlds. Here, only broken factories lurked, steeped in sullen disuse, abandoned dingy warehouses with a creepy vibe. The place seemed eerily deserted.

We passed only broken cement blocks and a corrugated tin watchhouse in the center of the yard, which looked, for all purposes, empty. We trudged up the back and around the side of the warehouse, our boots crunching on the gravelly asphalt.

They herded me along, pushing me in no gentle fashion when I lagged. I was desperate. My mind wandered to Wren. I had a sick feeling I'd never see her again. Glad she got away. Hoped she'd stay the fuck away from Mong.

The yellow sunlight hurt my eyes. Too much time spent in artificial light on ships and space stations.

My blood quickened. I knew once they got their grubby hands on the amalgo they'd waste me. At all costs, I must find a way out of this, throw a monkey wrench in their shit plans.

But how?—I had no weapon. Four against one. Mong and his telekinetic powers were unbeatable. I looked down at my throbbing hand, a comical pretzel of fingers that didn't work, and might never work again.

More flashbacks. Those silly dreams of how I'd wanted to be a rocket engineer as a boy. Before my parents and friends had been wiped out by warmongers storming our planet, before I'd been passed from refugee camp to camp. How I'd resolved to get myself out of that ghetto, ultimately becoming a gangster, the only way to get ahead fast. Look at where it got me. Now I was back on Brisis with a Star Lord up my ass...

"Move, Rusco."

"I have to take a piss," came my sullen growl.

"You can piss later. I want my amalgo."

"I'm going to piss my pants, if that's any concern of yours."

Balt laughed. "Go ahead. We won't much mind."

Mong looked over and cast me an impatient glare. "Go with him."

Balt took me over to the watchhouse, the smug fuck, some twenty paces away, nudging me with his rifle. Weeds and long grass blades poked up through cracks in the tarmac, caressing the tin siding. If I could fake the barbarian out, get one solid hit to the balls or some sensitive place, smash his nose, maybe I could make for that rusty fence and hop it over to the thickets.

With that limp of yours, Rusco, you'd be lucky to make it twenty feet before getting gutshot. And that hand? Good luck getting over a fence.

But they're going to kill you anyways. You want to die like a pig with lead in your brain, or die on your own terms?

Does it matter? Death is death, Mr. Rusco.

Mong seemed to be reading my thoughts, hovering around as I unzipped and heard a heavy boot fall behind me.

"Any problem here, Balt?" his deep-throated voice rasped.

"Nah, just Rusco being an old woman with a finicky bladder, slow as dogshit." He came close and smacked me on the shoulder, breathing down my neck. "That pecker of yours sawed off or something? Hurry up."

I held up a hand. I let warm spray sprinkle the tin siding, sniffed the sulfury air, maybe my last polluted breaths yet. As I zipped up, I darted eyes around the desolate yard. Death inched closer.

"Get going," Balt grumbled. They herded me up to the warehouse, then busted through a boarded up door with the ends of their rifles.

We came into a gloomy equipment bay that I remembered opened up to a loading area. The place had maybe an extra layer of dust and rat dung, cobwebs and reek of spilled oil. Several grubby rooms spread out along the wall. I could see activity here. Bootprints etched in the dust. Somebody had been storing cargo here, and then moving it from time to time. Large wooden crates, dozens of them. They lay stacked against the wall.

"Anything familiar?" grunted Mong.

"There," I lifted a mangled hand to the first room on the left. Toward a battered door, leaning on its broken hinges. They prodded me along, cursing and wrinkling their noses at the musty stench that hit them when they entered the room and thrust me forward.

"Search through that pile," I said.

They kicked through the bags and broken pieces of wood and metal strewn in a corner. From the likes of the broken machinery and tubs, at one time, I guessed, this had been some sort of meat grinding facility or canning factory.

Balt's face lit in a sick grin. The tech was still there—in that pile of junk amid the rat dung and the mice piss. A U-shaped contraption with thin, flat base and parallel plates standing waist-high on either side. Now it was covered in fly shit and rat dung, but still glowing with that dark, sullen greenish hue and emitting that disturbing low hum.

Mong practically fell to his knees in adulation of the precious artifact. "At last!" he rasped.

He held it up in his hands with reverence, lifting it to the grubby ceiling, and I could see the primitive, feral madness in his eyes.

The gunmen looked at him with odd curiosity, but I could see something of the falseness in those grins, as if they too thought their master was more than a bit off.

We came out of the warehouse and set out toward the ship, a man beside Balt carrying the prize.

A voice like a crow's caw echoed off the stone behind me. I staggered in my limp, my good right hand slapping involuntarily to my hip—for a weapon I did not have.

"Hold it, you fucks," came the voice. "Yeah, you!" The voice called louder.

Mong and his men kept walking as if deaf. I turned, saw a thin-faced security guard training his R3 at us at the edge of the watchhouse.

"I'm talking to you!" The man's rifle came up with a click.

One of Mong's men whipped out his weapon and plugged the guard in the brow. He fell in a crumpled heap.

In detached curiosity Balt swaggered over, treading over the body and grunting without a backward glance.

I licked my lips.

Mong beamed. "Mr. Rusco, you've been a good boy. You should be proud of your achievement today. I offer you my congratulations. This is history in the making."

"Yeah, seems so, and I bet that dead guy is cheering you on."

Mong sniffed. "That man will rise again, in another life. Long is the cycle of painful lessons to learn in this life and the next."

"Is it? A little rabbit once whispered in my ear that the call of the screech owl isn't to be considered an invite. I don't buy into your spiritual jabber, or your warmed-over bible shit."

Mong shrugged. "Your loss, Rusco. It means little to me."

"Yeah, well—"

"And now, for the second part of this operation."

"Let Blest go," I urged. "He's innocent in this." I braced myself for annihilation.

"Nobody is innocent in this world, Mr. Rusco. People must learn to accept the consequences for the company they keep."

I tensed, my teeth gritted for bullets to fly.

"Relax. I see you think I am about to snuff you out. No. On the contrary, I have plans for you. I reward those who bring me opportunities. I am not an ungrateful man. I am the angel of death. The ones who get in my way are blood sacrifices who are crushed under the boot of an enlightened future."

"If you say so." I let out a breath of contempt.

"Phase two may cure that defiance of yours, Rusco. If not, there is always phase three."

"Just can't wait."

Mong chuckled, a grunt at the end of an evil threat, a throaty, brooding sound, the closest I've heard to a laugh. In truth...my bluster was pure bullshit and I felt a cloying fear rising as a crest of warm bile in my throat, bursting at the seams, on the heels of a repressed scream.

Chapter 15

Back on the *Vulpin's* bridge, I looked down with wary distaste on Brisis 9, that slum planet of my nightmares as it slowly receded into the background stars. I wished the hell I'd never gone down there with Marty, my old co-partner in crime, and heisted that alien tech some months ago.

Our resident Star Lord seemed a changed man, all ebullience and bright smiles as he directed affairs from the captain's chair. Now that he had a working amalgo, why shouldn't he play captain of the universe? His despicable lieutenant Balt had dropped hints that the other amalgamator never worked, that its green glow had fizzled out long ago and the few attempts at exploration of its powers had denied him access to the alien worlds he so coveted. The box of small, disc-sized transporters given him by his erstwhile captain Baer had likewise yielded zippo, only toxic places of doom.

My hand ached like a bitch, my fingers skewed at unnatural angles. Torturer Balt had seen to a maximum of pain.

"Instruct your men on the amalgo," boomed Mong in his resonant baritone. "Any who so much as touches the device, shall be skinned alive. Is that clear?"

Lieutenant Balt nodded, grumbling an acknowledgement. He beckoned Hadruk forward, the security officer, looking a cross between a bulldog and an ape, given his stoop, glinting baboon-like eyes and the bristly hair on his cheeks and the back of his hands.

The bridge, a dim-lit place with high ceiling, black panels, viewports and holo displays, showed various state-of-the-art equipment. The setup made *Bantam* look like a toy. As Mong directed operations from his raised seat, a crew of nine of his men hunched around various consoles, operating computers and monitoring sensors.

I'd not seen hide nor hair of my shipmate Blest since we'd last journeyed to Hoath. Mong had ignored all my attempts to wrest information on his status. He assured me he was being taken care of.

Mong kept me on the bridge right next to him, like a pet hamster, flashing eyes my way every minute, along with his precious amalgamator, that blood diamond of treasures he'd forced me to uncover for him at Hoath. Mong had stationed it by the weapons console where he could keep an eye on it. The device glowed with a baleful purpose, a sickly green, its parallel plates inviting vistas into nowhere. Exactly what this fuck Mong planned to do with it was beyond me. But I'd visited one of those alien worlds some months ago via the phaso that the Skugs had destroyed—jolted there in a dangerous split of a second—to some freakish landscape with barely breathable air and desiccated bodies. I remembered the sallow dawn lit with strange clouds and aphid-like shapes crawling across the horizon. For all I knew they could have been far-off alien spacecraft—either way, I had no desire to experience such hell again.

Two long-haired men with war helms crested with eagle wings stood at attention by the U-shaped contraption, gripping R3s. Six more manned the bridge, all well-built soldiers wearing deep scowls and leather breastplates with firearms at their hips. My chances of taking any of them by surprise were zero given my crippled hand. As for Mong, well, I'd never gotten used to his intimidating size and strength. His leather and fur-clad bulk, some mythic incarnation of Genghis Khan, cast a cold shadow and exuded a magnetism that never failed to give me the creeps.

"How are our campaigns going in the frontiers?" he barked.

Balt shrugged. "They are going tolerably well, lord. We have puppet figures dancing Azron a tune in the Denista system. Funds and raw materials trickle in slowly from conquests in Bagrish. We grow our Beryllium plants there and on Phenix and other worlds in the Veglos sector. Captain Yisil is producing more warships every week on Susol's moon."

Mong gave a gruff acknowledgement. "Anything else?"

"A continued resistance on Melinar, sir. We have Guptaon under control, her sister planet. We'll blast them to compliance, if needed. But the Melinarians pose a worse threat. I propose we exercise extreme military force, move in on their planet with prejudice."

"Melinar?"

"They have cunning spies, lord. Also advanced tech which seems to have jammed our signals."

"Ingenious bastards, eh? Rebels?"

"More than that, sir. They rile up the neighboring worlds, the Vendecki, who are pooling forces with the Jaiwils on Xistris."

Mong slammed his fist on the console. "This is unacceptable, Balt. We must quell this budding rebellion and crush them all. We'll fly to the Azileus system immediately. Assemble the armada. Full speed. The kid gloves come off. No mercy."

"Very well, my lord. And the jammers?"

"I doubt they can jam an entire fleet." Balt nodded and barked orders into the com to the war captains.

"Prepare the enhanced fareon beams we received from Trellian," Mong instructed. "Have our vanguard outfitted with our most impenetrable armor. The insurgents will learn not to meddle with my plans. They'll be slaughtered. They've ignored our terms for too long and flout our authority like sharp-toothed badgers. I've offered them every reasonable alternative."

Balt grinned. "Too true."

I felt the ship lurch as we warped into Melinar with an armada that would make General Krod's historic fight against the Fineus rebel strike of 2401 look like a baby shower. Mong's ships materialized from the ethers, ships outfitted with augmented tech and now deployed. A thousand strong.

My mouth hung open. I'd never seen such a force of warships. They must have warped in from all over the galaxy.

"Look at their pitiful defenses," gloated Hadruk. "Two hundred Vendecki warships and a smattering of Melinar skyslips—That against our *millardian*? Paf."

Mong spat a wad of phlegm on the deck. "We'll overpower them with our superior firepower. Our armor is better and our new shields juiced with neutron boosters. Strike at will."

The ships sped forward to meet the defending vanguard. The first squadrons branched out in complex, crazy spiraling loops, each army trying to outflank the other. Mong's, of course, having the superior numbers. I cringed at the sight of the Melinarian forces surrounded and crushed.

Mong barked a command, "Order the left wing to bank and wipe out that Vendecki wedge."

"Signals jammed, sir," the weapons engineer cried.

"What?"

"It's bizarre. Like the last time. We were sure it was a temporary glitch—"

A Warhawk went up in flames beside us, now a smoking fireball, prey to Vendecki fire. Another disintegrated in a cindery ruin to our starboard.

Hadruk swore. "We cannot communicate with our fleet, lord! Jamming signal at 90%."

"Where's the source?" Mong bawled.

"We don't know. Conflicting reports."

Mong's face turned beet red. "Find it, you fools!"

The weapons engineer cried in vain, "Sir, they not only jam our signals, but scramble our weapon's systems. Fareons have gone haywire."

Mong blew air out of his nose.

I grinned a sour clown's grimace. Finally a world that could fight back against these mongrel war dogs. I rocked on my heels, relishing to see Mong fall, even if I were to die in the process. I stared down at my mangled hand. If I didn't get regen soon, the nerve damage would be permanent. I doubted dear old Mong was about to outfit me with another robot hand. I clenched my good right fist, the prosthetic, the robot implant, and ached to use it against his ugly face. Maybe drive it into his skull. Kill him in one last stand.

"Report."

"Weapons still jammed, sir. We've traced the sources to two small moons, Twidor and Anxaste, orbiting Melinar."

Mong hissed. "So fast? You knew this before? Why the hell didn't you say something earlier?"

"We ignored it because the signals ping-ponged back and forth, confusing our sensors." The engineer clacked keys on the pad nervously. "We thought they were malfunctioning. I now believe they have dual jammers going."

"Of course they have, you numbskull. How can they jam our signal and keep their channels open?"

"We don't know. They must have penetrated our encrypted messages. Some new phantom tech." The weapons engineer's heavy jaw clamped then quivered under the heavy boom of more strikes on the hull. Multiple enemies were encircling us. I jerked about and snatched a look through the viewport. Melinar and Vendecki craft swirled in dive formations to bomb the hell out of Mong's flagship. "If we destroy any station down there," the engineer quavered, "we destroy any chance of using such tech in our own campaigns."

"If we do not wipe out that jammer, Verlioze, we'll *lose* this fight."

"Shall we retreat, sir?" Balt suggested, his eyes narrowed pinpricks of feral intensity. Bombs erupted around us, though shields for now held.

Mong glared at him as if he were a poisonous toad. "I never retreat, Balt. Never. I win every battle I fight."

"The losses, lord, they could be catastrophic."

Mong's hand came out and grabbed the lieutenant's neck. Balt choked, clutching at Mong's wrist. It was as if the lieutenant'd swallowed a lizard. "Catastrophic, yes, Balt. But risk is inevitable and to be expected. We will win this battle, as I said. Find those damn transmitters." He threw Balt down.

"Take the ship to the nearest source," the lieutenant croaked, massaging his reddening neck.

Another wing fighter caught in flames and disintegrated in atomic ruin.

Hadruk and Verlioze muttered, then Verlioze raised his voice in a hoarse bray, "Our fleet, lord. We cannot communicate with them! Do we just leave them here? Our last command was to attack with prejudice."

Mong's face remained impassive. I looked to see his reaction. He bared his teeth, then said in a dangerously low voice, "For all your sakes, where's the exact source of those transmitters?"

The weapons master shook his head. Confusion clouded his face. "Sometimes they seem to come from Twidor's *Ghost Mare Valley*, other times from Anxaste."

"Triangulate! Send a probe in to investigate and fly back out. We can manually scan its databanks."

"We've done that before, sir—"

"Do it again!" Mong snarled. "Wait! Scrap that idea! Bring *Vulpin* into Twidor's Mare Valley. On the double!"

It was a gutsy move. We left the war front, unable to reach by signal the rest of the fleet. To Twidor we sped at full impulse, leaving the fleet behind to hold the line, or sink against the lockspring tide of resistance. In their glee at targeting Mong's gigantic front line, the defenders failed to notice *Vulpin's* absence.

Within moments, we were passing through the threadbare atmosphere of Melinar's closest moon, skimming across the surface, a grey desolation of changeless hills and valleys. The ship roared across the pitted craters and low rises of crumbled rock and layers of moon dust.

Mong advanced to study the holo readout as if oblivious to the damage his shields had sustained. I wondered what went on in that rattrap mind of his.

"There! In that thin ring of boulders! I see a weak signal pulsing on the scanners."

Hadruk, twisting about his stout, ape figure, said hoarsely, "Our probes must have missed it prior. That, or their signal is now operating at full strength and traceable. Helmsman, turn us about. Make another sweep!"

The 3D projection shifted to higher resolution. A clutch of displaced boulders rose on a low rise. A thin rod nestled inside, its tip poking above the cradle of its rocky protection.

"There's an antenna! Are our weapons up?"

"Fareons are inoperable, sir, but traditional drop bombs are active."

"Blast the transmitter to dust."

"With pleasure," Hadruk grunted.

The landscape incinerated below us and Mong stared in triumph. The ship soared upward into space. The communication static had diminished. Now only the thin garble of screams of dying men carried across the black gulfs.

"Move quickly!" Mong ordered. "To that shithole Anxaste. Since we can't reach our scouts, impulse over to Anxaste."

Vulpin's heavy–duty Vega 8 impulse engines roared under our feet, bringing us to Anxaste, another dead satellite of Melinar—the place of the second illusive triangulated signal.

Sure enough, a high-energy transmitter lay cached within the rocks on some barren moon hill.

"Fire at will," Mong bellowed.

I saw a mushroom cloud erupt on the desolate horizon. A dozen breaths tensed on the bridge. If they undermined the communication jammers, Melinar fate would be sealed...

Seconds passed and communications systems came online.

Mong's lip curled in a vindictive leer and my heart plummeted. It was clear what would happen now—another world lost to Mong's mad vision of galactic supremacy.

Orders were shouted across the com and traded across the air waves as *Vulpin* raced to the battle front.

It was as I feared, his ships, the bulk of which had survived the onslaught of the smaller forces, now united in full assault and communication, drove in a wedge, firing full on into the defending ships, which up till now had held the advantage. Mong's remaining ships, some seven hundred strong, blasted a hole through the thin line of defense. A dozen assault fighters impulsed at max speed down toward the orange globe of defenseless Melinar. The defenders, stunned by the sudden downturn in fortune, brought their ships back to meet the strike. But fareon beams prevented them from making any difference.

I winced as a new contingent of Melinar and Vendecki ships ignited and blinked out of existence. Long range fareon beams made mincemeat of the underpowered craft, firing at double strength.

Our flagship rocked to gunfire, but Mong merely grunted. He knew that his shields, electro-juiced to the max and built for disaster, could dispel any threat. The rebel leader of the resistance, a large Melinarian cylindrical cone with wide brim and tapered stern, flared, its shields at capacity. A sudden red poof lit against the backdrop of stars and the ship disintegrated in a ruin of cinders and twisted metal.

Mong's men on the bridge howled in triumph.

Mong forced me to watch that one-sided battle. The thousand ships he had assembled from lord knows where, all attacked in wide loops, evading fire or absorbing it with their electro-shielded armor, surrounding the relatively few dozen of remaining Melinarian craft. Nothing but wholesale slaughter. In his flagship *Vulpin* he oversaw the destruction, his muscled arms crossed on his barrel chest. As he barked orders to his crew, I saw a whole planet brought to its knees. Bombs fell on the cities of Jezuan and Narsilie—millions dead. Visuals showed green forests and parklands, tenements, roads, bridges, towers exploding in ruin. Suddenly I realized just why no one could defeat those armies, led by that madman. He knew his tactics, was meticulously informed, ruthless as an armored viper. No detail escaped his attention. Almost as if an inner angel whispered in his ear, or some inner sense guided him to victory, complemented with an unerring confidence in his invincibility, even when doom should be his reward, as the present glitch in detecting the jammers had demonstrated. Such sociopaths were beyond domination. Was it even possible to take down a monster as this? I knew without doubt, no one in this galaxy would have any peace or security until Mong was destroyed. Without him, his empire would crumble. His lieutenants did not have the nerve or the spark in them to keep such a bestial war machine alive—Balt, Hadruk, Verlioze, the lot. They were surely all evil, but not of the same stock as dear old Mong and his Machiavellian mind.

The hours passed and were like blows to my senses. A ghastly blur of death toll and destruction. My aching hand was but insignificant compared to the losses suffered that day.

Struggling shapes were at last brought to heel on the bridge and forced to their knees, to grovel before Mong.

Hadruk, the security officer, announced in a triumphant tone that the resistance leaders were dead or being gathered up. "We tractored the remnants of their pitiful army aboard, lord. Caught them trying to escape our net."

"What a surprise," said Mong. "Good work, Hadruk. What's their story?"

"Ambassador Zaud from the world, Melinar, meet Lord Mong, your new master," he announced tonelessly. "And here is Lady Volia who was shuttled off to preserve the civil aristocracy. Some Baroness or Countess or some fool thing—queen or slut to the dead Prince Athrean."

While Zaud bowed his head in cowed defeat, Volia crouched. She was defiant, clad in her silver and red brocade. A limber woman with fiery, hazel eyes, red-gold hair spilling from under a diamond-encrusted tiara. A silver sickle was tattooed to her brow above an elegant face. That face, pinched with anguish and tear-stained, brought a pang of sadness to my heart.

"You've killed our people, slaughtered my Prince and husband. What more do you want?"

"Oh, everything, my lady," said Mong.

"You beast. You've destroyed—"

"I know, destroyed your air defenses, knocked out your communications systems, laid waste to your beautiful planet."

She spat a gob in Mong's face. "I curse you for the end of time!" she wailed.

He wiped his cheek without haste. "You may do that if you wish, Lady Volia. Accomplishes nothing."

"We will not give up! We will never surrender to your crude domination and brutishness. Our people will fight in the streets, though they be broken. They will run guerrilla warfare in the cindered forests till the end of time. You will not last forever, Mong. Sooner or later you will fall!"

"Where are your feckless allies now, Lady Volia?" Mong jeered. "The Vendecki? Who abandoned you at first sign of bloodshed?"

She stiffened and a sullen scowl lit her strong features.

"You can resist," continued Mong, "but you will end up with buckets of blood on your hands. I urge you to speak to your surviving citizens. Advise them to surrender peacefully and these war tolls will stop. Maybe you can even spare some of the war hounds you have hiding in the hills painful deaths. We'll ferret them out eventually."

She turned away, her glistening lips and mouth working. She lashed a contemptuous glance my way, as if I were one of Mong's motley brood. I opened my mouth to protest, knowing the falseness of it and knowing any words would be useless in light of her despair. A wave of nausea and animosity blossomed in my chest, then remorse for her loss and her defenselessness. I realized the full weight of my impotence in this affair. A helplessness that shamed me, being as useless here as a trussed deer before hunters.

"I will lay bare all your secrets, Lady Volia, like your puny jammer circuits. You will learn a new meaning of the word 'invasion'." Mong's lips twisted in a sinister sneer. "Sift through the slave-prisoners, Balt. Bring me all their engineers. I want to know the secrets of this jamming technology. It may be a weapon I can use against other renegades like the Melinarians."

Balt croaked some words into the com.

Mong went on, an explosive exclamation whistling through his teeth. "I have no time to waste on defiant females. You show a spark, Volia, that your husband didn't, dead as he is in his metal coffin, but I think I will hand you over to my lieutenants. They will teach you a lesson in humility. My personal guards have been restless of late. Part of their training is to practice abstinence. Though they balk, it makes them stronger. The odd time I do throw them a bone, they light up like candles. Hadruk! See to it."

The security officer approached, nodding, grinning.

Mong flourished. "Have Lady Volia taken to solitary. She will serve as a useful adjunct in the Temple of Light on Othwan."

Volia struggled but such efforts were useless in the hands of Mong's guards. I surged forward, hurled my hard-muscled body at them, but brawny arms held me back. Fists smacked me down to the metal grates. Mong glanced my way, scoffing in passing amusement. "Rusco, you do have a chivalrous streak in you. Another weakness I must cure you of." He sighed and dismissed me and the woman without a backward glance. Now that the bloody battle had been won, the Star Lord would land his warships at the capital city of Jezuan and secure his toehold, as he had so many other worlds across the galaxy before. Of the Vendecki, I had no clue as to their fate.

"Set a course for Othwan," Mong murmured. He had moved on to other matters, the testing of his amalgamator.

Chapter 16

Vulpin dropped out of hyperdrive and I looked out upon a green planet. A wide river flowed through a peaceful valley. An ordered colony, set straight out of a page from history—Old Earth? with its Oriental peaked roofs, red and white pigments, stucco and wood, set on the lush bank of the winding river? Rice paddies loomed farther back at the base of the hills from what I could see, dotted with workers in the fields, both men and women who clutched hoes and carried baskets.

We banked low and settled on the wide tarmac at whose near end rose a complex control tower prickled with antennae. Several other Warhawks sat docked. A giant hangar loomed about a half mile away, likely harboring a fleet of warships of similar menace to *Vulpin*.

We debarked and several figures met their leader on the landing ground. All wore curious helms of bronze and robes of various ornamental dress, reds, yellows and gold. He waved them off and strode on, beckoning his henchmen to take me and others from the ship, and what looked like several selected prisoners. Balt and Hadruk personally attended to the amalgamator, handling it with utmost care, under Mong's critical, watchful eye.

My step landed lighter here than on other worlds, so I assumed Othwan to be a smaller planet than the more earth-like worlds.

We passed an armed gate and entered the colony, or whatever it might be, and strode past a towering bronze statue: of Mong with forbidding face and arms crossed on chest. We hustled down a main avenue of flawless asphalt flanked by transplanted palms and rare, ancient banyan trees then headed toward an edifice with a red-tiled roof of many dips and valleys mounted with turrets and spires.

I blinked under the warm sunlight, not used to the stark dissonance cooped up in starships and space stations, to this ordered greenery of an unexpected oasis.

What was this idyllic place? It seemed incongruous considering Mong's brutish character. Could it be a haven of his?

Mong seemed to read my mind. He turned his heavy smile of amusement on me. "Not what you expected, eh, Jet Rusco? This is the only settlement on this planet. I discovered it years ago, wild and pristine.

Perhaps you'll revise your opinion of me. Every man can have his many faces, and alter ego—mine is one of the aesthete."

I grunted and shrugged. I had no use for scum mass murderers like Mong.

Othwan then, was a private planet he had made his own. An oasis amongst the stars. Lush forest on low-domed hills of green firs mixed with ancient yellow and rust-colored banyans, sheltering a temple community nestled along the banks of a slow-moving river. Odd and surreal. A haven too bucolic for warmaster Mong.

We passed some rock-strewn gardens with fountains, trickling rivulets of water purling through a maze of exotic plants and flowers: cacti, succulents, azaleas, daffodils, bergamots, a myriad of unnameable wildflowers in yellows, reds, oranges, blues and whites. Several pagodas lurked off to the side, decorated in orange and white plaster and wood with eastern motifs patterned after Old Earth architecture. A quiet, hushed atmosphere ran among the trimmed lawns and the manicured bushes. Monkish figures, dressed in violet robes, some trimmed in brown, others in white, moved in respectful gaits. Some from building to building, carrying supplies, foodstuffs, or what looked like prayer books. All tuned to order and perfection, much like Mong's military mind. Though I struggled, given the man's barbaric proclivity, to comprehend how he had the aesthetic impulse to mastermind such a complex.

We came upon another open iron gate, straddled by large sculpted heads, mean-looking, eighteen feet tall, staring down at us from the corners of what appeared to be a grand temple. Not Mong's face, these heads, but some related figure, possibly an avatar, with a look of rapture in his big, bulging eyes.

The temple, raised on low pillars, proved an awesome sight indeed. The mere gravity of it was enough to instill awe in the casual spectator. Perhaps a hundred and twenty feet high, speckled with stained-glass windows. The massive double doors were open. Mong marched up the steps and ushered me inside, as if I were an honored guest. I blinked, stared at him in cold contempt. I inquired about Blest but he ignored me.

The peaked ceiling was eighty feet high, carved and paneled in what looked like rosewood. Pale light shone from both clear and stained-glass windows high above. White marble floors led across a great open space— an auditorium, I guessed, to a raised altar. Cushions for some audience to kneel or sit on and listen to discourse, ranged in piles to the sides. The massive stone altar near the back wall of the temple stood flanked by square columns rising high to support the peaked roof.

Mong strode in with authority. I took reluctant steps after him, that or suffer the painful jabs of his guards.

A fresh balmy air blew from artificial air circulators. Palm trees grew inside, along with other potted plants sporting green and yellow leaves. All in all, a pleasant environment, but the reek of depravity hung heavy. I could taste it, smell it, feel it in my bones, as I paused to absorb it all.

"How do you like my victory shrine?" Mong inquired with a leer.

I could only shrug. I saw men and women coming in through the door to bow before the altar, monks or nuns or some mindless worshipers.

"Don't look so surprised, Rusco. These residents are just showing their respect and allegiance to the new order—the Power of the Light of Ages. As custom dictates, they obey without question. In fact, it is customary for all visitors to bow before the great altar. I don't recall you having genuflected yet." He lanced a meaningful glance my way.

I stood there, stone-faced.

"Bow," he said in a cold voice.

I licked my lips. Coinciding with my better judgment, I gave a slight gesture of head, hating every moment of it.

"Very good, Rusco. A grudging bow is better than none at all. Acceptable at this juncture, but in need of improvement. Ritualistic prayers and acts of devotion go on here daily in assurance of a better future."

"What is that exactly?" I growled.

"A unified universe governed with strength, peace and order."

I snorted. "Under your rule."

"Of course—under who else's rule? Strength must be wielded by the most capable man."

I had to admire Mong for his supreme arrogance. Not a shred of doubt in that feverish brain of his with its vision of manifest destiny. Lunacy at its most depraved. Insatiably cruel, but a mathematical beauty lay in its simplicity. I shook my head. Shut your mind off, Rusco, you don't want to get brainwashed like these others.

I looked above and saw alabaster statues raised on high amongst the columns flanking the altar—half man, half demigod with wings spread wide. Angels of doom? Avatars of destiny? They all had R6s clutched in enlarged hands and maniacal grins carved on angel faces. I shuddered. The rifles had barrels large as bassoons.

Mong nudged me forward. I had to wipe my eyes to ensure I wasn't hallucinating.

Two glass tanks flanked the altar, each with a human male floating suspended in pale greenish liquid. Their eyes stared out from behind the glass, as if they were alive. The tanks reminded me of those I'd seen on a derelict Ring Station out in the Muridon Belt.

"What the fuck are those?" I croaked.

"Watch your language, Rusco. This is a hallowed place. Those tanks are the wave of the future. I've been collecting them, like curios and scientific curiosities. They are like nothing else in this universe! Strokes of genius from a dead race like no other. Once I discover how to harness their power, I'll become supreme ruler of these jaded worlds while you and other dissidents will go to feed a nation."

"I have no doubt about your vision, Mong, and yet, I'm glad to know I will serve the empire in some small way."

He huffed at my sarcasm and breathed in a heady sigh. "Those two tanks I discovered in a remote, abandoned mine station, a Mentera factory, if you will, on Perseus. A rare find."

"No doubt."

"The grim, vacant-eyed fellow to the left is the Lord of Evenness. He defied me at Jaro. The one on the right is Vanxus, a skulking rogue if there ever was one. The blackguard betrayed me at the battle of Brog. Now the two are sacrifices to the Temple of Light."

I moved closer to study the victims and saw Vanxus's lips move in a small curl as a fish might blow bubbles. I recoiled. The blond hair hung suspended and moved with the imperceptible currents in the pale green liquid.

"Are they alive?" I asked in morbid wonder.

"In a way, but perhaps it is better to be dead than grace the waters of the Mentera tanks."

It became clearer to me now Mong's infatuation with the alien tech. These fucks worshiped the technology of the tanks. Maybe they worshiped the whole dead race of the Mentera. I'd heard of them, even seen evidence of them aboard that Ring Station. Mong and his crew must be one of these old Mentera cults still floating around the universe in fly-infested corners…which explained his obsessive fascination with relics, memorabilia and acquisitions of amalgamators.

I stepped back to stop from reeling. He had made some ghastly shrine out of these pickled occupants in the tanks. The dazed cultists wandering about this temple worshiped them on their fancy daises near the altar like statues of Zeus, while their high priest, the mighty Mong, fed on the living within and became the all-powerful sorcerer. It made twisted sense. In a skewed, monkey-brained world. My head ached.

"Sorry to bust in on your parade, Mong, but what about my hand? Am I supposed to walk around with a bird's claw for the rest of my life? It's throbbing like a banshee. Some regen would be helpful. That or a basic medic."

He waved a palm. "Don't sweat it, Jet. A minor wound, some small inconvenience in the overall order of the things. Distractions as these are fodder for disciplining an aspiring mind. Makes a man worthier to rise above a modicum of pain. You seem a bit squeamish about pain. I had my man Balt go through a heavy rigor on his journey to lieutenant-dom. Now he could care less if his balls were on fire."

"Very good to know. I'll remember that next time I'm applying for position of lieutenant."

"Good rejoinder, Rusco. I like your quick mind. But your creeping cynicism, I don't like. Speaking of which, seems you got your other hand back. Pity I didn't blow the other one off back on Trellian. It would have had me devising more creative tortures than bent fingers to convince you to reveal the location of my amalgamator. But I have better plans for you. As much as you've sabotaged my plans, I've taken a shine to you. That last scheme you pulled off on Belisar One was a bit of genius. Oh, don't think I didn't know about your part in orchestrating poor Captain Baer's demise. I was just fucking with you earlier, drawing you out, seeing what you knew, hoping you'd let something slip about my amalgamator. And you did. I see potential in your hustling and roguish mind that may serve my ends quite well—as much as I'd like to see your hide roasted and blown into a thousand fragments. I'd take as much pleasure in personally torturing you myself."

Mong's true colors shining again. I knew his aesthetic side was too good to be true.

"I spare you this painful indignity," he went on, "because you delivered me my amalgamator." He reached over, gave Vanxus's tank a loving caress, then flashed its victim an affectionate leer. "The Mentera used these tanks to siphon out the life energy of their victims. They had some fancy apparatus for it, hoses and pipes and circuitry and other gadgets beyond our current science. I haven't figured them out yet, but I hope to soon, and use it to augment my own, above-normal strength."

I stared at Mong as if he were an instrument of lunacy. "What sick fuck would even think of doing that?"

"You judge me, Rusco," said Mong. "Remember, judgment is a dangerous thing."

"Where's Blest?" I growled at him. "You plug him in one of these tanks?"

"Blest is currently occupied, redeeming his sins. He raised firepower against me. For that he must suffer."

I winced at the implications. So, Mong's hints suggested that Blest was beyond saving.

"Move out," he commanded.

Hadruk and two others motioned me away from the altar and we trudged down a windowless corridor located behind the altar. Guards prodded me from behind. The light dimmed. I could feel Hadruk's rank breath on my neck.

I heard then a woman's scream. A man's hearty laugh followed and a heavy slap. I turned to see a flash of reddish-gold hair, a figure like Lady Volia's suddenly pushed through a half-opened, double-door in carved teak.

Mong grinned. "Perhaps if you are well-behaved, Rusco, you may experience some of my Orpheum's pleasures one day. 'Tis a novelty."

Almost at the same time I saw a figure who looked like Blest hauled into another room. I could only guess that each victim would be taken to task in the most practical way. The Temple of Light... What a fucking joke! Temple of Pain. Fane of the Loony Tune.

"Perhaps you'll want to rename your hallowed shrine to 'Temple of the Deranged'," I said.

"Deranged. Very good, Jet Rusco, perhaps that is one way of seeing it, but I hope you will be convinced otherwise." He brandished a fist. "Come! The hour is late." He beckoned with a sweep of arm, his voice resuming that cordial earnest mockery that I'd come to detest about Mong.

He drew me aside, his jaw working as if dissatisfied with my attitude toward one so great.

"You have potential, Rusco, but your sly sneaking and vindictive brooding erodes your sense of reality. You are like an old woman trying to get one up on everyone she thinks has slighted her. It's unhealthy. It has made you gaunt and unlikeable, like an old crow cawing for the cheese it cannot have. Withdraw from the past and embrace the future." He raised his hand in a righteous flourish. "'Tis a healthy, healing attitude. My program can help you on the path of your journey toward enlightenment."

"Gee, Mong, would you do that for me? And I only wanted a nice ride away from a nuthouse, on a starship, at first available convenience."

He tsked, shook his head with a screwball gleam in his eye. "Impossible, dear Rusco, I'm afraid you're quite disillusioned into hoping for such a fantasy. Once a guest's landed at Othwan, there is no going back."

I swallowed, the thought chilling me, even more than a prolonged death at the hands of this psycho, a lunatic of lunatics.

"Let us test out the amalgamator. I'm sure it will be of interest to you."

Chapter 17

Mong's men transported the amalgo to the farthest room at the end of the hall and set it in a prominent position against the back wall. It looked like a new-fangled electric radiator. Didn't seem to require any mechanical tweaking either; the flat facing plates continued to radiate their infernal green glow. The plates were wide enough to fit three men striding abreast, no more. None of the others spoke as Mong remained deathly silent for a time. He stared off into space like a Sphinx. "Ever am I searching for their lost worlds," he intoned. "I can use this device to find them. Maybe acquire more samples and apparatuses that will help me resurrect their hallowed race."

A sick feeling grew in the pit of my stomach. For what purpose and at what cost?

Mong nodded to Hadruk who withdrew a light oxygen mask from his side pack. Then he tossed it to me. "Put it on."

Mong inclined his head to Hadruk. "Give me gauze."

Hadruk handed him a roll. Friend Mong tore off a strip, spat on it and tossed it at me. "Look after that hand, Rusco."

Grumbling foul words, I wrapped the stuff around my left claw. Hadruk accelerated the process by forcing the mask's straps around the back of my head with no gentle hands.

"Hey, watch it," I warned.

"Shut up," he grunted.

"As for what lies on the other end of this warphole—" Mong shrugged, held up a palm. "It is a gift, I give you, Jet Rusco, to be first to venture to an unknown realm. The first to explore a new world, a place of vast potential, or perhaps terror and eerie surprise. A crap shoot. Perfect for a hustler like yourself."

I gave a mocking salute while managing a sick grin. "I know, Mongo, why risk your own balls when some expendable stooge can risk theirs?"

"On the contrary, Mr. Rusco, Balt will accompany you on this important mission."

"Good ole Balt? Really? Is he up to it?"

Balt stammered, licked his lips. "Sir, I'm hardly the best choice for the mission. Hadruk is much more qualified—"

"No arguments, Balt. I have thought the matter through. Are you ready?"

"I must prepare my war gear, lord—"

I put on a sour face and pushed forth. "I must freshen up and take a few things with me, like some Black Dog ale and a pint of regen—"

Mong shoved me through with a vicious snarl. I staggered between the space enclosed by the parallel plates and was gone in a second.

Harsh, strident sounds buzzed in my ears as if bees swarmed me from all directions. The eerie plates lit in full amber and an electrical surge passed through my body, hitting me square in the temple. I gave a soundless cry. A white light practically blinded me as I was sucked across gulfs, whole universes, unfathomable distances, through black holes and out the other ends.

I fell an incalculable distance then landed with a thud on a hard surface. I felt disassociated from my body as if I had been atomized. But somehow I was whole and very bewildered, staring out from googly eyes, not knowing where I was. Everything was dark here, with only the sound of the raspy air whistling through my mask. The air felt warmer than before, though edged with an acrid, dry tinge of decay. The mask only assimilated the alien air, processing the surrounding atmosphere as best as it could. My lungs pumped air, but my brain struggled to catch up with the impossible reality.

A tickle of electrical energy played at my back. Balt materialized behind me, like some amber ghost. His electrical signature jolted me forward, spiking me with a stronger current. I lurched to the laws of physics, sprawling on my hands and knees on some type of concrete floor. Balt's form shimmered back to visibility, his atoms reassembled, and I saw that he wore a mask like mine. He kicked me aside, his weapon raised, trained to kill.

We crouched there like white-eyed zombies, breathing in the sepulchral darkness, waiting for some horror to come out at us. But it did not.

We'd left Mong's temple far behind. We were in some new dimension. Behind us, the sister amalgo, companion to the one on Othwan, buzzed with a bee's hum and shone a grim amber. We were in some medium-sized room with a low ceiling, carved out of pure rock—no, it was metal of some sort. I reached out to touch it and it gave back a hollow, tinny, reverberating sound when I knocked. Only the ethereal glow of parallel plates of the transporter gave us any illumination.

We edged our way to the room's end, which was empty save for the amalgamator, perhaps fifty feet away. We passed through some U-shaped doorway with no visible door. I sensed we had moved into a vast space, like a cavern of giants, or some immeasurably large hangar. I looked down upon a frightening scene:

A vast pantheon of rectangular tanks standing upright, like old telephone booths out of Old Earth all assembled in a V-shape, or some deformed star shape. How many? The numbers were uncountable. Hundreds. Thousands? Some tanks were larger than others, and sported a dim green glow, perhaps large enough to hold some large lion or elephant or alien creature.

Balt prodded me along down the walkway that spanned the rim of the depot or hangar, whatever it was in the gloom. I discerned several aphid-shaped ships scattered amongst the masses of those tanks, much different from the Skug vessels, larger, bulkier, like praying mantises, with cruel prows and grotesque, chitinous flukes in their sides.

Christ, what was this place? Another Cyber Corp, some enormous crypt of the past?

Balt nudged me on. We wandered down a low ramp that gave access to the hangar below. I use that word loosely, for I approached the first row of tanks as a man would shamble in a sleepwalk. Ages of dust and grime coated the panes of thick glass. I wiped off a section and peered within. I saw only death. A human skeleton, stoppered, entombed, honeycombed like some primordial honeybee. The saliva in my mouth suddenly tasted dry and sour. Another victim was in no better state. A grinning skull, slumped at the bottom of a glass cage, some relic caught in time. The glass had cracked in several places, as with all of them, as if a foul liquid had drained from the glass sarcophagi ages ago.

A glow of green water radiated up ahead. Balt pushed me along with surly impatience, a hoarse rasp deep in his throat. Two neck-high tanks, stood side by side. Intact. We wiped the glass. I sprang back in horror, recoiling with a snarl on my lips. That tank contained the most repulsive creature I'd ever seen. Some jet black insect, as high as my shoulder, floating on its hind legs, suspended in some god-awful brine, light green like that back at Mong's temple. The red eyes blinked back at me with feral intensity and a claw pincer lifted to touch the glass a few inches from where I stood. As in a trance, I raised a hand and my right finger mechanically touched the same spot that the insect had touched, suspended in that horrible brine beyond the glass. The insect's lips parted and a bubble rose, as if to say something. *Peekaboo. I see you.*

No, this couldn't be happening. Like some lunatic on a funny farm, I laughed at the mad absurdity of it. Balt licked his lips. "Pipe down. So, they do exist. They didn't all die out."

"Does what exist? What didn't all die out? What the fuck are you talking about? What are these things?"

"They are the Mentera. The mutant locusts. Overlords of the galaxy."

I stared again. The hint of wings, the faintest silver on the chitinous back, glinted back at me, as if long ago over the course of its evolution those dwarfed appendages had dwindled to stubs, depriving the thing of its power of flight. "Doesn't look like that to me."

"You wouldn't understand, Rusco. Mong can tell you all about it."

"Fuck Mong," I sneered. "I'm sick of that crazy bastard and his airy hints. Let's get the fuck out of here."

"Shut up."

"We've done his scouting, god damn it. Dead humans, a bunch of tanks, and a couple of weird bugs—"

"I said, shut the fuck up!" He gripped his R6 with a white-clenched fist. I could see the sweat dripping down his bull neck. He was spooked too.

That dome far overhead, it allowed those mantis ships access to the universe. Sealed now. Perhaps that power grid, or control board, whatever the fuck controlled it at one time. I glanced at it again, to the side, with all its knobs and dials. Could it still work? If I could make a break for it, steal a ship—

Balt prodded me with his R6.

This was a graveyard, a mausoleum of death.

This depot once, was a vast factory of something, some repository of human specimens. I knew it, from what Mong had maundered on earlier about. But where in the hell was it? With no windows or portal to something for reference, it was impossible to gauge where in the cosmos we were. We could as easily be inside a small moon as on a space station, or in some madman's dream. The green glow of the weird water of the few intact tanks was the only source of light.

I noticed a cable dangling from the stopper at the top of the insect's tank. It hung to the floor, as if hinting of some feeding apparatus that Mong had described. To feed what—the Mentera? Or the trapped insect to feed something else? Why was one of their own kind imprisoned in the tank?

It was enough to make me retch.

I turned to back away and kept backing up, my entire being sickened by it all. I kept backpedaling, only to smell a more pungent odor of decay. I lifted a hand to shield my nose, nearly stumbled over a body, caught myself at the last instant.

I balked, did a double take, for in that withered face of the human figure, I thought to recognize a person of the past. I gasped. "That's Mitch! I knew him. From way back on Brisis 9 when Marty and I had heisted the amalgo. Poor fuck must have starved here."

"Yeah? Well, he's maggot food now," muttered Balt.

There, at his side, lay the crumpled black and white cap Mitch'd last worn. I remembered how he'd gripped one of those phasos and then poof, was gone, blasted into some forsaken dimension with no way to get back. The phaso ride he had taken back in Baer's warehouse must have plopped him into this complex. Never occurred to him he could get back via the amalgamator in the other room. Then again, how could anyone have known that, or even how to use it?

This amalgo was tuned to the same destination as the phaso that Mitch'd touched. However long he'd clawed his fingers bloody trying to escape this place of lunacy, only the goblins of the past knew. Mitch had no inkling the magic U-shaped amalgamator in the other room could have transported him back.

I scanned the ships that lurked in the dim peripheries among the hundreds of tanks and skeletons. Mantis-like prows with big smooth, curving hulls like monsters of the deeps waiting to pounce. Perhaps one might offer a chance of escape? Yet the beetle-like turrets with their bug eyes sent shivers down my spine.

The place was dead. Not a flutter of movement. It had lain dormant for centuries. A part of me swayed, as if suddenly ready to fall head first from a high mountain. I bolted, trying to chase that image from my brain. Tanks swept by me like phantoms.

Balt gave a sharp yelp and caught up to me and ground me to a halt, pushing the R6 in my ribs. He prodded me back toward the two intact tanks. "Where the fuck do you think you're going? Dimwit. Playing hide and seek on me in the dark? Another stupid move like that and I'll plug you full of shells. Mong will be interested in these tanks."

"He'll likely want to play grabass with old Grover back there."

"Shut up and move. Don't waste my time. Mong should've blasted you from the start. Help me haul these two tanks back over to the transporter."

I blinked as if he were speaking another language. "Your crazy master already has a couple of these."

"So? Not with bugs in them. Move!" He struck my shoulder with his rifle, causing me to wince and gasp.

He kneed me toward the nearest tank, forcing me to start pushing it from behind. I leaned my shoulder into it, groaning in agony as the glass brushed against my mangled hand. The water inside the tank sloshed. I could hear the thud of hard chitin of the insect's shell knocking against the side. It creeped the hell out of me. "Pure insanity what we're doing here."

"Quit your bellyaching." Balt snapped me again with the end of his gun. "You're such a baby. Mong can be a real hardass. Be thankful you have me. He had me lifting concrete blocks with a broken ulna."

"Bully for you. Maybe you two can suck each other's dicks as return favors."

He sprang at me with a snarl of rage, pinning my arms down on the floor with his knees, shoving the barrel of the gun in my mouthpiece. "Only reason I don't blow your fucking head off, Rusco, is Mong'd have my balls for breakfast. Consider this: 'So, Balt, why'd you waste, Rusco?'

'Because he was a dumb fuck.'

'Well, I wanted him kept alive.'

'Yeah, easier said than done—'

Bang—"

"So, consider yourself lucky. Now help me move this piece of shit out, and keep your mouth shut!"

He took an end and wiping my stretched lips, I helped him lug the bulky tank back the way we came.

We got it up the ramp and I pleaded for rest, hissing breath through my teeth through my awkward mask. I shook the pain out of my hand. Balt ignored me. We pulled it the rest of the way to the transporter room. I stepped back. I could see the trapped insect's gimlet red eyes following us in something of rabid interest, as if after so many centuries it had something finally to entertain it. The thing was definitely alive. I could feel the vibrant force of its alien existence pulsing through the glass. Whether it breathed or shat like humans I could barely guess.

Balt prodded me back to fetch the other tank. Hard work. We crouched before the amalgo, gazing at our cargoes, Balt with satisfaction, me sweating and grunting with agony. We pushed the first of those eerie tanks between the parallel plates. The thing fit between the plates with only inches to spare. A flash of light almost blinded me, a sizzle, a flare, then the tank and alien vanished. The plates resumed their familiar dull, greenish glow.

Balt grunted and jostled my shoulder, a signal to help ease the other tank through. We did. It vanished with equal alacrity. Gone. Obviously such cargoes were meant to travel through these transporter highways. Balt pushed me through next. Vertigo hit me like a hurricane. Again that tickling sensation clutched my nerve ends and the dizzying freefall marked a dark journey through some wormhole. Not a bon voyage.

I came too, blinking in exhaustion back in the room on Othwan. Balt shoved me aside as before. It was as if I'd been gone only a second. Balt, the glib fuck, appeared to suffer no side effects. A half dozen eyes raked over us as if we were lab specimens. Hands snatched at the tanks, sliding them to the safety of the nearby wall. Mong, muttering in boyish excitement, gave a sharp exclamation. He pushed by me and embraced Balt in a bear hug. "You're a hero! You'll be awarded medals for this historic salvage, Balt. Those are live specimens—real Mentera!"

"I knew you'd be pleased, lord. Hundreds more tanks are back there. Maybe no more of these live bugs that I could see. The other tanks are cracked and drained of their life-giving fluids. There was a fleet of mantis-like ships." He filled Mong in on all the gory details.

Mong stood rapt and hungrily drank in the information like a kid learning about the birds and bees. "It's a food factory!" he rasped. "A human-processing plant. We'll assemble teams to investigate. The technology is staggering. Look at the accessories on their tops. Full-fledged feeding cables with intact circuitry."

The Star Lord's fleshy lips pursed in satisfaction. Mong was in high spirits. "A gold mine out there. Enough to study for years. Enough to defeat my enemies and ensure my rule of the galaxy."

He let his gaze pass over the nearest Mentera, the black, hulking locust with red eyes, quivering antennae and sharp pincers. His jaw hung in awe. "Incredible. They are such beautiful specimens."

I gazed in horrified incomprehension. Walking, mutant grasshoppers which enslaved humans for centuries and this fuck worships them like some totem god of the past? It was beyond lunacy.

"Excuse me, but am I missing something?" I croaked. "How can a vampire that fed on countless humans be 'beautiful'?"

"They were an advanced race," he declared in a defensive voice.

Was it adoration I heard in that tone?

"They were scavengers. Soul-sucking parasites."

"So you think," Mong sneered. "But they knew how to establish their supremacy and become all powerful."

"As you intend? You're insane!" I peeled off my mask and threw it on the floor.

Mong flashed me a sadistic grin. "Perhaps, Rusco, but I prefer to think of myself as a visionary. Your opinions of me mean less than dogshit. Congratulations on your first salvage. There'll be more to come."

Chapter 18

Hadruk had two lackeys escort one broken-fingered Rusco out across the common grounds. Pagodas and prayer halls nestled amidst banyans, garden fountains and trim lawns. We waited at the stone terrace of a minor shrine for some time. I couldn't make heads or tails of the archaic deity to which it was dedicated. We traded no words and they kept me under close watch. Mong met up with us and dismissed his men. He beckoned me with a gracious hand toward the main lecture hall with its red-and-white peaked roof. I studied the man's swarthy face, wondering what went on behind that complex skull of his.

"What now?" I asked. "No new journey to locust land?"

"Since you have shown sense," Mong said, "you'll get a bonus. I invite you to attend the lectures of the 'brotherhood', the brotherhood of the future."

"Where's Blest?"

"Your comrade's being taken care of. Quit asking about him. I plan to make a better man of you. That's what you're here for…for that you should be grateful."

I snorted air through my nose. None of the residents ambling about, monks or nuns or whatever they were, seemed to have any official status here or occupation. They wore no weapons at their belts. All were plainly dressed, in smocks and robes without frills and for the most part quite ordinary. But I could tell something was wrong with them. They walked funny, like stilted starlings, and they looked out of their eye sockets sideways, as if something had been done to their brains.

"No guns?" I muttered.

"Firearms are prohibited at Othwan," Mong explained, "with the sole exception of me and my lieutenants."

"Hmph." I absorbed the information. "Not so good when a disciple goes ballistic and clips the headmaster in the forehead."

"You've a morbid imagination." .

"Well, you can thank my mother for that. Her genes."

Mong ignored the remark. "Step up the pace, Rusco. We've a big day ahead of us."

I noticed loudspeakers strung up on every building. From time to time a singsong voice would come over announcing the time of day:

"One o'clock and all is well! Residents of the Brotherhood, please proceed to Prayer Hall #1. Seva duty, as a reminder, will commence an hour earlier, since the Celebration of Silence is slated for 2100. Brothers and Sisters must observe absolute silence until 0900 tomorrow morning."

I chortled.

Mong turned me a scowling look. "I run a tight ship here, Rusco. Schedules, rules, strenuous physical activities, group sessions. Discipline invites obedience and cultivates an ordered mind."

I gauged the territory, its lush opulence, careful attention to detail. Not a grass blade out of place. Ever an escape plan brewed in my mind. We stood roughly in the middle of the grounds. The odious 'Temple of Light' sprawled behind us, about five hundred yards to the east, laced in fine mist from the river. About the same distance to the west, the elegant prayer hall of acolytes loomed. Various pagodas with peaked roofs and ornate wooden scrollwork carved on their lintels, spread across the grounds; residents or followers milled about in numbers, steadfast in their business which seemed solitary and internal, judging from the glazed-eyed faces and the bird-like mannerisms.

The background whine of cicadas dulled my senses, as did the odd hoot of a grey tree monkey, or something like it, swinging in a nearby banyan. My mind absorbed the various-colored birds and the large butterflies flitting from bush to bush. All a so-called utopia.

The common ground or lawn, with its various bushes, terraced walkways, white-walled shrines wrapped in ivy, small gardens with fountains and ornamental boulders, created no less the illusion of a peaceful community. The final, definitive touch, the small, burbling creek that bisected the oval grounds and ran down to the river. Behind us terraced paddies rose before the domed hills of Othwan.

Mong beckoned me. "Here we are, Rusco. You'll like it here." We approached the prayer hall where a group of individuals stood, conversing in hushed tones and holding books.

"Listen, Mongo, I don't want to swap bible stories with your hermits and balding pilgrims."

He touched finger to lip. "Is that what you think of them, my *meslars?*"

"What in the hell else are they?"

He nodded and snapped his fingers at one of the members of the group—a brown-skinned woman with hand drum and small, wizened, chipmunk eyes. "Kazu, come here please."

The shaven-headed lady approached, all gleaming pate with stubble bristling from her chin. The drum vanished and hands pushed together in a loose scarlet and green robe.

"Yes, lord?"

"Take Mr. Rusco to the 'inauguration' pagoda. See that he's cleaned up and outfitted properly. I'm thinking it's time he learns the Seven Serums like the other recruits. Truth, Pain, Vice, Love, Hate, Renunciation, Emptiness. How they slip off the tongue. I have a feeling, *Pain*, with a capital P, will be Rusco's bugbear."

"As you wish, lord." The *meslar* bowed. She had a glazed look of emptiness, as if juiced on something. Myscol? Some happy drug? I hated that pervasive hush about these men and women. Looked like a bunch of busy little badgers. The men probably hadn't gotten laid in a decade, if they'd ever been laid before. Judging from the look of 'Kazu', I didn't blame them.

"I think you're proud of that hair, Rusco," remarked Mong. "We'll take it off today sometime. You will wear simple clothes—an acolyte's smock, gown and garb and say goodbye to your 'streaked purple' look. Acolytes undergo strict ordinance, ritual, fasting once every ten days and every day only one meal and no food after sunset. Toughens a body up. Needless to say, no extracurricular activities among males and females, as it dilutes the power and purity of worship."

I gawped. What a bunch of baloney. "How do you expect to win over any recruits to your pagoda club under these strict rules? What if I have the hots for Kazoo?"

"It is traditional, Rusco, the way it has always been. Study the religions and sects of the past. My advice for you is to follow the ordered regimen. The penalties for disobedience are severe, as you can guess. I hope this gives you enough of an incentive to take the program seriously. I expect nothing but enthusiasm and acceptance of the teachings."

Mong turned to leave, but paused with a thoughtful look. "I'll let you in on a secret—because you gave me the amalgo, I tender you this 'gift' my master told me about years ago. It was about emptying one's mind, going deep inside and probing the deepest layers of being. I laughed at my master, disrespected his mystical message. The last laugh was on me. I tried out this 'spiritual purification' and my mind became empty, one-pointed, a powerful instrument of execution."

"Sure, Mong. I believe you. I really do."

He clapped his hands. "So, shall we? You're first up in the Medicine Wheel. Really this is a favor I'm doing you. If you do well, you'll rise high in the realm of the brotherhood."

I wagged my head in bright enthusiasm. "It's everything and more I've ever wanted to do in my life."

Mong slapped me on the back. "Excellent! Sister Kazu will brief you on the technique. Please keep your eye off her behind." His expression grew dark, and the Mong I knew returned in full force. "Do anything you want here, Rusco. But do not ridicule the teachings. My wards do not appreciate it. They can be downright nasty when due respect is not bestowed."

I gave a nod, seeing no need to goad Kazu or these other fucks into torturing me as Mong already had.

Mong strode off. Was the man confident I wouldn't get into trouble? I laughed. I heard the chanting deep in the prayer hall. Low, guttural sounds rendered in monotones in some language foreign to my ears. A shiver of unease ran through my body. The rumbling unison of the subdued figures portended evil purposes and practices, endorsed by Mong.

"This way," Kazu said, a singsong lilt to her voice. She beckoned me toward that house of chanting prayer.

I held up a hand, trying to keep my eyes off her wonderful ass. "I need to take a dump badly. Where's your crapper?"

She frowned, then nodded, pointed to the communal facilities back behind where Mong and I had come from. I took my long-legged strut there but she stalked along with me, her busy chipmunk face working hard.

I turned and leveled her a cold glare. "In private please, Kazoo."

She pinched her lips in a frown. "I'll be waiting back of the facility hall. No funny moves, Rusco, for your sake."

"As you wish, Kazoo. I'll be the embodiment of purity and chastity."

She scowled and stared at me with hard eyes.

I shuffled off down to the patio-stoned terrace bordering the communal facilities. When I was around a bend, I gave a grunt of satisfaction and tossed off my polite bearing.

I peered at my broken hand, grabbed my index finger, counted to ten, pulled hard, yanked it straight. "Motherfucker!"

I waited until the ripples of pain had subsided.

Sweating in profusion, I left the background agony behind and hissed air through my teeth. I waited a full two minutes, then yanked on the finger next to it, straightened it as best I could. Then the pinky. More waves of pain. I dug through the dense shrubbery, gritting teeth and cursing, then found some tough twigs, enough to make a crude splint so my fingers would at least not move. Some of the stems of these green leafier plants I could use as string to tie my fingers together. I smelled like grasshopper spit afterward, but it was better than suffering from chronic, crooked finger syndrome for the rest of my life.

I scanned the layout of the grounds once again. The compound's gates and six-foot-high barbed-wire fence were well-monitored. There was some ringed tower over to my left behind the prayer hall, a lookout post that likely housed sentries on the eye alert for wandering, recalcitrant acolytes. I caught a glint of movement there, rifles, binoculars? Mong had said no weapons were allowed here, but then again, what did that mean? He said his lieutenants bore arms. Maybe he wasted precious lieutenants guarding the place, gazing out on the yard, on the watch for troublemakers like me.

I doubted I'd have an easy time reconnoitering the hangar some mile or more off. Though something told me, I'd have to discover what was inside, at least use whatever was there to make my escape, like a ship, for example.

Not much I could do now, with old Kazu pacing and gnashing at the bit a few dozen yards away.

After slashing cold water on my face, I returned to the dutiful *meslar* who led me across the lawn to the chambers adjoining the prayer hall. Four *meslars* took me to a room, some sort of dressing room, and off came my ponytail and purple-dyed hair. They garbed me in orange and brown robes like the other novitiates. I ran my fingers through my crop of bristles, whistling through my teeth. Last time I had a buzz cut, I think was in my rebel years. Or perhaps when I had to jack that space trailer out in Gazeus, posing as an energy monitor or some damn thing. Could have been both. Did it matter? A blur now. Change, Rusco, change. At this point in your life, you're due for some. What's a little hair gone, compared to a broken hand and some torture?

Kazu shoved a book in my hands then flashed me a stern glance. "You are looking better, Rusco. These are the first Five of Seven Serums on the Path of Attainment. Please memorize them and adhere to the strictures."

"Says who?"

"Says Master Mong."

I scoffed at that. "Be a cold day in hell when 'Master Mong' gets me to—"

"Silence. Your opinions are of no value here. We have a 31 hour day on Othwan so you'll find our program especially strenuous. We will proceed to the inauguration. You may join the current group of acolytes."

The loudspeakers emitted a gong-like resonance, a call to attendance at the prayer hall.

We assembled in the auditorium. I saw figures from all quarters gathering, moving like robots. I could only think of moths fluttering toward a bright light. Perhaps a hundred and fifty initiates, men and women, mostly men. No children. Kazu shuttled me inside and gave me the once over while passing me to the ten monitors dressed in long white and brown robes, then she took a place at the front.

I grabbed a cushion from the side like everyone else. We sat in cross-legged silence. Plunked on our cushions facing the front in an ordered grid, with exactly two feet between each novitiate. The spaces were marked in red tape on the polished teak floor.

The prayer hall was smaller than the main Temple of Light, one third I'd say, with a proportionally high ceiling and white stuccoed walls with varnished pine beams scrolled with ornate eagles, falcons and majestic birds, none of the disturbing, warlike elements of the former temple and its lurid glass tanks. In fact, this hall stood in stark contrast, following the old Zen tradition of minimalism I'd seen on other terraformed worlds. I put on my best smile and mask of cooperation, listening to what old Kazu had to say.

"Close your eyes," she said gently over the lightly amplified speakers. "Focus your attention on the third eye point. Empty your mind. Let your spirit relax and slip into emptiness. Let your breathing come to a placid rest. Relax into a deep state of inner silence."

There were sighs and shifting of legs, noseblowing and coughs. I looked around with a crooked grin.

A stern monitor eyed me and approached with a sharp gesture. I held up a hand, nodded, squinting as if to comply.

"Focus, pilgrims, focus," Kazu said. "Mong's mission is a bright blip on your horizon. Your future is at stake. Let the inner tranquility transport you to a higher dimension."

I yawned. It was nice to get a breather after all the intensity of the past days, hunting aliens and killing Skugs, but after a while I could not help my mind from wandering. I kept wondering how I could garrotte Mong and flee this nuthouse while these fucks sat in their mental masturbation with eyes closed. If I could sneak out and make a break for it... I opened one eye. A simpleton's plan, Rusco. Monitors ranged the hall, scanning the rows of acolytes with cane whips in hand. These whips had metal-edge flails. I could see them glinting in the dim sconce light. One poor schmuck at the front had the bad luck of wavering in his seat and a flail came slashing down on his shoulders. He let out a miserable wail. The female attendant who had administered the blow grunted then raised the weapon again. The guilty aspirant sat up in rapt attention. A painful lesson on the path to enlightenment.

The others stood with backs ramrod straight, keeping silent, maintaining equanimity, if not in more rigid attention now. They pretended as if nothing had happened. A weird scenario, if you asked me. Gave me the chills. Suffice it to say I stayed quiet and played the obedient monk. I did feel a new strength come over me as if there were a concentrated force of mental power in that hundred and fifty or so gathering doing their mediation, but soon a thousand qualms plagued my brain. Where was Wren? I doubted Blest or Volia were sitting as comfy as I was.

Twice I caught myself nodding off, barely saving myself from a cane-lashing.

The session came, thankfully, to an end, though after what seemed endless hours. We filed out, many of us blinking like owls and looking very zoned out. I had to admit I did feel refreshed, more than after a good sleep. My ears buzzed with the sounds of silence. There was a peculiar alertness to my brain as if I sensed every sound around me, even the cicada huddled behind the manicured boulder. Maybe, just maybe, I needed more sleep and this tranquility was my natural state?

Or maybe Mong had some subaural brain stimulators or brainwashing devices running on half power in that Zen cult room of his? What the fuck did I know?

The sun hurt my eyes after coming out of that dim lighting inside. I sure couldn't wait to get back to prayer session for more breath-taking excitement. The romp through cricket world on amalgo transit seemed almost a letdown compared to this nail-biting adventure of sitting with pins-and-needle ankles for hours on end. That said, I would not want to trade places with Lady Volia or Blest any time soon.

Chapter 19

There was a lot more going on here than just passive monks going about their business, conducting hokey prayer habits. Activities abounded… Climb a ladder and stand straight on the top of a high pole, teetering with vertigo. Then jump from said pole that towers over the cement below. The bungee cord would catch you before you mashed your face in free fall. Anyone with a fear of heights was dead meat. I was about a six on a scale of ten, so was not as unfortunate as some. Men and women blubbered like babies, bawling their eyes out, retching their guts, white as ghosts, fighting tooth and nail not to go up that ladder and stand on that one foot square pole with the wind blustering. But Mong's enforcers shuttled them up and pushed them over if they chickened out. Somehow it shattered their nerves. Did it accomplish anything outside of breaking those individuals' spirits? I doubted it. Just another form of torture.

The activities continued. The browbeating, the physical conditioning, the brutal hand-to-hand combat. The repercussions high in cases of cowardice or failure. Also of interest, the fire walk. Walk slowly and you were doomed. The undersoles of your bare feet scorched by red hot coals. Move fast and keep an eye ahead on the target and one has a chance. Slip and fall in that 8' by 30' pit of ash and cinder, as one poor schmuck did and had to be carted away yelling with agony, the whole left side of his body charred and smoking, and you'd be sorry for not taking better care. Those who thought to dodge off the path were cane-whipped along by *meslars* on either side. Nowhere to go but forward. Mong had an endless supply of new recruits, so he didn't care if a few got damaged beyond repair or lost their minds. "It's the warrior's way," he quoted at a prayer session he had come to attend on one of the following days.

I growled under my breath. "Sick fuck."

"Anything to add, Rusco?" Mong's ears perked up with interest like those of an alert hound. "Please share with your brothers and sisters."

I remained sullen. How I'd like to put a fishhook in the mongrel's brain.

There was *Seva* too, a term he had coined from some ancient term of spiritual service. Out in the rice paddies, watering and weeding in the hot sun. One to two days a week, working for the common good.

A soothing voice rang over the loudspeaker, announcing that a time for rest had come—one hour, and that evening prayers would resume after.

A small grassy rise set back from the fire pit caught my eye. A solitary figure sat with a grass blade stuck in his teeth staring off into space. I approached and plopped myself down beside him, hoping to find out his story. He squinted up and I sighed. "I think of all the he-man exercises, the pole is the scariest of all, on account of my fear of heights. Something about plunging off into thin air. It unsettles the soul. For a spaceman I reckon that's a bad thing."

He replied in a dead voice, "This fire-walking stuff's not too bad once you've got it under your belt, or done it once or twice." He looked at me with minor curiosity, assessing me with his bushy brows lifting and a scar over his left cheek twitching under his skewed eye. Something about him tipped me off—I knew he was not like the others. A glint of deviancy showed in that skewed eye.

I stared in earnest at the bald man they hauled off from the fire. The bottom of his feet were fried, smoking. "Certainly he'd disagree."

"He didn't listen to Sister Kazu's instructions."

I laughed. "Name's Rusco."

"Zan Vulder. What brings you to Othwan?"

"Oh, a little birdie chirped in my ear, told me about this little utopia out here in nowhere-land. Mr. Mong took a big shine to me. Practically made me his bed mate since the get-go."

"You don't say?" Zan sighed. "One of those?"

"Yep, and you?"

"Master Mong's captains initiated me into the pleasure of the brotherhood quite a while back. Recruited me from Bagrish when they 'assimilated' my home planet. Broke my brother's legs, raped my sister. They told me I'd be next if I didn't join his brigade of zealots. Said I had 'all the qualities of excellent battle breeding'. 'Fine-quality soldiery'."

"That's quite a compliment. Guess we all are indebted to Master Mong for some reason or other, bringing us here together." I tipped my head at him. "Long live Master Mong."

"Yeah, long live Mong." His voice was edged with venom.

The exercises continued into the evening after the final prayers and picked up again the next day until we were a battle-weary and sleep-deprived bunch. Then we were shuttled back to the prayer hall to listen to those monotonous liturgies of Sister Kazu and her company of *meslars,* chiming off items of dogma that Mong called Teachings.

We settled upon our usual cushions and I steeled myself for the usual rubric of dogma and drawn out lectures.

"The soul and spirit are one. They must be fed by constant purity and discipline.

"The mind that is weak and the body that is impure are ones that languish and die in a state of sloth.

"We must vanquish evil. Must hear no evil or see no evil! Let us put forth our vows and learn the moral conduct of warriors! All in favor say 'Aye'."

"Aye!" came the crowd's forced, automatic response.

"Open your heart and mind to the path of wisdom as espoused by Master Mong!"

"Aye!"

"Cherish the teachings of the elder age. Let the brotherhood envelop you!"

"Aye!"

"Work hard, be humble. Serve and be faithful! Never let the darkness or the temptation of deceit enter your heart!"

"Aye!"

And so on. Maxims after maxims and mantras and affirmations with it, a vestibule of brainwashing, enough to come slopping out one's arse like diarrhea on demand. I wouldn't give a wrap of dirty baby wipes for half this stuff. Hours upon hours of slogans and half-baked spiritual syrup, until I was bug-eyed and my ears burning and wanting to shut out the world around me and put a blanket over my head and curl up and die.

Mong had a nice little setup, I'd give him that. A brain-washing crib as cute and cuddly as any unofficial, high-end think tank engineered by any autocratic government. He'd select the most promising recruits, make them lieutenants, train them to fly those nice little Warhawks out into the wild blue and blow planets to shit and nuke any suckers who didn't want to play ball with him, cede their native land and governments. People who'd die for the cause, grinning, faithful to the end to dear old Mong. How could a man demand so much loyalty? In the same way all the dictators, did it, through personal magnetism, an iron fist and classic conditioning. Genghis Khan, Nero, Stalin, Wasgon, Farseid, a hundred others, though my tired brain couldn't conjure all the mad, sick fucks throughout history who'd done it, and succeeded, for a time.

Grey skies graced the horizon that day and the following day. Zan caught my eye and approached me at the refectory as I cleaned up my tray of standard beans and rice fare. I gave him a dutiful nod of acknowledgement, tired and exhausted from the day's rigors.

"If a man were to think of getting out of this place," he hissed, "he'd think fire in the hole." He jerked his head in the direction of the prayer hall. "Some wild animals must have made a gap in the fence, been in and out eating from the garbage bins filled with all that delicious food you just chucked out."

"You're suggesting burning the joint down?"

He shrugged. "Just saying." He walked off.

I rubbed my chin.

As I was well on my way away from the refectory, Mong came sauntering by to check up on me. I gave him a salute. "All well on the battle front, general? Enjoying your little batch of insects from a new dimension?"

"You know, Rusco, we found an alien species there never before seen. Trapped in one of those tanks. To describe the creature would do it no justice. Suffice it to say it had six tentacles attached to a greyish-black bulbous body with no visible face that we could see. Even I have the good sense to stay away from it."

"A wise choice. These little nuggets of wisdom come from long experience. They leave one in the best of health."

"Too true, Jet Rusco. Now to your health? Are Kazu and her people seeing to your comfort?"

"Kazu is simply marvelous. Couldn't be better, especially my hand." I held it up, showing my makeshift splint.

Mong gave an ear to ear grin. "I'm glad of that, Rusco. I see you have used your ingenuity to accelerate your healing. Bravo. That's testament to a man of resource."

We both laughed in our own dark way.

"What do you think of our program?" Mong asked.

I drew in a slow breath. "Where to start?—unique? Rigorous? Zany? A wild ride? A jaw-dropping experience? Bullying, invasive, a blatant mind fuck?"

Mong cleared his throat. "Privation, torture, hardship, renunciation, spurning luxuries and passion is a means to an end. If a man can see with a crystal clear mind, without frivolity and excess, he will rise above the rest.

Burdened by them he will be distracted. You show promise. That's why I spared your worthless hide. I could use someone of your multi-talents. Purpose can focus a man's will, one-pointedly on a goal. Anything else may fail."

"You're a hypocrite, Mong. You indulge in these power-mongering no-nos on a daily basis. Who is it who controls vast wealth gained from war and plunder? Do you not waste worlds as if they were fly paper?"

"I need not justify anything to you. I've passed my tests. I've dug my destiny. I can do whatever the hell I want. That's why I can wield power from anywhere I stand, and why you are in the monk's robe."

"Good point," I jeered. "Just playing devil's advocate."

Though I wasn't and Mong knew it.

Just keep playing this stupid game, Rusco. Dial it back, or you're going to get yourself killed. You're still alive and if you can keep your brain intact, you may get out of this tin can in one piece. Look for a way to get out of the pickle jar and save your ass.

Mong could see the gears working in my head and gave a moody scowl. "Rusco, I'll not insult your intelligence. Most of this structure is set up as a conditioning farm, like what Pavlov did with his dogs." He held up a hand. "I know what you're thinking. A certain primitive part of the brain responds well to conditioning. The reptilian brain, the primal core of what drives us. We drill our initiates into obedience, so that when I tell them to act, they move without question. If I tell them to jump, they ask how high. I give them basic proficiency of body and mind through rigorous training then a diminishing confidence in themselves by forced association with the group and affiliation to our cause. I make them what I want of them. After training, they respond favorably to stimuli; good deeds prompt rewards, bad deeds prompt punishment. It's a formula quite tried and true; maybe even dull and monotonous, but in truth, quite effective."

"So simple that even an ant can follow it," I added.

Mong exhaled. "Study the ant, Rusco and you'll learn something. A creature that never gives up, never! Even when 90% of the hill dwellers are destroyed in a fight with a rival horde, they go on biting and gouging, protecting their eggs and territory. Such tenacity, such strength!" He lifted a hand. "If only humans could exhibit such concentrated power and competence. We humans would do well to study the insect species, Rusco. If a mere ant were the size of one of us, they would rend us limb from limb, crush us in their mandibles like soft fruit. Like these dormant Mentera, you have seen. They—"

"They lost the war."

"You are mistaken, they didn't. They are merely hibernating, biding their time in their cocoons, safe from the ravages of war before they will be resurrected. I may be the only Star Lord to resurrect them as my minions. You'll see. The Mentera left enough of their technology behind to preserve their species forever."

A cold shiver prickled my skin. I hoped to hell Mong was far off in that assertion.

He gave me an odd, faraway look—the look of the fanatic—as he strode off to confer with his prayer monitors.

Dumb bastard. I'd drive an ice-pick in his brain before this was all over.

Maybe not tomorrow though, Rusco. As illusively innocuous this place looked, it was a regular Fort Knox. Sneaking out at night from the barracks would not be an easy task…in fact, it proved downright foolhardy. One sod tried a sleepwalking gag and I recalled the dull wails and whimpering as he was caned from head to toe. He later revised his story to 'getting out for a breath of fresh air' which earned equal whaps and slaps. Night time was an obvious no-no to make a getaway; the grounds were then at their most heavily guarded.

Rotten pricks. I reflected on the week's activities with a grimace. The Seven Serums—what a bunch of shite. Seven Validations of Reality: Truth, Pain, Vice, Love, Hate, Renunciation, Emptiness. Each day of the week we'd visit one meditation, or 'Serum', centering on the profundity of existence. *"Focus your tiny brains, miniscule ones. Focus on one spirit medicine."* I couldn't take much more of this shit. Soon I'd be spewing Mong's dogma. It was time to act.

Chapter 20

Three days passed with much brooding over escape from this prison. Early in the day, I heard the roar of fifteen Warhawks buzzing overhead. They vanished in the clouds, their engines fading to oblivion. Seems as if Mong had taken a significant number of his warships with him.

Perhaps a good time to initiate an exit plan.

I contrived to scout near the fence Zan had mentioned earlier on pretext of a morning walking meditation. Sure enough, the wire mesh had been pulled back and a gap about a foot off the ground gaped for a lean man to worm his way through. Very convenient, especially for a man who had lost much weight at this fat farm. Good on you, Zan.

An easy enough diversion, Zan's scheme—torching the prayer hall. Any of the other structures in the compound would be too minor a distraction, so would sabotaging the Temple of Light be a call for suicide.

The nagging voice in the back of my head warned me about how hackneyed such a plan was, but for the life of me, I couldn't think of anything better. Hard to come up with a quality plan in a micro-controlled environment with a mangled hand.

The refectory would be teeming with its regiment of robots at midafternoon, precisely 3:30. The prayer hall would be empty, or near empty. If I could sneak out, do my deviltry and be off with none the wiser, I might be able to pull this caper off. Shamble to the hills, any hidey-hole would suffice, better than being stuck in this madhouse, captive to Kazu, the meditation-meister.

A section of the west fence was unguarded from what I could see. There'd be fewer *meslars* now as the lunch bunch tucked into their flavorless fare, seeing as it was the only meal of the day—one of Mong's innovations to make recruits more disciplined, and better fighting, loyal, iron-willed machines. Or half-starved, sleep-deprived zombies eager for scraps and any chance at betterment.

I took an early exit, chucking out my beans and rice, grimacing with distaste at the soggy paste. Didn't doubt Mong spiked the food and water here with a brainwashing compound. I snuck out to the prayer hall. The doors were always open, for keeners who wanted to get in some 'extra meditation' or some shit like that. I crept to the front altar where Kazu usually delivered her guided meditation. Long burgundy tapestries hung from ceiling to floor behind the altar, starched and stiff. A kerosene lamp burned away amidst assorted knickknacks: candles, incense, medallions commemorating Mong and other soul-stifling memorabilia. Very convenient. Minimal electric lights outfitted this place. Old school.

Snatching a glance over my shoulder, I grabbed the kerosene lamp and kindled the fabric behind the prayer altars. The wood paneling and spray-painted stucco would go up like tinder. Because the devotees loved this prayer hall so much, they'd naturally not want to see it go up in flames, so they'd come running to douse it in a bucket brigade. A perfect bit of cover I needed to get away from this funny farm.

I paused at the door long enough to see flames licking up the wall. My lips curled in a grin. In minutes this place would be a raging inferno.

I turned and ran across the green, my stumbling feet taking me to the west fence and the gap I'd scouted earlier.

I wasn't half way there when a figure came sprinting up next to me—must have seen me scurrying away. I turned, baring my metal fist for a strike, halting in midstride.

Zan hissed at me. "You actually did it, Rusco? You're crazy! Mong will skin you alive."

"You only live once. Are you in on this, or do you want to go back to playing disciple at prayer meet?"

He grinned. "Hell no. Let's blow this scene." He charged after me.

We hurried to the fence and squeezed through the hole, Zan first.

Shouts and activity drifted from behind.

I looked back to see a bright funnel of flame eating at the prayer hall's roof. Frantic figures scurried around the doomed building like beetles, waving hands and shouting commands. Fools!

We took off toward the river, abandoning the plan to strike out for the hangar.

We didn't get a hundred steps before Mong's security people were all over us like muggers in a back alley. Intercepted us from a place down the fence. Didn't take them three seconds to figure out who'd pulled the fire stunt either.

I took down the first wanker with my bare right fist, though two more came at me with truncheons. I kicked out with fury and lashed out with my metal fist, smacking down a big brown-robed figure, elbowing another in the teeth with as much Jet Rusco street fighting 101 as I could: keep your head down and keep punching. Never let up on your guard, unless absolutely necessary for a winning hit or you're going to get creamed.

Three of them surged in to smack us down, but not kill us. A significant detail. Three more lay groaning in the grass with broken bones.

Yet my fucked up left hand would not win me this fight and with no weapon I could seriously do little against these shitheads' superior numbers. My strong right hand made contact with another face and I relished the crunch of cartilage and bone. I lost track of Zan in the melee. Floundering arms and legs were all around me.

"Get him down," snuffled a robed figure. Blood dripped from his cheek and flattened nose.

Four of them overwhelmed us at last and twisted my arms behind my back, smacking me hard in the gut. Another whacked me a couple of times in the face.

"Don't damage him, Paneu. Mong'll want to have words with him when he gets back. The last time some new recruit got frisky and made a break for the river, Vorcox roughed him up good and Mong brutalized Vorcox for playing the overzealous policeman."

Five more came huffing and puffing to our side. I saw Zan pressed in the ground a few feet away. The *meslars* hauled us gasping and cursing to the refectory, now a place of operations for dealing with the fire. Armed men stood around trading bitter words and questioning *meslars* and disciples.

A half a day must have passed, maybe more. I wallowed in a blur of memories, hazy voices coming in and out of my fuzzy brain.

Through vision half blurred I saw Master Mong stride in, wearing a Star Lord's crown and nursing a lion's snarl. I guessed he'd preempted his mission just to try to save the cindered prayer hall.

One of the captors who'd taken me down jerked a thumb in my direction. "Fire boy here and his crony tried to get to the rice paddies. Likely wanted to loop back and make a break for the hangar. Figured if they'd made it past the first fence, they could double back and steal a ship."

Mong shook his head. "You never cease to amaze me, Rusco, with your juvenile antics. It almost makes no sense to me."

I looked over at Zan, crouched in a ball, cowed against the wall. Why'd I listen to that shaven-headed idiot?

"Sometimes I think there is some genius to your moves but mixed with these dumb, rat-brain schemes makes me pause. How are you even still alive? Did you actually think you'd be able to make it past a battalion of trained men not a mile away? I thought you a man of some resource, that you'd devise something more innovative?" He frowned, a heavy sigh pulling down his lips.

I shrugged. "Well, desperate times demand desperate measures, don't you think, Master Mong? You would know something of that." I grinned, spat out a chipped tooth and a thin spray of blood. I remember regurgitating some dumb line like that back on *Bantam* when Noss's hand had been chewed up.

Mong clicked his tongue. "It saddens me to think you've corrupted innocent minds into committing arson. Brother Zan is a loyal member of our Brotherhood."

I broke out in a laugh. "Brother Zan would cut your heart out and eat it if he had the chance."

Mong stared at the rebel who sat crouched, scowling with a sullen gleam in his black eyes. "Perhaps. The truth will be ironed out in time. I am confident in Zan's loyalty despite your claim."

I shrugged. "You can keep on believing your fantasies."

"I see my tests have failed," he cut in. "I expected you to try to escape—I was wondering when and how. Surely not some lackwit effort from the master of mayhem, Jet Rusco."

"Well, now that we know the truth, it's cause for celebration. Just a dumb grifter in need of Sister Kazoo's teachings."

"Get them out of my sight," he barked. "Take this wiseass to the Chamber of Redemption. Zan too."

Chapter 21

They dragged us to the Temple of Light, several doors down the hall from where Blest and Lady Volia were held prisoners. I guessed Mong kept all his subversives here.

Before a lofty iron-bound door, Zan and I slumped with armed guards on either side. Balt and Hadruk were among them.

After a time, Mong arrived in a black mood, murmuring curses through his teeth. He stared at me, as I looked up at him, sullen and red eyed.

"You disappoint me, Jet Rusco. I told you about my rules—no escape. What do you do? Try to escape." He exhaled a caustic breath. "I've been far too lenient with you. It's been an expensive mistake. I fear I've done you a karmic disservice by not counseling you properly."

I grinned in a crazy daze of unreality. What the hell was he talking about? I contemplated his words in my hazed, beaten-up condition as Balt kicked the grin off my face and a new level of pain tingled through my nerve centers.

"A few prayers first." Mong declared, beckoning us curtly into the main chamber of the Temple of Light.

Rough hands hauled Zan and I forth through marble halls, high-ceilinged as a basilica's. In truth, an odd and surreal display of opulence not generally known in these depressed times. As if I saw it for the first time, the Temple of Light's apse loomed before me. Seen from another angle, graced with dreamy, multi-colored light filtering through the stained-glass windows, to illuminate the altar screen gilded of only purest gold inset with pearls. Paintings were strewn lazily on its walls of war scenes, inspired by works of art from long ago Earth.

Before the altar, Mong muttered a few desultory words at the macabre tanks. "I must clear my mind of this fiasco. Balt, Hadruk, be my witnesses. Bow and meditate, Rusco, all of you. Pay obeisance to the old gods!" He bowed his head in silence. Minutes passed. At last, marching footsteps drifted to our ears behind us and a massive, square-shouldered man dressed in leathers and furs like Mong swept forth stiff-legged. He had a troubled frown on his flat-nosed face.

Mong tilted his head up. "What do you want? Why disturb me now?"

"It's the planet Sargon, sir. It is—"

"What of Sargon? Full report."

"Seems they took the Vendecki lead and fired by propaganda—"

"What, Freduk, what? Spit it out." Mong glared at him.

"I'm afraid, the Sargonians triumphed and managed to seize Keryutti, the capital city."

"What of our outer defenses?" Mong barked.

"Lost. Bastions crumbled."

The Star Lord's fist clenched. "I gave you full command. What of the squadron of attack ships I deployed under your leadership?"

"Repelled, sir." Freduk winced, his lip downturned. "By some unknown force field." He quivered. "More Vendecki tech. We believe they were colluding with the Melinarians."

At the mention of the name, Mong sucked in a long, slow breath. He moved toward the altar on tired feet, his boots echoing ominously on the marble. He stared at the memorabilia there for some time, the medallions, incense holders, the hallowed cups and carved, commemorative bowls, lit a candle and looked up into the ancient, dead face of his stone god lost in the mists of time. He murmured a few words then withdrew, turned his weight full around. "You idiot! May Yrzin punish you for your incompetence." He lifted a hand and in barely concealed wrath, the guilty lieutenant Freduk's eyes bulged. Blood pooled around those lids and his face shriveled, crimson with fluid.

Freduk slumped in an unruly heap. "Clean up this trash," Mong said with disgust. "Throw his body to the eagles and buzzards on the other side of the river."

Balt nodded.

Mong scowled. "If I had have been there, Balt, instead of playing policeman to Rusco's stupid high jinks, none of this would have happened."

"Agreed, lord. Give the irritant to me. I will kill him, slowly and painfully. We will be rid of this pesky canker."

Mong swelled in irritation. "No!" He gave the explosive order with impatience and walked away, waving Balt off. "Rusco will come with me. He will not get off so easily."

The Star Lord seemed to master his anger; once more he resumed the warlord in control with a face of relaxed manner, if such could be said for a psychopath like Mong.

"Come," he said to me in a curt voice, "I will show you what you could have been and what you both could have had."

I traded glances with Zan. Mong took us to the *Orpheum*, that garish chamber decorated with barbaric fountains of gold and animals carved in marble and twined around the legs of its statuary. Pearl-gray waters were stocked with rare tropical fish. Amongst the splendor, lounged a dozen diaphanous silken-clad beauties of all races. I saw Volia there, drugged out of her mind, sprawled on silken cushions with her mouth and legs open amidst tropical plants. Others, men and women, drank from golden goblets or fanned their dainty faces with exotic feathers. Mong's concubines? Or perhaps for the general use of his privileged captains?

He mustered a sly smile. "Yes, Rusco, sloe-eyed nymphs from Alphanor, geisha girls from Nashene, courtesans knowledgeable of a hundred pleasures and tricks of the trade to drive a man out of his skull. Pleasure, ecstasy beyond his dreams." He grinned, an animal grin. "And you thought I was a eunuch. Pah!" He shook his head in wonder. "Yet you have disqualified yourself from all this." He swept an arm in a grand, mocking gesture. "You have repeatedly broken rules and proven yourself unworthy. Phase 3 is now upon us. I must take necessary action."

We returned in swift order to the hall sporting the iron-bound door. Hadruk unlocked it and set it creaking inward, then he and Balt thrust Zan and me inside.

Balt held back my flailing fist while Hadruk secured Zan. This secret chamber I guessed was Mong's inner sanctum, only the privileged few got to witness it. He'd set up a mini altar here, though several degrees creepier and more sinister than that of the Temple of Light. A strange primal drumbeat echoed from deep within the candle-lit gloom.

The man seemed to have a thing for altars, pious sod he was. Here he had not only his two tanks with live Mentera on display but two extra ones, one which contained Blest, staring out of his glass cage like a deflated grouper. My jaw sagged in dismay. Likewise Zan uttered a croak of despair. I almost had to turn my head, seeing Blest like that, but my own morbid curiosity would not let me look away. His dirty blond hair floated like seaweed from his scalp; he hung suspended there like an underwater scarecrow, his legs floating a few inches off the floor, one leg turned a deep shade of yellow where the parasite still clung, his thin lips parted in a O. That blank expression, the eyes staring, his unblinking gaze all unnerved me. Slowly his pale hand lifted and a small bubble rose from his open lips. I gave a crow's squawk of panic, struggled for sanity to return to my brain and stop the dry heaves from coming. A grisly sight, yet, truth be told, the scene didn't surprise me.

Breathe, Rusco, breathe.

My gaze flickered to several ropes suspended from a beam above. Light chains too looped around that high beam and dangled from the ceiling. Some of the rope ends were frayed and bloody.

I licked my lips. Did Mong do public hangings in this dark crypt? I rejected the thought. That Zan and I were worthy of such an easy death seemed unlikely. I sucked in another breath and willed myself to be strong. How much worse could it be than a few broken fingers?

Much worse…stuffed into that spare tank.

I stared at the usual assortment of adjuncts and curios spread on Mong's altar. Candles, incense, sacred texts, mortar and pestle for grinding alchemic substances and aromatic herbs or other odiferous things to toss on a candle flame. Secured in a glass case sat the bulb that Follee had coveted and had once clutched in his trembling hand. A brown, fist-sized pod with rough skin like a coconut's. A reminder to me that Mong kept all his weirdest curios here—relics, grotesques, commemoratives—a place where he inflicted the utmost pain upon his favored residents.

The drumbeat grew louder. Without warning a big brown-faced man, looking totally stoned out of his mind, came ambling forward, tapping what looked to be a deerhide drum with his tanned palms. He sat before us wearing a trance-like grin. Bristly, black-matted hair spread from the scalp—Oriental, like Mong, of some mixed race of old Earth lineage.

Glaze-eyed, I opened my mouth to speak, but Mong spoke first. "Boauk is a faithful servant of mine, don't mind him. Listen to the drum beat, Rusco. Let it draw you toward the inner world of mystery."

"I'll get right on that," I said.

Mong chuckled and flashed me one of his hideous grins. "You jest, Mr. Rusco. But maybe you will not be joking an hour or two from now."

I motioned to the two grisly tanks of Mentera arranged at the front. "Running out of space to put your pets?"

Mong smiled. "The Mentera demand further study. As do these tanks, before I install them as permanent fixtures in the Temple of Light. I hesitate to release the creatures, knowing their diabolic tendencies. How to study them without emptying their tanks? A little conundrum that troubles even my formidable mind, so for now they will remain tucked away in this little cubbyhole."

"How fitting. I suppose we could use the company."

Mong stared at me, a sullen grin twisting his face. "I see my Redemption Chamber has not fazed you much. That shall change. Your meddling and sabotage at Othwan has set back my research a month or two."

"Sorry to hear that."

"Condolences acknowledged. Now to our program."

"Wait!" I grumbled. "I still don't get why these bugs are in their own tanks. Didn't you say they fed on humans?"

"I did." Mong sighed. "These specimens were likely criminals, punished to serve as a type of cannibalistic nourishment for their fellow locusts. Sacrifices—given as sluts to the state, so to speak—not peculiar, if one studies history. The irony is, these prisoners have outlived their overlords, cruel jailors they were."

My skin prickled. Not unlike others I knew.

Mong motioned. "Blest, as you can see, is cooling his heels in one of the feeding vessels."

I nodded. "I imagine the waters are quite chill there. So, Blest is dead. Does it give you a particular thrill?"

"On the contrary, Blest will return to the land of the living soon, as shall you, to continue the rigors of my discipline. Blest's penance is not yet up."

A cold ball of fear knotted my gut. "Death is death, Mong. Why mince words?"

Mong flashed me an enigmatic glance. "You don't believe in the other worlds, do you, Jet? The life after death?"

I snorted. "Do you?"

"It is not for me to preach. I know the truth. Whereas you do not."

I gave a grunt of exasperation. "This ancient religion you market to your stooges and that you model your 'learned' teachings on does little to convince me of anything. Nor is your unreal world of drugged up cultists and yes-men you've recruited to fly your warships and carry out your dirty work, credible."

"Is that what you conclude?" Mong inquired with amusement in his eyes. "How's this then?" He clenched his fist. The walls started to shake. He closed his eyes. A rumbling as fierce as any earthquake grew. The tanks rocked, their glass panels jiggled, waters sloshed and Zan started to whimper and whisper prayers in all the languages he knew. My eyes darted about in instinctive panic. Did the man have control over the elements?

"Does that interlude not convince you of its reality?"

"I do not understand any of these voodoo tricks of yours."

"Not voodoo, Jet Rusco. Science and physics. Intelligence and power mixed as one. I am the first of the true augmented humans." He saw my skeptical, grimacing look and smiled. "These circuits I've implanted amplify my telekinetic powers. I've had many engineers working on the ins and outs of the problem for some time."

"An augmented arm then."

"Yes, Jet Rusco."

He pulled back the brown leather on his right arm and exposed bare skin. He peeled back a flap. I saw dense circuitry there that went up and probably past his elbow.

"As well as being left-handed, I have ESP and psi power. I am considered demonic and a warlock by my own people. My mentors recognized my potential from an early age on my home planet, Vasgon. Some of them worshiped me, others persecuted me. I had to slay most of those who became too ambitious and tried to use me for their own ends. Their mistake. I had the augmentations custom-built to my needs." He raised his augmented hand, flexed it, and I heard a clicking from within. "You marvel?" asked Mong.

I gave a curt shrug.

Mong closed his eyes. Flicking out his finger, he sizzled a small hole in the far wall. Black smoke billowed out from the indentation.

"A nice parlor trick."

"It's more than a trick, Jet Rusco. I see you have a machine hand too. But much cheaper than mine."

"We all don't have access to unlimited funds." I stared at his flexing hand, feeling a wave of nausea as he made to demonstrate more.

"I think it's time to see how you fare in the lower realms, Rusco. Prepare for an awakening."

Quicker than a snake, he smacked the palm of his hand into my solar plexus in sync with the next boom of the drum. I felt a tingling queasiness in that flat fleshy part of my gut below sternum and centered between my rib cages. It sent an avalanche of pain through my nerve ends—taking every breath out of me. Something else with it—my tenuous link with reality. My waking state world disintegrated as I was thrust into an altered consciousness.

Chapter 22

I could only vaguely discern the past privilege of having a body, gasping, sweating, feeling the pain of what it was like once to be human. It made Myscol seem like a kindergarten field trip.

Visions swam before my eyes. Souls of the dead. My dead mother in her shroud. The guy I killed with an ice pick back in that bar out in Brefus on a chop job. The dozens of others who had perished by my hand. All crawling around my bug-infested skull, floating out of mists of nightmare. All the close scrapes in every hole and seedy dive. My hand exploding into bloody bits. The hundred climaxes with nameless flings on the road. The infinite light years travelled through the star highways—the restless spirit that followed the body of Jet Rusco. All peaking in one final climax. Then nothing.

Blackness. No body. Jet Rusco, effectively dead.

But a vestige of the old Jet Rusco still remained, drifting soundlessly in some freakish ether on the gulfs of time.

Somewhere I was still alive, like being in an obscene tank perhaps, but not connected to anything, or any reality. I was everywhere at once, but nowhere at once, and it scared the living bejesus out of me. I couldn't get out. I couldn't flee anywhere. Only the basic truth of existence was laid bare before my mind's eye.

Cold…empty…space.

For how long I floated in that caustic vapor, a dead, spiritless zombie, I do not know. I could have floated there for a million years. What meaning does time have in such bodiless realms? A human thought, some mere idea, or figment of imagination, as insignificant as a grain of sand or a single atom, floating in space and time which might become a thought bubble of tomorrow.

Maybe only a split of a second was I in that realm. The mind can be a funny thing. The conscious reality that we cling to in this waking life is tenuous, that stuff we take for granted in our pitiful drop-in-the-bucket existences. The merry-go-round soup bowl we live in.

I'd never really understood it so clearly until now. I could still not describe it, since it was so abstract and timelessly alien as time itself—and so frightening. The expanse so enormous that it brought to light in chilling clarity how puny the individual awareness truly is.

In a blur, I came back.

"Wha—"

"Easy, Jet Rusco."

I came back into my body, sucking in a rasping breath. Mong sat before me, grinning at me like a grim reaper. "How did you like your little ride?"

"What the—fuck are you?"

"I am the angel of death."

"You're a psycho-demon."

"I was already well-versed in the forbidden arts before you were sucking on your mamma's teats." Mong's jaw worked in satisfaction. He blew air through his nostrils. "I had hopes for you. But it's time for you to die. Maybe then you'll understand the truth of it all." He nodded to Balt and had him plunk me on my ass and hold me steady.

He stripped off my monk's robe to the waist. With my hands lashed behind my back, he stepped behind me, brandishing a glinting bowie knife. Without preamble, he cut deep into the muscles of my back.

I howled with pure agony. He took no notice of my squeals. He merely threaded leather cord into my slit flesh and looped the strips round my chest, tossing their ends up over the high beams above. As an afterthought, he wound my ripped robe around my back to contain the flesh and blood before he pulled me up like a stuck calf with his massive strength.

Regrettably I came to know the reason for those ropes now hanging in front of his obscene tanks.

Dangling and twirling like a slaughtered buck, I gasped and gurgled. How my flesh could withstand the pressure, I did not know. Perhaps a testament to Mong's setting of knot and cord, looping rawhide around my chest to take off some of the pressure.

He stared at me in a mode of abstract curiosity, as an ever inquisitive scientist would who wonders how his lab experiment is faring. Not with eyes of sympathy, but of detached interest. How long could Jet Rusco handle the pain? How long before Jet Rusco wailed, shit his pants, cracked, gibbered like a lunatic, convulsed, cried? Most curious of all was Mong in seeing where my edges lay, the thresholds of reason before the other world of lunacy and death.

"Surrender to pain, Jet Rusco," he murmured. "'Tis the only way to survive. Fighting will only get you deeper in the mire."

"F-Fuck you, you shit fucking bastard sadist," I spat out between my gritted teeth, the pain rising to indescribable levels. I closed my eyes. Utter agony had my eyes rolling backward in their sockets like a crazed yogi, hoping that a split second's death would release me from this flesh-tearing, mind-numbing pain.

But death would not take me. Mong knew it as he knew his brutish handiwork and he was master of torture.

That figure of doom withdrew from my flickering, darkening vision, but my sense of reason knew a monster was still nearby. Next came Zan's turn, the recruit who had shriveled to a husk, shrunken to a worm in some crab shell of fear. He thrashed and whimpered but there was no getting away from Mong's bestial justice that would envelop Zan in seconds. In less than five minutes, we were like two stuck hogs twirling slowly and gently from our fishhook, rawhide lariats in Mong's special house of horrors.

Through pain-streaked eyes I could make out the clear glass tanks below us. The trapped insects inside looked like black-tarred puppets, much different from this vantage: toy specimens out of a cartoon lab. So did Blest's blond-matted head appear like a comical jack-o-lantern as he floated in his pale brine a dozen or so yards away.

Mong loosed a moody sigh. "Let me tell you the story of my mentor, Rusco. He was Zastras, a cruel man and practical man, with many innovations. We had a particularly grueling time one fine day in late summer. I remember how he strung five initiates up, one by one, dangling from rawhide straps like yours from the stout branches of certain cypress trees.

"I was one of them. A time like no other—brimstone and fire stretched across a limitless fire plain; pain and pleasure mixed as one in a long silent continuum. Suspended over the fire one minute, then dunked in ice-cold water the next. Some of us he dunked in pools of fire weed; others, he incited flesh-nibbling fish to bite at our toes.

"You can see I am much less imaginative than Zastras. I saw men with ankles bared to the bone. Zastras was a dark humorist of his time, assuring that his victim would live, that the skin would grow back. Strung up there like beasts, we would believe anything.

"Oh, Zastras was a funny man! One of the old guard. There will never be another like him, rest his cursed, black-hearted soul. Lucky I have not so macabre an imagination, Jet Rusco. Still, you will beg me to stop, you too,

Zan. Both of you will beg, and I will smile and watch you squirm like maggots."

Mong burned loathsome incenses, clouds of sickly sweet vapors, rank as mushrooms from some jungle hell, and his doped up drummer beat those skins with ever fiercer force and wilder intent while the Star Lord stood by, nodding with much toe-tapping and finger-snapping as the fumes of myrrh and absinthe, cinnamon and sage struck my nostrils in a vague fury of madness during my time of torture.

Cold water dripped on my brow now from a tap he had installed high above. He lit a crackling fire underneath my toes. Both sensations were eerily approaching the threshold of pleasure now. One counterpoint to the edges of sensory overload of the other. Reaching such places, he tapped new regions that the pain-pleasure sensors could not reach. All the while his mellifluous voice swirled in my hazed brain, spewing out dime-store philosophies, cheap, preachy aphorisms, endless lessons, patronizing, hackneyed teachings, moralizations, sermons, which hovered on the edge of my consciousness.

Every sin I'd committed roared back to me in full technicolor during those moments of pain. I screamed them aloud in a hoarse voice, as did Zan, who was half dead while Mong nodded, explaining in quiet tones that this was perfectly normal.

He gave a snorting sigh and rubbed his temples in thought. "I will leave you two for some time. But I will return to record your progress. My interest waxes high in this affair. I want you to reflect on a basic point. What drives you? What is your purpose in this universe? To what end will you go to fulfill your lives? Men and women have pondered these basic questions since the beginning of time, when we rose from the lower species and became masters of the planets. Still, we have no more clue of an answer to these questions than when we rutted in primitive caves as common beasts. Questions perhaps much too abstract, Jet Rusco, considering the direness of your current situation. At a base level, you'd be thinking, when do I get cut down from here? When do I take some regen or narcotic to dull the heart-ripping pain? But life is pain, Jet Rusco and Zan Vulder. When do we ever take time to contemplate these grand questions? Maybe in our darkest dreams and most intimate moments of pain. I leave you with these questions."

Mong's words echoed in my beleaguered brain. The pain had gone far beyond any sane man's threshold and yet we hung there like freshly slaughtered deer, our bodies numb. I saw a giant man-insect in the form of Mong leave us in that godless torture chamber, a place of windless darkness that had no windows showing vistas to skies or stars. My vision blurred and before I lost consciousness, I cursed Mong and all his breed of *meslars* and monkey-guards to eternity, cursed them to suffer the worst hell that this universe could offer.

Chapter 23

Light years later I remember strong hands prodding my body and testing me to see if I were still alive. Those hands stopped my slow twirl around magnetic north. A fatherly figure with compassion in his eyes peered into mine while capable hands lifted me from my swinging perch and unlashed the hated leather from my pierced back. Those same hands cradled me as if I were a baby, popped off the top of the nearby empty tank and let me fall into the chill green water with a plunk. Struck dumb, I floated there for some time, unable to move my arms hardly an inch, and my body a wall of stiff rubber while an unfathomable pain racked the mutilated flesh of my back. Those hands pushed my head gently under the pale green water while I choked, struggling weakly, like some limp shrimp beached on a lonely shore. My lungs filled with water. Muscles spasmed as all muscles do when faced with perilous conditions, or in my case, death. My legs and weakened arms thrashed, struggling to raise my head above water and gulp life-giving air. But the arms of that impossibly tall figure held me firm and with his fatherly strength and ever compassionate sense, drowned his deformed child with no future.

Twice I died on that day. Jet Rusco, twice deceased.

I hung there suspended like a jellyfish, or some unlucky crustacean in the sinister water. It was eerie, but magical. The numbing pain that had once burned my body like a firebrand subsided to a dull ache, then to a warm tingle, some soothing balm of long-lost techno-science. A background elixir of warmth and massage. I was on a blessed Myscol trip!—to the far stars!

My eyes flickered open. I looked out upon a dim panorama of opaque filminess, blurred shapes, distorted distances, much different from when I came in. Through eyes not my own, it appeared a grainy world out there. The Star Lord stood idly by as he watched me with detached interest, as a father does his child caught with his hand in the cookie jar, as if nothing could be more natural than watching a child drowning in alien brine.

The water on my lips tasted terrible, salty and fermented, a peculiar rancidity, impossible to quantify. I saw my arms float up. My hands looked as if they had starfish-like fingers. That's because they were broken. The splint had come off, the wrappings peeled off long ago. My fingers were not as crooked as they'd been on entering the tank. Knob-knuckled, yes, like some old codger with severe arthritis. But remarkably whole. I could move them, barely. The water seemed to act as a paralysis agent, making my nerves sluggish and unresponsive. But I could think, and the mind of old JR was as active as before.

What to think? Well, a million things. Dwell on the past. Be stuck in a cage of the mind forever. Remember those medicine teachers of Mong's somewhere back in the pagoda babbling on about the endless chatter of mind when one first sits down to meditate? I was a drowned man floating, but alive. A punishment worse than death.

All sorts of random items flitted across the landscape of my mind as I stared out from behind the glass.

What were these plant tendrils wrapped so tenaciously about Blest's leg? What was that bulb that hatched the flying cricket? The thing that killed the Skugs and Mong's mercs.

The alien plants must have given birth to the flying things—the dragonfly and the eel-lizard, then the flying cricket. How? A poignant mystery. I shuddered at the implication, thinking again of the gross leaf twined about Blest's leg. The poor sod must be going out of his mind.

I closed my eyes. Shielded whatever remained of JR from the demons that would eventually take him. I let my mind travel inward, like those insistent monks had instructed me back in the prayer meetings. I flashed back on old memories, truths, lies, to past lives. Or were they past lives? Or just tricks of the imagination? The images, compelling enough, entailed fighting enemies with swords and gunpowder and electric wands then R4s, enemies so cruel and detestable that they threatened to bring down the empire. One minute I was a hero, then a broken-legged soldier, next a traitor, then some nameless beggar wandering the ghettos, slumming for scraps in back alleys. Was that this life, or a previous one? All a blur. My lingering dream morphed into the boy wanting to be a rocket scientist and save the world, then it flickered out like a candle flame to something else. The bombs of the warmongers fell ravaging my home planet, leaving thousands dead, and the camps and the flight of madness occurring afterward, a nightmare like any aftermath of war, but it all started to make sense. I saw the dance and drama of my life multiplied a million times over in the lives of countless others. Just little puffballs of existence flashing in and out of time, with little significance to speak of in the overall picture.

The quintessence of me was but a tiny drop of water dribbling down on the vast leaf of time. Dripping down into an immeasurable pool of life, to be drawn out, consumed, reborn, recycled into some new matter and new phenomenon. Humbling to see this, and yet disturbing to catch a glimpse of what could be reality.

And I thought and I dreamed and brooded in the green liquid as the days and the weeks drifted by.

Out of my suspended animation I sprang up in a groggy rush. The sounds of murmuring voices and the sensation of touch drifted nearby. I flexed my hand. The fingers moved with full power. No more did my knitted flesh or my bent fingers throb. As the water had the power to nourish the occupants in the tanks, so could it heal flesh and broken bones. As long as the individual wasn't dead, the liquid could perform the miraculous.

I felt rough sandpaper hands slapping at my moist cheeks. Words struggled to come to my nerveless lips.

"Steady does it," said the figure who pushed finger to my lip. "Well, Jet Rusco, how do you feel after your first rebirth?"

I stammered.

"It will take some minutes to readjust. It won't do to talk. Look at Zan over there. Comatose. Afraid the poor lad couldn't cope with his suspension. Alas," Mong sighed. "I will have to throw the wretch back in the tank for a while to regain his wits."

"Wha—" I sputtered, my lungs heaving with the effort of taking breaths of life-giving air.

"You have questions, I know. We will repeat this exercise, until you are cured of your insatiable desire to defy me. Blest is up next on the ropes. Each of you will take turns in the Mentera bathtub. The liquid heals all wounds, no matter how grievous. We will start the process all over again, then the pain will run deeper. Much deeper. Treat it as my gift to bring you to a level of awareness higher than what you have already attained. It is written in the Budo scriptures that enlightenment can come through pain."

"F-Fuck you, Mong," I croaked. "You rude fucking sadist. I s-shit down your throat and piss on your scriptures."

The Star Lord sighed. "Blasphemy. Disrespect for the wise ones. Very bad. Behavior as this demands cleansing." He signaled to Balt.

The fucker lieutenant grabbed me up like a sack of potatoes and tossed me back in the tank, making sure my head was sufficiently underwater for enough time. I struggled, screaming bubbles from my lips. No use. They drowned me, again.

Whole days passed in snail-crawling increments. The prolonged immersion had me fading in and out into weird and grotesque, infathomable worlds.

Again I contemplated the truth of the universe in an alien tank, an irony that did not escape me. For all purposes, I should be dead, physically and spiritually. Then it hit me...as that voice from deep within the psyche broke through the filmy layers of encroaching darkness and spoke in an echoing blur:

The Star Lord will destroy this universe. Such is the duty of an angel of death. He is a cancer that must be excised, hit in the most vulnerable place—through his adulation of the crickets. Your life's purpose is not to sit encaged in brine, Jet Rusco. Do you not see it? Do you wish to suffer torture indefinitely like a chained beast? You must kill him. You must kill deftly. By striking at the core, the weakest link...

I'd come to believe Mong was invincible, but the monster had a weak chink in his armor, as did anyone else. It was those damn bugs. Mong worshiped them. They had no love for him. Why should they? I'd seen the evil glint in their eyes when he came sidling into the room and their brooding red glares trained on him. If I could escape, loose those creatures upon the compound, maybe there'd be a chance...But how, Rusco? You're in a tank with half your back ripped open.

All those ruined worlds out there, all the people crying for emancipation from slavery, death—can you help them?

So the devil sat on my shoulder, whispered in my ear. *You have to take a stand.* So drenched in cynicism I'd been for so many years, shooting my mouth off and myself in the foot with all my breezy sarcasm and my clowning around, I hadn't seen it. I thought being a rocket engineer was my role of roles. A hustler not long after? Scammer? Gangster? Big man with the big ship?

Your purpose lies before you, Jet Rusco.

Even if it kills me?

You're already dead. Twice remember?

But I'm in a tank.

So, get out of a tank.

And there was a flash, a glimpse, of some reckoning between me and

Mong, a final showdown, just me and him on a distant planet. The details were crystal clear. My mind, lucid as a ten megawatt bulb saw the rocks, boulders, the fields and the peasants hoeing their onions and yams in the fields, eking out a meager existence off the impossibly arid land. These past lives, these future lives, whatever they were, they were a hell of a trip. I'd stick to Myscol if I could.

So, floated to the surface, one of those crazy visions and conversations one has with his alter self, which make a lot of sense in a storybook fantasy but not in real life.

The tanks, the failures, the fuckups, the slits in my back—all these were the universe's way of forcing me to see reason, to do my duty, and fulfill my life's purpose. The voice spoke again. What are you, a crazy bastard? Yes. But the path burned clear as a lighthouse's beacon before me.

I'd have to bring down Mong if it was the last thing I did.

Chapter 24

I must have floated there a lab rat for hours, days. Who knew in this artificial, freaked-out world?

When Balt next removed me from my tank, Blest was out of his watery prison. He sat trussed like a wet hog, his back tied to a square wooden post. Zan twirled in my place hung from the beams, his shaved head lolling on his chest.

"Time to dry for a bit," Mong remarked, rubbing his chin in earnest thought. He motioned to Balt. "See that they're taken care of. I have tasks that require attention offworld. Blest's punishment will be less severe than Rusco's, so he'll need time to dry out some more."

Blest's leg had turned a deep green from shin down, a source of amusement for Mong. He studied the strange creature, the flap of leaf wrapped around Blest's shin and tsked his tongue. "Old Greenie seems to be still latched on for good, Blest. Aren't you a lucky one? He's taken a liking to you. Pretty soon we'll have to start calling you Mr. Greenfoot, or 'Jolly Green Giant'. Or how about Plant Toe?"

Blest moaned.

Balt gave a chortling laugh.

"Let's leave our sleeping beauties for the time being, Balt. They need to catch up on some well-needed rest."

Before Mong left, he turned and raised his hand. As I blinked, thinking to hear a sound behind me, he whacked me in the solar plexus again, hard with the flat of his palm, that magical palm that sent me spinning into a world of oblivion. Some new universe, some new dimension of pain, horror, and illumination.

Maybe it was angels I saw, or consummate devils. Winged beings, half anthropoid, half alien, with voices croaking like frogs, breathing sighs of wind, whispering horror in my ears. They hissed macabre tales of the universes we know not of, both unseen and the seen. I protested in a voiceless murmur, wishing their voices would leave my mind, but they did not. Only laughed and carried me far away to realms unheard of, places beyond the sphere of time and space that defined the witchery of the amalgo. Call me a liar, Jet Rusco, but this was real! Perhaps it was the same place where the filthy locusts built their diseased technology. I wished for no reminder of that terrifying world, that other world that Mong brought me to again and again.

I died another time, and I knew the power of Mong's devils. His depraved gods. And I wished to hell I hadn't.

* * *

My waterlogged brain woke again, struggling to drive sense back into the flaccid cells. Mong and his minion were gone. Only Blest and Zan remained where I'd last seen them. I guessed this would be one of the last times we would all be together in any conversable ring, so we'd have to take full advantage of the situation.

I hissed at Blest who lolled about eight feet away. "Pst...can you hear me, Blest? Are you still conscious?"

He moaned. "Go away whoever you are..."

"Blest, dammit!" I cried. "Look at me."

He stirred. His eyes blinked and gained focus. "Oh, Rusco. I must have died and gone to heaven. It's you. Are we back in Bantam yet?"

"*Bantam*?—you idiot. The ship's dead. Remember?"

"Oh, right. Where are we then? Oh, I'd better not ask. Why are you tied up like that? Wait, I'm tied up too." He shook his head, struggling to make sense of the physical evidence, as if he were an amnesiac, his eyes goggling every which way.

I gave a wretched sigh.

"Rusco, you wouldn't believe it," Blest said in an excited cackle. "The funniest, damnedest memory. Me and my buddy Rog were out cruising at Pegri's tavern. We'd just come off training shift, wanted to let loose, hit the pubs, and we had this bet, see who could get laid first...old Rog, braggartly bastard sicced himself on this quiet, solemn-type sitting in the dimness o'er by the window. Real killer broad. Turns out she was a robot, can you believe it—"

"Shut the fuck up! You're rambling, Blest! Focus! Can you reach your bonds? Twiddle them with your fingers?"

"Don't rightly think I can, Jet. Why, you want a hand job? Ha ha."

"Would you knock of the hillbilly shit?" I gave a sigh of impatience.

Blest started to slip back into his delirium. Drool dripped from his lips. His head lolled.

"Snap out of it! For Christ sake, Blest. No time to die yet."

"Wh-what?" he grunted. "Go away. Fuck off, Jet, I want to sleep."

"Plenty of time to sleep in your damn tank, dumbo. Listen to me—"

"I told you to bug the fuck off, Rusco."

"Listen!" In a fit of sudden anger I focused the brunt of my frustration at him and there came a sudden zing, like an instrument popping strings. Blest's head jerked back then he snapped alert with a sharp cry. "What the hell was that? Rusco, you don't have to get sore. Stop chucking things my way."

As my eyes darted around, I was as startled as he. I shook my head. This chamber was booby-trapped, beyond a house of horrors.

I turned my focus toward Zan, who seem to have roused from his painful hangman's hell. He hung up in the rafters, dangling from the beam. "Zan, talk to me," I hissed.

As Zan twirled, his one skewed eye bulged my way, blasted me with a look of despair. "D-did I ever tell you how I made it to Othwan, Jet?"

"Think you did."

"Nah, the real story." He winced and took bite-sized breaths as he hung from those cords knitted in his back. I empathized with such pain, like a pork loin dangling from a butcher's hook.

"We were on an attack ship. Mong ordered me to blast the small ship that my mother and father were escaping on."

I closed my eyes and looked away.

"Yeah, that bad, Rusco…Well, Mong—basically, he killed my family, my brother and sister. The man has means…technology, influence, black magic."

Zan was preaching to the choir. I'd witnessed too many bouts of Mong's black magic. But I needed to keep Zan talking, engaged in the present, if he were to be of any use, which at the moment, didn't look likely. "How'd you get that scar under your eye, Zan? What happened?"

Zan snorted, grimacing. "Mong's guards cut me to make an example of me."

"What'd they do that for?"

"I violated the bell rules."

"Really?"

"When the bell rings…we're all supposed to…assemble for teachings. I was a little slow."

"Got us all jumping like trained seals."

"Seems so." Zan's face curled in anguish. "What about you, Blest?"

Zan croaked. "Seems you've dropped out of the—conversation. Nothing more to say about Rog and his sexy robot?"

"Forget Blest," I grunted. "He's out of—"

"Quiet. Someone's coming," Zan hissed.

There came a clinking at the door. Hinges creaked and Balt, the sick fuck, came in, carrying a large bowl, which might have held food.

"Dinner anyone?" Balt called, sauntering forth with a breezy chuckle. "Oh, I see you're occupied. I'll just leave these fine treats here on the bug tank. Fresh owl gizzards, chicken liver, raw snail. Mmm-mmm. Whole bowl of it. Prepared raw for maximum protein."

"Why don't you try some yourself, Balt?" I suggested. "Mong's prayer circle always emphasizes sharing and goodwill."

"That's true and mighty kind of you, Rusco, but I'll pass on the victuals. My stomach's a little off today. I'll stop by for a little chat though."

"Mighty neighborly of you."

Balt frowned. "Those thongs look infected, Vulder. Think the skin on your back can handle it? Might rip off more of your shoulder."

"We're all getting used to it by now, Zan included," I broke in, hoping to cut Zan off and stop Balt from getting riled up.

Balt huffed out a grunt. "No fun here, Rusco, this is boring. Think I'll be on my way now. Good luck, kiddos."

He left, closing the portal behind him with a loud thud.

"Fucker." I pinched my eyes shut with a sigh. "Where were we?"

"Ready to die, Rusco, what else?" Zan gave a horrible groan. "Let's lay off the chatty Cathy stuff. I'm dying over here."

"Listen, we can defeat this Star Barf. We have to—"

"What? Scream a little louder?"

"Listen, Zan. Blest, you too. Dammit. Let's dig in our heels here. We can beat this fucker if we cooperate. But if we whine and grouse about it we're toast. There's three of us, plus these ugly bugs in the tanks, that makes five."

"Now you're—the one's sounding—like a lunatic," Zan croaked.

I gave a hiss of exasperation. "Blest, are you with me? Blest?"

Blest had slipped off into some lotus land. His head jerked up with a jolt.

"Rusco, I had the most brutal, fucked up dream."

"Another?"

"They come at me a mile a minute."

"Lucky you. Must be the fluid in the tanks."

"You think? This one was of me drowning in a swimming pool. Bugs—fishes—they all were nibbling at my toes, eyes, arms, legs, taking bites out of my ribs...except it was no dream, Rusco, it was real, and my buddy Rog and the rest of them were all bagged up in that tin can of a space capsule on a training mission. They'd crashed-landed. There was nothing whole left of them when the rescue unit came after they'd washed up on the shore, capsule and all, Rusco. In the middle of nowhere. Damn it, that really happened! Rusco, are you listening? Don't look at me like that. They all died in that crash. It's in the report. They found the ship crumpled up on Maelstrom's beach. Rog, Ven, Peri and Noose. Should have been me. Earlier when our ship was cracking up, we drew straws to see who'd live. I got the lucky straw, took the single chute, there was only one left after the explosion.

He shook and shivered like a man suffering from dengue fever.

"Not much left of Peri and Rog after they got eaten up by those fishes. They nibbled at them, man—those fishes ate them like corn meal! Damnedest thing. But here's the weirdest part. This time I was the one who got all chewed up and Peri was the one who escaped...as if the scene played a million times over in my head in every possible combination of survivors and losers." Blest convulsed again, and this time his eyes rolled back in his sockets, his mouth agape, showing white teeth and drool spilling down his chin.

I grimaced, remembering the glimpses of past-lives flashbacks during my own time in the tank, much less with Mong's whacks to my belly, and I didn't doubt that what Blest was saying was real. Each scenario a new alternate reality in some dimension somewhere. Blest's tragic tale was as close as I'd ever get to the real Blest and any clear understanding of his haunted past.

When Blest slipped off into unconsciousness, I heard the recurring moans and cries of a woman in a chamber somewhere down the line, possibly through an upper air vent. Perhaps they were Volia's or perhaps other pleasure victims of the Orpheum.

Chapter 25

Mong had gotten a tad more creative lately and rigged an interesting variation of the hook and hang punishment. This one had me hanging from my toes, with my back to a pole, strapped at the waist. He claimed it would make me smarter, in a crude way, all that blood flowing to my head, plus seeing the world upside down. Did a man a world of good, he said. A party bag of laughs, Mong was. Hadruk had done the tying, not Balk who was the designated rope man. One of the rawhide knots ultimately slipped while Mong was out on errands, the one on my big toe, which allowed me to thrash with one freed-up foot against the knots of the first.

A significant breakthrough. With that foot I scraped a hell of a lot of skin off the other toes in the process, but after a painful amount of cursing and grinding, I managed to get the other foot free.

So, I was swinging ass over end, trying to worm my way free with waist still tied to the post while Zan was cheering me on in his hoarse way, practically dying up there in his hangman's noose. While I was practically choking from being bent over double at the middle, my hips like a pivot with my spine still stuck to the pole. I did manage to squirm out of that hold with the extra leeway I had with my legs free.

I was squatting on the ground now like a pinched toad, panting, with only my arms bound behind my back. Not too bad for an old timer. I staggered up painfully, pushed my back to the post, rubbed the leather cords against the corner of the wood, all drenched in a feverish sweat, knowing that this would be the only chance I'd get to get the fuck out of this mess. Snap, snap. Enough friction to cut one of the cords then the other. Freedom!

Not too shabby. Some torn flesh, scraped toes and wrists, nothing I couldn't handle. My ears perked to a fumbling at the door. I ducked, swearing as the iron frame groaned inwards. I hobbled the best I could behind the nearest Mentera tank, dreading the proximity to that vampirish creature and hoped whoever was coming hadn't seen me.

It was Balt and his eyes flicked to the vacant post. Up came his rifle. "Rusco? Where are you? Come out, wherever you are." The torturer grinned, aimed his rifle at the posts, peering crosswise.

I clenched my prosthetic fist, trying to stay hidden behind the hunched form of the locust suspended in the tank. Whether I got shot up or I didn't, old Balt was in for a bit of rough and tumble.

This Redemption Hall went back quite a ways into darkness. I didn't know what was back there. Didn't want to find out either. That was Balt's business and his first guess as to where I'd fled. He probed the silence, squinting into the dim shadows with a bulldog's scowl on his face. "The more games we play here, Mr. Rusco, the more painful it gets for you. Big Mong's not here to protect your silly ass. He gave me full license to use excessive force should there be civil disobedience."

Good for you, Balt, you smug fucker. You can call 'civil disobedience' on me all you want. *It ain't over until the fat lady sings.* I came scuttling back like a land crab from behind Blest's tank, hoping to get closer to Zan who hung like a bug on flypaper.

Balt must have heard that scuffle of movement because he came beetling back like a scarab, clutching the end of his gun and using it as a club to take a big whack at me. He missed. I ducked the butt end of the rifle that came smashing full into Blest's tank.

The glass splintered and water spilled out in a tidal rush. A whole side of the tank fell outward and Blest came sloshing out on his knees, gasping, choking and spewing putrid green water out of his gullet.

Balt charged me with a deep-throated roar. His full weight caught me head on, and I grunted, bowled over, croaking, smacking my metal fist in his face, jamming fingers in his nose, his eyes. The man was not human to have a grappling force like that. Any other strike would have split a man's skull. I struggled with him. The man's ape strength was enough to make me crumple and I could feel my backbone starting to give. I saw Blest out of the corner of my eye, staggering woozily to his feet while I fought on with less and less hope.

"Kill him!" I wheezed. Blest suddenly came stumbling like a straw puppet with the feeding bowl clutched in a fist. He clocked Balt on the back of the head.

Balt grunted. I felt his grip slacken. It gave me time to get my fingers into his eyes again. He roared, grabbing my wrist. I chopped him in the throat. Blest smacked Balt again with the bowl just above the ear. Balt went raging maniac and charged Blest, rolling on him like a bear. The alien plant leaf which had up till this time been stable, suddenly unfurled, doubling in size, whipping out like a serpent. It latched onto Balt's midsection like a cincture, squeezing the breath out of him. He writhed and howled, clawing at the thing, only to get more wind sucked out of his lungs.

I kicked at his head. Blest stayed well back from the constricting force that had plagued him for so long. The sudden intrusion on its stable habitat had pushed the plant parasite to violence.

While Balt twisted and howled, I hissed out a vindictive laugh. "Never forgave you for busting up my fingers, Balt. Not too smug now are you, you fucking bitch-ape? What's that, can't hear you?" I ground my boot heel into his flailing hand, stepping on it so hard I heard it crunch. He grimaced in agony while struggling in the wet glass.

I motioned to Blest. "Here, help me drag this fuck over to the tanks." Zan watched the battle out of the corner of his eye in a groggy haze.

We dragged Balt by his heels, taking care not to touch the alien plant. Under no circumstance did I want it to leapfrog to either of us. We upended Balt into the tank formerly occupied by me. He sputtered foul brine and splashed like a fish but he slipped under water, having no more will to fight, clutching feebly at the constricting leaf robbing him of further strength. Before the lieutenant sank to the bottom, his lungs filled with water and he stared out of his glassy cage with lips parted in an O like one of those black bugs in the vessel beside him. Oh, how Balt glared out from behind that glass! If I could only snapshot that scene.

We crouched on our haunches, panting. I reached over and patted Blest on the back. "Good work, friend. You came through as I knew you would. We were always a team."

Blest babbled an incoherent word. "This is fucking madness, Rusco. Where are we?"

I slapped him on the back. "Madness or not, seems your vine critter came in handy after all."

I gathered up my boots, then snatched up Balt's weapon, gripping it in a sweaty palm with an air of triumph. There'd be some serious payback for old Mong now.

Blest stared at me with suspicion glinting in his eyes then at Balt's twitching form in the tank. "Why put him in there? Let's kill the fucker and get out of here." He grimaced as Balt convulsed in his watery prison.

"He's already dead, Blest. No way to change that."

"Don't like him swimming in there, Rusco. He ain't dead, and you know it."

"I know what you're thinking. Let's not mess with things that aren't broken."

Blest shivered, as if recalling an odious memory of his own tank experience. "That damn plant thing constricted me like a bitch, Rusco. The green devil water gave it more strength."

"Yeah, well be thankful you're out of there and rid of it now."

"For how long?" He started to shake like a recovering Myscol addict and I had to grab his shoulders and shake him like a wet blanket and slap his cheeks a few times.

"Snap out of it! We have to move, Blest. First, let's gather up Zan. He looks to be in a bad way."

We cut him down from his swinging post, then unwound the leather from his wrists and got the groaning man up onto his feet. His back was mangled up, sure, nothing we could do there. But Mong had spared him the usual agony of extra deep slits this last time. Zan swayed on his feet, moaning, looking around in confused horror.

"Amp up your game, Zan," I said. "We've got a journey to make." I shook him as I had Blest. Seemed it helped. Zan wasn't in great shape. I considered dropping him in one of the spare tanks to heal him up better but I grimaced at the idea. No time, and even if I could hold him by down like a rat in that witch water, by the look in his eyes, I knew he'd not go in easily.

"Steady him, Blest. I've a little last minute business to take care of."

"Like what?"

Over to the remaining tanks I hobbled and took the butt end of my rifle in a firm hand. With all my force, I smashed the nearest Mentera tank.

Blest's eyes bugged out in horror as the glass cracked and green fluid trickled down the side. "Are you fucking insane?"

"Chip and Chong are inseparable," I declared. "We separate these bitches and we create a whole new dynamic, don't we? It'll sharpen up our old friend Mong. He seems to be a big fan of trials and tests." I leaned in and smashed the glass again with triumph and rage.

"What about us?" Blest croaked. "You plan on getting snipped by their claws?"

"I'm not messing around here any more."

"Easy for you to say, Rusco, you're—"

The next strike hit the cracked glass square on and the locust came spilling out in a spray of green water and glass. The thing rolled then coiled up in a dense, black heap. It lay there sprawled, its antennae quivering before the broken tank. Then the dwarf wings fluttered in a burst of movement. The power of flight seemed lost over the passing ages. It scootched up on its hind legs into a beetle-like crouch, making weird clicking noises with its mandibles.

Blest recoiled. Zan's mouth moved in a hoarse scream.

"Let's get the fuck out of here," I cried, "before Chip starts to get antsy."

We hobbled like three broken musketeers to the exit.

On the way, I caught a brief glimpse of the glass case on the altar, the one that housed Fol's alien bulb. A brief hesitation had me wincing before I smashed the glass case and snatched up the bulb, the same that Follee had taken up on a whim from Cyber station.

"What are you planning to do with that?" croaked Blest.

"Stuff it up your ass, what do you think?"

"Rusco, these things are fucking dangerous."

"Exactly. Now move."

We thrust our shoulders to the door. Nothing. Tight as a spinster's crotch. Locked. Why wouldn't it be?

Blest sighed, blowing spittle past his dry lips. "You could have tested the door before you woke up Chip."

"Hindsight, Blest, hindsight. The key must be in Balt's purse. Guess that's what his firearm is for." I lifted the gun barrel.

"But the noise'll—"

I blasted the fuck out of the mechanism before Blest could argue. The door sagged open.

"There, see? Now shut up or I'll put you back in the tank with Balt. Everything'll work out." I grinned in satisfaction as I used the rifle to widen the gap to reveal a dim-lit hallway. Broad marble tiles sheened in the sconce light. Zan huffed out a laugh then hissed a breath between his gap-teeth.

I nudged the others out into the deserted hall. Thank Mong's ugly gods there were no guards. I risked a glance backward and saw our little bug friend, Chip, righting itself, staggering over to his cricket buddy in the nearby tank in a bent-legged crouch.

Time to bug out from this crib.

Chapter 26

Shadows crawled where I motioned the others down the temple hall. Fewer wall sconces lit the broad passageway. Only portraits of Mong and his warriors and ancient warlords adorned the walls. A small air fan chugged away. I started to move toward the exit then recalled a face devoid of hope and a woman's legs splayed over silk cushions. I halted, mumbled a curse, and backtracked.

"Where you going now?" croaked Blest. "The exit to this shithole is back that way, isn't it?" He stared around grimly then rolled his eyes. "Oh, Rusco, you've got to be kidding? Don't you get enough skin from Wren?"

Blest and Mong had me pegged, yes, I was a stupid, chivalrous sucker. My true colors coming out. "More than enough skin, Blest. But for now, move."

He flung off my arm. "Who the fuck are you to give me orders?"

Maybe I should have pistol-whipped Blest for his insolence long ago or left him on Gainor. My brain wasn't totally sharp-edged this moment, nor was I the greatest tactician. Too many rival emotions, desperate plans and hopes, crossed signals. Too many damn things that could go wrong. Good to see that Blest was returning to his normal obnoxious self. But dammit, we had one chance at freedom and seeing blue skies again! I didn't want to blow it or lie awake at night, thinking, well, Jet, if you had only tried to save the noble lady who had the guts to stand up to Mong, instead of scurrying off like some damned coward with tail tucked between his legs intent on saving your own skin…

I heard the staccato rap of gunshots ahead.

"Down!" I cried.

The roar of ship engines surfaced above, then sounds of explosions rocking the temple's massive roof.

"What the fuck?" Blest stared white-eyed at the ceiling. "Mong got a little fireworks celebration for us?"

"No, those are fareons," rasped Zan. "Attack ships."

"Maybe Mong's got a little training exercise then in motion?" I mused.

Something smashed into the roof and the whole temple shook down to its foundation.

"Maybe he's made himself a few enemies?"

"Come on!" I squawked. "No better time than now to get out of here."

Commotion reigned up ahead. Three figures came running toward us, rifles in hand. Two trailing—youngbloods. They cast tense glances over their shoulders, at the *meslars* who pursued them. I halted, Balt's confiscated weapon trained, reluctant to fire on them.

Good thing I didn't. The foremost, a tall, shadowy figure loped up out of the dimness, moving like an agile cat. I recognized her at once. My God…my heart leapt. Could it be?

It is you, you glorious sight for sore eyes.

She turned and aimed her R4. Mong's *meslars* came waving truncheons at the three. They crouched and spat gunfire back at them. Two fell. One of the fanatical survivors kept running with truncheon raised. She blasted him to shit.

Wren tossed me a better rifle. "You look cute in bald, Russy. But you're harder to find than a beetle in a barnyard."

My jaw dropped. Not the grim affirmation one'd expect, but the lean figure was a balm to my beleaguered spirit. "Good one, Wren." I rushed over and gave her a fierce embrace.

"No time for kisses, Rus. These temple laymen are all lambs but Mong's hard-boys are out, crawling all over this place with guns."

I motioned them forward. "Back down the hall. How'd you find out where we were?"

"I asked the hired help, nicely."

"Yeah, I'll bet."

"They're still picking their teeth up off the ground," said one of the youngbloods, a curly haired gunman garbed in grey khakis and kevlar.

I gave a curt nod. The short-barreled R6 I'd taken from Balt I tossed to Blest.

I made a signal to move on with quicker speed. Wren blinked, indicating the exit was back the other way. Blest just sighed and shook his head. Knowing time was short, I herded the others on, urging them to silence. The corridor curved in a bow around the back of the temple. Stairwells led to lower levels. I bared teeth at those places, wondering how many more torture chambers Mong kept in this ill-begotten place.

We crept down the hushed halls, Wren, Blest and the others at my heels. A vengeful leer was carved on my face as we halted before the iron-bound door worked with ornate inscriptions of naked bodies plunged in orgiastic positions. I gave a quick nod. We blew the mechanism and burst through, our guns hefted. The place appeared deserted, but through the thick billows of reeking incense, I perceived goblets of stale wine and ale lying strewn all over the marble floor amidst the decorative fountains. I caught a shiver of movement in the back. Cushions and embroidered blankets sprawled on plush divans; heads turned at our approach and naked bodies twisted.

Amid the rank haze, I stared and found her spread-eagled under a drunken captain whose croak rose to a bull's roar of defiance.

The naked, struggling figure underneath him kneed him in the groin. The man groaned, one hand groping for his weapon. Wren opened fire and he fell in a rapidly-spreading pool of blood.

Frenzied shrieks echoed about the stone chamber. Several of the dazed women rolled off their couches, uncertain what to do. Volia staggered up, pulling a fleece cover around her half-naked, olive-skinned body. She looked broken in some indefinable way, but I glimpsed a defiance still burning in her hazel eyes and a growing contempt for her captors and a raging desire for vengeance. I shuddered to think what those animals had done to her in here.

I moved forward to gather her up, snatching up a long fur coat draped on the side of a couch.

"Who's she?" grunted Wren, motioning her gun. One of your girlfriends?"

"It's Lady Volia—"

"Leader of the Melinar," Volia croaked. She coughed, staggered up to her full height, fumbling to accept the garment in my hands. She leaned heavily on me and I caught the musky smell of sweat and sex. She wrapped the black-furred garment tighter, hugging the trim contours of her body, the smooth round of hip and curve of breast I'd glimpsed earlier. She was half drugged with something, still zoned on local poppy or some drug no doubt. Probably the least of what Mong had forced on her. Her eyes stared funny, all glassy.

Wren seemed to pause. "Your people are here, Volia, trying to rescue you."

She nodded, gave a weak acknowledgement.

"What of these others?" Wren motioned to the scattered few in this smoke-hazed, degenerate orgy grounds.

A half dozen other women shied away from us. The riddled corpse spooked them and had them cowering back against the wall in even greater fear. "If you want to come with us, hurry your asses!" Wren called in a crisp, no-nonsense voice.

None of them responded, only quivered in doubt and fear, retreating to their shadowy corners.

"Broken as whipped dogs." I shrugged in resignation. They were too far gone, too brainwashed and terrorized by Mong's sadistic abuse. It was sad. I took a few halting steps toward the exit.

Blest's moon-face blinked; he started to shiver again, still prey to convulsions.

"Blest, snap out of it." I slapped him then gave him a reassuring pat on the back. "We have killing to do."

"Yeah." He shook off whatever was buzzing through him and took a firmer grip on his R6. Zan was doing better, though he was looking terrible. Pale-faced, bloodshot eyes, jittery hands.

Wren looked the epitome of health. Ready to take on a small army.

I shuddered to think what I looked like. Probably a ragged scarecrow with a shit-eating grin pasted on his gaunt-ugly face. I rolled my eyes. Quit mucking around, Rusco. You auditioning for a beauty pageant here? A second's daydreaming and it's graveyard time for you.

Another half-baked sot sprang to life from under a blanket on a nearby divan. His hands clawed for me. I kicked him in the gut, whacked him with the butt end of my gun as the snarl died on his lips and he fell in a soundless heap.

I stepped over the body and motioned to Zan. "Forgot to make the introductions. Wren—meet Zan. Zan, Wren."

Wren waved her gun at the two young recruits. "These ugly mutts are Voj and Grild." The whites of their eyes showed against camo-blackened faces, matching toothy grins.

Zan shook his head in confusion. "Rusco, who are these guys? What gives?"

"This is my swat team, can't you see? If you want out of this prison, follow her lead."

Zan gave a low whistle. "You've got friends in very high places. Or some guardian angels protecting you."

"I followed Mong's meditations, remember?"

"What's our plan?" Blest growled, facing Wren.

"Get to the ship," she said. "Noss is out there waiting for us. I told him to hide the ship not far away, on the other side of the river."

"Good," I said. "What is it, *Alastar*?"

"No, a new one."

I shook my head in wonder and could have laughed for joy. "Wren, I applaud your resource. Good play. Can you reach Noss?"

"Of course." She tapped her invisible earset. "All on a safe channel."

"A bold move, considering Mong's ruthlessness."

"It was the only opportunity we had. Paid some mega yols out of your drug money for secret intelligence. I'd been watching Othwan like a hawk for weeks, then I saw the Vendecki move in. They must have used some force field to penetrate Mong's defenses and used it to repel the host."

"Heard them surge in," I mumbled. "Sounded just like Mong's bat fighters making a stealth swoop on a defenseless world."

"The Vendecki can't hold these brutes off forever. We'd better hurry."

In that moment I realized the fortuity of Wren's presence and loved her all the more for it. The gal was saving my ass again. All of our asses. She'd been watching the planet. Liquidated the assets to buy and equip a ship and track down Mong's movements. The Vendecki strike had been a bonus, providing the perfect cover to move in. Probably by trying to spring Volia, they'd gotten neck deep in Mong's murderous warships. I hoped they'd stay alive long enough for us to get to our new ship.

We slunk with speed down the hall.

The sound of sudden bootfall thundered behind us. I swore. Angry voices, shouts of doom followed. Somebody must have gotten wind of the expo of carnage back at the Orpheum. I turned to level fire at the pursuing figures, a half dozen or more.

"Rusco!" I felt a sharp tug at my arm. Wren.

From up ahead, two ghastly shapes scuttled straight for us. Anthracite figures out of a ghoul's nightmare. *Chip and Chong*. I almost shat my pants. Wren raised her gun to blast them to atoms. I elbowed her gun wide.

"What did you do that for?"

I pulled her off to the side and we hugged the wall. Blest, half out his wits, lifted his trembling rifle.

I slapped his gun away. "Don't kill them!" I barked. The two locusts scuttled forth on their hind legs, antennae twitching, but as anticipated, they fled past us as if having a definite mission in mind. I could see in their red glinting eyes the malice and vindictive wrath, armed with centuries of old animosity for whatever the fuck else. The ancient memories that brewed behind those insectoid skulls, could not be known. They were infathomable.

"Let them face Mong's guard," I hissed.

"Why, they're—"

A crunch of bone precluded words. The two black shapes pounced on a defenseless *meslar* armed with a truncheon.

The first locust's strike was lightning fast. Lashing out a slimy appendage, it hooked the man while its partner snapped off the man's arm at the elbow. Another pincer reached for the man's jugular. The victim gave a blood-curdling shriek as his life blood spurted on the marble floor.

The creatures sped away on their hind legs, heading toward the Orpheum and the place where I remember Mong kept the amalgamators…almost as though they were drawn to a homing beacon like moths.

I had to turn my head away as more crunching sounds came drifting back to the tune of men's screams and hoarse wails of agony and terror.

The insects scuttled on, leaving a trail of dead in their wake. Feisty and efficient devils, I thought.

"What are they?" hissed Grild.

"Come on!" I rasped. "Let's get the fuck out of here before those bugs decide to beetle back and bring a horde after us." I waved my R4.

"Where did those things come from?" Wren called.

"You don't want to know, Wren, believe me."

Blest was too dissociated from pain to do anything but mumble doom and gloom. Volia, paralyzed with shock, was having trouble registering any of it. Zan had already inured himself to such unnatural violence, having seen and experienced enough grisliness to last a lifetime back in the Redemption hall.

Events were fast sliding out of control. I knew I had to get a grip on reality and get the fuck out of here.

No such luck. Fierce shouts issued from down the hall—Mong's men, perhaps even Mong himself. The heavy tread of clopping boots and running figures came to our ears. We were blocked in. Enemies in front, enemies behind. Too many to deal with, even with our guns. Some of us would die. Maybe most of us. I looked around in utter desperation. Where's your bag of tricks now, Rusco?

On a sudden inspiration, I shuttled Volia and Zan to a door and into a room, hoping to hell there was nothing lurking there to cut us to ribbons. Blest and the others loped behind; Wren brought up the rear.

Nothing. Nobody. Just a shrine room dedicated to some obscure god, one of Mong's pantheon of creepos.

We crouched in the murk, the whites of our eyes showing and our breaths held. The shadows were thick at the far end of the chamber. A lone, sputtering candle set on a low altar cast long and wavering shadows upon a grim warlord's face carved on the stone wall.

We passed precious minutes hunched in the dark, crouched like mice, trying to stay out of the cat's jaws. Weapons trained at the door, we prepared for violence. Blest tried to hiss out some unsolicited advice, but I waved him to silence. Too many bloody amateurs spilling ideas in the stew pot. Too many foes around us. I could hear harsh, enemy voices echoed from under the crack of the door. We couldn't hide here forever. Decision time. I was about to give the order to head out and let us take our chances in a mad scramble in the hall when I heard more voices and figures doubling back this way. I winced and waved the others back, though they huddled close at my shoulders. I stuck my ear to the door.

"The locusts, sir. They've escaped!"

"What do you mean, escaped?" Mong's voice rumbled in a throaty roar. "How the fuck did that happen?"

I heard the man groan then another groan. "There's more, sir. Balt's in a tank. Drowned."

There was a pause until Mong bawled, "Rusco! I'll kill that fucking bastard. Go, look for them."

Now the proverbial shit was about to hit the fan.

The sound of running feet echoed up then the sound of panting breath. Another harbinger of doom?

"They've killed six men, sir! With pincers and claws. One guard mauled but still alive, told a gruesome tale. They fight like demons. The Mentera. Hooks, claws, squirting venom from pointed teeth. The *meslars* died badly."

I opened the door a crack and saw Mong's eyes widen with fury.

"Find them," he hissed through gritted teeth. He flung out a hand and the wall sizzled as if acid had been thrown at it.

I scowled and pulled my head back. If those fiends could keep chopping up Mong's brigade, we might have a slim window of opportunity.

Staring back through the crack, though, I swallowed hard. This was a precarious situation. Multiple enemies. Nowhere safe to run.

Another voice panted and huffed in fear in the hall. It sounded like Verlioze, Mong's weapons master. "The Mentera have slipped back through the transporter tunnel, sir, the sacred amalgo."

Mong gave a bleat of rage. "Go in after them then. Get them back!"

His henchman swore. "Can't. The device's jammed. It's inoperable."

"Those fucking grasshoppers." Mong clenched a fist. "They must have shut off the amalgamator from the other end. Now we can't go in after them. Can't even visit that wondrous world again."

Another voice, sounding like Hadruk's, jeered. "Still think they are the greatest thing since sliced bread, Master Mong?"

I heard a slap as Mong backhanded him. Probably Hadruk. Though I couldn't physically see Hadruk. "Shut up, you ignoramus. Until we know the Mentera did it purposely, we'll give them the benefit of the doubt. Maybe the device just jammed and it can be fixed."

The struck man sneered. "You're a bloody fool if you believe that, Mong. Hypnotized by this ancient bug cult of yours and this brotherhood of 'light'. You're losing it and you can't see it."

Mong pulled out his weapon and smacked Hadruk hard across the mouth, drawing blood. Hadruk grinned and jumped him. The security officer got a good grip on Mong's face, clawing at nose and lips, before Mong, with his bare hands, grabbed Hadruk by the throat. Hadruk sagged, struggling like an ape, but was no match for the Star Lord's unnatural strength. With the crushing brawn of ten men, Mong's augmented arm lifted him off his feet. There came a sudden crunch and ripping of flesh. Mong snapped the man's neck like a rotten branch and tossed the security officer's corpse aside. I winced. So much for Hadruk.

If those fiendish crickets could get one of those ships running…I balked at the thought.

Mong bellowed, "Don't stand there like a bunch of stuffed dummies, you fools! I want that amalgo fixed and I want Rusco brought to his knees. Find him and bring him to me. Someone will answer for this and die."

Verlioze licked his lips.

Mong gave a feral roar. "Now, you fucking idiots!" The Star Lord's orders rebounded off the stone and wood like the boom of a cannon.

The temple roof rocked to new blasts.

Mong looked up and he shook his head in frustration. "Leave the corpse," he spat. "Come with me. New plan. Those fools on defense are doing next to nothing to stop this inane attack. Let's make for the ships. We'll deal with the rest of this mess later."

The sound of echoing bootfall faded down the corridor.

We bolted out of the room, sidling in an opposite direction. Hoping for a back exit, we threaded our way like thieves through the wide, dim-lit corridors. Far too many of us though for stealth.

But stealth wasn't necessary.

Chapter 27

We burst out of the doors in a shambling crouch, our guns on the ready. Out onto the temple grounds we poured, with Wren in the lead, the roar and whine of jet fighters overhead and the scurry of running feet and anxious shouts all about. The light was fading from Othwan's opalescent sky.

Enemy ships ranged the sky. How they had penetrated warlord Mong's security net was still beyond me. More tricks? More last minute secret tech?

Volia and Zan were having a hard time. They had no weapons. I stayed back to cover them. Wren instructed Voj and Grild to move ahead and act as front men, clearing the way. It was their chance to prove themselves.

They hopped from boulder to garden bush, keeping their bodies low, rifles aimed. They motioned us ahead; the coast was clear.

The Temple of Light smoked behind us, a thin chute of flames rising from its caved-in roof. Now a gaping hole smoked in its nearest side, the once-proud spires teetering on drunken angles.

The grounds in the vicinity of the hangar writhed to a beehive of activity. Men in khakis firing R6s. Ships roaring overhead. Vendecki skyslips, smaller Melinarian fighters buzzing by. I could see Mong and his men scurrying away in an opposite direction while the Warhawks were on the move ready to pick them up. One landed and as bombs dropped, lighting up the green in crimson fire, they dove for cover. Mong's plan to board was thwarted.

I still couldn't believe the Vendecki had slipped through Mong's defenses leaving them this unaware and exposed. Must have been one hell of a force field.

I draped an arm around Volia's shoulder, seeing the white, dazed look of confusion in her eyes. Like another dream, Rusco, no different than the one hanging from Mong's torture rope or floating in his Mentera tank...

We made it to the open green, a few hundred yards just shy of the charred prayer hall. That was as far as we'd get. I could see Mong's men were converging on us, coming out of the woodwork like termites. Doom stared us in the face. So, it had all been for naught. Wren screamed orders into the com. Maybe she couldn't hear over the roar of the destruction. Where the fuck was Noss?

The savage sweep of heavy engines blitzed the compound. Cone-like shapes and elliptical hulls of the rebels drew up and away while others landed air strikes.

A grenade clattered six feet away from us in front of a ruined fountain. Wren tackled Zan out of the way; I pulled Volia down behind a statue. Shrapnel webbed the immediate area; splatter hit the marble base behind which we crouched. The blast nearly took out our ear drums.

Vendecki and Melinarian ships roared across the sky, deafening us further. A fierce dance of death played before our eyes with pursuing Warhawks which numbered in the dozens. Selected rebel craft dropped paratroopers to extract Volia from the temple. What a colossal fuck up! Brave souls, those would-be rescuers. I saw they hopped from cover to cover like us and the terrified cicadas and rained fire into the fray. Volia gestured frantically. None of them could see her. I debated trying to do a kamikaze run across that no-man's land to tell them we had her, but it'd be suicide.

Wren shouted into the com. "Noss, bring Eagle 4 around to temple pickup! Now! The back door!"

"Can you signal the Melinarians?" I rasped at her.

"All their channels are blocked."

I shook my head in frustration.

Groups of rebels sprang from blackened shrines to trade fire with Mong's defenders, with the rebels intent on storming the main temple to rescue Volia. Bombs dropped from above. The tops of pagodas disappeared. We crouched, hoping we could last without getting peppered full of holes until Noss could bring the ship around. So much for Mong's halcyon, idyllic world.

So much for us too, if we didn't get away from here fast.

Clutches of men fought guerrilla style, launching grenades and spraying fire, ducking, scrambling for new toeholds of cover. It was Resus all over again.

Fareon beams lashed out of the sky. A sleek ship with gleaming hull roared down from above.

My heart leaped. An Alpha 9 fast runner? Could it be? My old ship, *Starrunner*, back from the dead?

No, only a copy.

'The next best thing," Wren rasped.

I shook my head in bewilderment. No time to ponder. The ship landed a few hundred yards away, trim and grey with ox horn-shaped prow and rough diamond shape at stern.

It might as well have been a thousand yards away though. A squad of ground troops identified me among the company and moved in with guns booming.

A hoarse yell hovered on my lips. I turned kamikaze and leveled R4 mayhem into the figures that came charging us. I waited for oblivion to snatch me, riddled with fire and the force of energy pulses. But it did not. In a last defensive move, I fell flat on my stomach. Fire clipped the earth all around. I plugged round after round into the noise and confusion. Through the smoke, I saw Mong striding amid those running figures, a gigantic, barbaric, black-clad leather brute with furred cap. I knew the jig was up.

Gunfire grazed my side. Not possible to escape hits. I reached down, felt a wet stickiness at my ribs. The pain was minimal compared to the animal agony of Mong's hangman's torture. Still, I'd need regen soon. I saw a dream image of Blest hobbling behind me somewhere, catching some shrapnel fallout in the burst of fire power.

He and Wren jogged together, or rather tottered, lurching ahead to dig in defensive positions closer to the descending ship. They dove into low shrubbery. They would get eaten to bits in seconds if they didn't find better cover. Volia and Zan, weaponless, hunched like whipped puppies behind them, white-faced, resigned to death while *Starrunner's* engines blew dust and grass all over the place. Voj was down, riddled with bullets. Blest's leg had caught a slug. We were not going to make it. *Starrunner*, resurrected, loomed a hundred feet away by my estimate, near some broken fountains and a sizzling stream. The ship lifted and tilted. Seeing our plight, Noss angled her in to shield us from the savage fire of Mong's militia. I realized we had missed the narrow window of rescue by mere minutes, despite Noss's clever maneuvering. Bigger ships loomed on our rear horizon; they came chugging toward us.

The alien bulb lay at my side, slipped from my waist belt. With my head tucked low, I launched it, mumbling a prayer that Mong and all his deranged brood would taste bitter death. The frightening thing left my fingers, lobbed like a grenade at the first group of running figures only a few dozen feet away. They lay into it with fire, thinking it some freak grenade come to shred them to bits.

A big mistake.

The bulb exploded in ruin and fragments of its coconut shell bubbled like lava. They turned away to shield their eyes from what they expected to be hideous shrapnel. But from within came unimaginable horror. A winged, misshapen creature, some demon spawn with six starfish arms equipped with sucker pods of sandy-brown color, emerged from the chaos. It was different from the other birthlings, nothing like the dragonfly killer or eel-lizard that had attacked and munched through the Skugs, or the black cricket horror that had burrowed into Mong's gunman's face.

What spawned the endless variation of this creature from its plain Jane bulb, none could ever know. This one was like some cross between a sea urchin and a bat, if such were possible.

Fully grown and buzzing with anger, it now dove like a demon possessed upon the hapless minions of Mong's troop, slicing holes into them with its barbed-suckered appendages. It tore through a gaping man and came out his back, leaving a fist-size hole where his heart should have been.

"Holy fuck," I gasped.

Mong shouted orders, barely ducking and dodging a lunge and slice and dice by the creature. "Stand down! Don't fire at the thing! It's one of those alien freaks. It'll only kill us if we attack. Kill Rusco over there—kill all the fugitives."

Mong lifted his augmented arm. Immediately I felt a sharp tingling surge course through my joints, rattling my nerves. I flopped about like a fish, but such was my hate for Mong and all his sadistic powers that I vaulted up, gun in hand, spraying fire, cursing him for the end of time. I directed every atom of my animosity and feverish hate at the man.

"Eat buzzard shit, you bloody scumbag, fucking tyrant."

I watched his arm jerk in a spasm and then his figure double over. With a roar of rage, he straightened then I blinked in puzzlement because my rapid fire didn't come anywhere near the sod, but I was already stumbling to my feet toward the ship on the heels of Wren and the others, heedless of the gunshots whizzing around us.

I cried out in pain as more stray beams grazed me, but they didn't kill me—at least not yet. Wren was still shrieking into the com. The others were on the move. I staggered toward them, one hand clutching my ribs, the other my R4. We all raced to safety. In that fateful minute, death and life hung on a thread while the creature from another world made hatchet work of Mong's men. If not for its deadly savagery we would have been rat bait from the get-go.

We made it through the cargo hatch before it closed and Noss was fast in getting us airborne and the hell out of there. A squadron of Warhawks were on our tail. No doubt Mong was ordering his gunners to exercise maximum force.

We lurched inside and crawled deeper into the dimness, choking on the smoke and clutching the straps along the wall while Noss weaved us on a rocky tour with fareon fire slamming the hull.

I stumbled on duck feet toward the bridge, my ribs on fire, while Grild stayed behind to tend to Zan and Volia. Blest? I don't know about Blest.

Wren hissed in dismay. "You need regen."

"Screw the regen," I rasped hoarsely. "We need to save this ship—and our hides."

We staggered onto the bridge. Noss beamed at me from behind the pilot's console. "Welcome back, Captain."

"Get this bird out in deep space, Noss. Good to see you."

Reunions were short. We had bogies on our tail, deadly ones. Both Noss and Wren were on it. Wren slapped herself down before the weapons console. I assumed nav. Noss weaved us in impossible circles high over Othwan's forests and lakes as flash bombs spilled around us like confetti at a wedding. Wren blasted blue hell back at the warbirds behind us. I knew Mong had those superior shields installed, making his vessels nearly tank-armored, so our fire-power would do less than nothing. Dodge and dip was all we could do while we ran the dangerous gauntlet on impulse power. Noss was doing a capable job. This new, suped-up starship was ace, but I could see we were not going to make it through this hell unless we did something very damn tricky. I set the course for Veglos. My hand strayed to the Varwol slider. I pulled my fingers back at the last instant. Gripping my side, I was wracked by a sudden spasm and felt the crippling wooziness of shock threatening to tumble me into an abyss. A monumental bad feeling hit my gut hard—one flick of that lever and it could be the end of us. Planetary gravity and warp drive do not mix, cadet Rusco. Any junior flyboy can tell you that. There had to be another way.

The Vendecki line of battleships ranged the inner edge of the planet's atmosphere. There was a right, mean space fight in progress. A hundred

Warhawks stood arrayed against much the same Vendecki numbers. No other choice but the hard one. The reckless one. And that meant—

"Noss bring us into the eye of the storm."

"What?"

"There! Straight into the war zone." I stabbed a thumb at the holo nav.

Noss blinked, he hesitated; at the last moment he caught my drift. Steering *Starrunner* straight into the Vendecki front, he fought the controls, negotiating an obstacle course where hundreds of ships weaved in and out, firing fareons and launching bombs at Mong's Warhawks.

Volia came staggering onto the bridge. She'd bypassed Grild's ministrations and stood before us, her breath a hoarse rasp. "Where are we?"

"A million miles from nowhere soon, sister—or we're space debris."

She gazed at me, looking somewhat better than before, though her wide eyes teared at the number of her own Vendecki and Melinarian allies locked in heated battle with Mong's forces getting battered by Warhawks. She let out a hoarse cry. "Tell them you have me, Rusco! Innocents are dying in the air, on the ground—for me."

I grimaced. The rebels hadn't responded to us on secure channels. I swore and patched her through to the general emergency frequency.

A staticky voice rasped over the com, "General Azun here, Lady Volia, Countess of Melinar. Are you alright?"

"Yes! I am, General. I'm aboard *Starrunner* right now with a fellow named Rusco. Get your people out of there!"

"Roger. We've confirmed visual. All rescue teams are on the abort. Set a far course and tell Rusco to fly *Starrunner* to safe haven!"

"Affirmative. You too, find safe haven. Please abort this crazy assault."

"Negative. Operation Tiger is underway. We've committed and we'll never get a better chance to destroy Mong's hideaway, though many of us may die."

"You will all die!" she wailed.

"With all due respect, beloved Lady, we are all dead with Mong ruling the free planets. Over and out."

I grimaced and clutched the nav. Volia wrung her hands in despair.

The two Warhawks on our tail battered us to hell. Our shields dropped to near zero; a few more direct hits and we'd disintegrate. Before us loomed a phalanx of rebel ships holding off the attackers. We passed right through their great wall of defense, through fire and flame and roiling ships and the topsy-turvy madness of full out war. Fareons grazed our shields and had us buffeted around like puppets. Noss and Wren went skidding out of their seats.

Before the shields blew, I hung on to the console and engaged the Varwol. Death was at our doorstep. Our fate lay in the hands of Othwan, but Othwan's witchery was less risky than flying with our shields down. Never a good idea to warp out so close to a planet's gravity, cadet Rusco, but we were in no position to be choosy right now.

For a split second, the ship seemed to come to a dreamlike halt. Then we hung in space like time thieves. A brilliant white blast lit the cabin, like a small supernova, then a fan of multicolored light trailed behind us, shearing by our viewport as the familiar rainbow of an enormous light highway set us moving to the far stars.

Then only silence.

Free, at last from that bastard's clutches! It was almost too surreal to be true.

A part of me, a grim, primal part from way back in incarnations of my war-torn past, vowed that the next meeting with Master Mong, if ever there was a next, would not be under such one-sided conditions.

Chapter 28

We passed the metal tin of flesh-regen around our company. I could feel its magic working as I lifted my torn monk's robe and ladled the smelly orange paste on my ravaged ribs. The stuff was good for cuts, tissue tears, small organs like a missing ear, damaged tongue or even major skin damage, but generally not for regenerating bones. Except the heavy-duty regen like we had. The pulse weapon that'd tagged me left no lead in my guts, fortunately, only burns, so the regen worked at stitching the flesh together, sparing me the agony of pulling metal out my hide. Luckily none of us had heavy-duty bone issues, outside of Blest with his busted shin. We'd have needed Mong's tanks for worse injuries. We said little and were indeed a glum party, though we had everything to be grateful for—being alive. There lingered the secret fear that Mong was still about lurking like a ghoul around the next corner as we raced across the cosmos at hyper warp speeds. Where was the lowlife? Why had he let us escape so easily? What happened back on Othwan?

Grild sat apart from the others lost in a world of his own. I passed by and gave him the tin, wincing with the sting of my own wounds. "Dry up those cuts, Grild. Don't let them get infected."

He took the tin with a heavy grunt of little enthusiasm. "Voj bit it down there."

"I know. I could see you two were friends."

"He was a loyal ally and a brave man." The young man's eyes were bloodshot, his fleshy cheeks grime-smeared. Ordinarily, a youngblood like him'd be apple-cheeked under that camo cover. A definite defiance on that tough face with the flat nose and the flared nostrils—a kind of proud, physical fighting ancestry that went way back, perhaps to the stone ages. I could see why Wren had chosen him.

"How much of our booty is left?" I asked Wren.

She shrugged. "When you didn't show up at Gainor, our usual place, I knew you were either dead or they'd captured you. I really hoped not dead. The information came at a high cost, Rusco. There's virtually nothing left."

I gave a wheezing sigh.

"You've got your life to thank for it, so be grateful."

"I'm getting used to it."

"You're bleeding still," she pointed out.

"Ah, just flesh wounds," I mumbled. The regen was working, but slowly, and waves of hot pain stung my side, arcing from rib to rib as the flesh knitted together. I'd become almost immune to pain after Mong's long cruel sessions. Wren lifted my blood-soaked smock and balked at the scars building there. Good thing she hadn't seen me before the tank dunking.

"Forget it." I pushed her hands away. "We've other things to worry about. Throw me some more regen after Grild's finished, I'll slap it on and be done with it."

"As you wish." She took the tin from Grild's upraised hand and tossed it my way. "Got extra just for you, Rusco. Knew if we did find you guys in one piece, you'd be needing it."

If I came across as an unhappy man, it wasn't because I was not glad to see Wren. I just wasn't in an affectionate mood. No one could blame me. Torture and too much senseless death kind of does that to one. Deadens a person to the finer things in life, like a wholesome, caring woman. I looked over to Blest who had the look of a lost soul. Couldn't blame him either. Degradation and torture had made him a withered husk. Guilt hit me that he'd suffered too much for my sins at the hands of that sadist Mong. Follee dead too, Voj dead. How many more casualties before this was all over?

Wren reacted to my melancholy. "Going to take some getting used to you with no hair, Jet. The one and only Jet Rusco, bald as an eagle. Who'd have thought?"

"Yeah, well there're always changes happening in the universe."

"I take it Mong was not gentle with you?"

I made no comment.

Blest interrupted with a surly snarl. "Very nice chitchat, lovebirds, but how did you get the drop on us, Wren?"

She shrugged. "We gave it exactly twenty minutes to get you out and warp to safety before Mong got wise and crushed us like bugs."

"And you managed it," I said, "minus a few flesh wounds."

"Speak for yourself," Blest said, rubbing his slow-healing injury.

"With your funds from the Myscol payout, I purchased this new ship, an Alpha 9, as you see—" Wren swept out her arms "—also bought reliable intel that pinpointed your place of captivity at Othwan. We also learned some rogue planet was going in for a strike against Mong—at his monk's retreat to steal back the Countess. If it hadn't been for the Vendecki's diversion, I would have given up, thrown any rescue plan aside as suicide."

A dead silence. We were happy to shut up for once and just stare at nothing.

We took our time outs and rested in our cabins. Noss and Wren took shifts watching the helm as we sped through the light highways on our long journey to Veglos. Why Veglos? Well, where else? Volia still hadn't said much, staring in her vacuous way in a cloud of shock. Likely processing her part in the whole affair—the Vendecki assault, the conquest of her planet, the death of her husband and her old way of life. A chunk of the Countess's soul had died on Othwan and I'm reckoning it had for Blest and me too. She kept to herself, said little, nursing her wounds. Zan was Zan, still blank-eyed and a partial zombie after being strung up on Mong's chicken wire so long. He'd not had the luxury of a tank healing to repair his wounds and relied solely on regen. Blest had taken some serious leg damage, which was no secret to any of us. Like me, he'd been stoic about his pain and the regen recovery process. Luckily we had the extra duty regen, costly as it was, otherwise Blest's shin would have been a lot sorrier than it was right now.

Zan and Grild had bonded and played mindless games to pass the time. *Crockseye* and *Bad Leader*—computer board games with AI players to up the ante. Wren and I had a lot to catch up on, but there was a distance between us. Of my time with Mong I spoke little and was evasive at best. Though she managed to catch pieces of it from Blest who spoke in grunts and whispers from time to time but was at best unreliable. Next time she saw me she was all hushed up and our eyes did not meet, as if she were reluctant to trigger my depressed moods or broach any sensitive territory involving physical torture. I let it stand at that. I wasn't even prepared to talk about it to myself. I couldn't imagine how Blest was coping with it. His video games and rough-guy talk worked to some degree. As did hiding behind a Scroogely-curmudgeon persona and mask. As good a protective mechanism as any.

Volia later approached me and others on the bridge as we munched on assorted goodies in nutrition packs: veal alfredo, spacer's ghoulash, tofu teriyaki, all washed down with instant coffee. "I want to thank you for what you did, Rusco. From what Zan and Blest said, you went out of your way to get me, at risk to your own safe getaway. Is there anything I can offer in return?"

I shrugged. "Nothing I can think of."

"There must be something—"

"After being in the Mentera tank, there's nothing much matters any more, Volia. Materially anyway."

She frowned, confused at the tank reference. I gave her a ham-faced grin, opening my mouth to say something then thought better of it.

Volia touched Wren on the arm. "I am indebted to you too, Wren. If not for your dogged persistence and courage, we'd all still be slaves down there."

Wren nodded. "We'll drop you wherever you want to go, Volia. I'm guessing it won't be on Melinar."

"No," she said, with a rueful shake of her head. "The capital, Baki on Vendecki soil should be fine."

Wren hesitated. "Isn't that a little close to the war front?"

"We're still allies in the uprising against Mong. Like it or not, I'm leader of my people and the titular commander of this war."

Wren swallowed a mouthful of microwaved lamb. "Not envious of your position in life, nor eager to trade places with you, Volia. But if I were in your shoes, I'd keep up the fight for freedom. I'd do everything in my power to take down that murderer Mong."

She flashed Wren a moon-eyed stare. "It's as if I know you from somewhere." She blinked and shook her head. "All of you. As if we've been here before and done this in another time." She shook her head again, wiped her brow of sweat. "I must be losing my mind, or experiencing some major case of deja-vu."

Remembering my flashbacks in the tank, I guessed it was contagious. Maybe good old Mong'd plunged her into a tank and she didn't remember it?

A tear drifted down her cheek. "After all the tragedy, my people slaughtered, my husband..." She couldn't say more and turned a desolate gaze upon me. "I misjudged you, Rusco. When I saw you there on that ship of Mong's, I thought—only a brutish thug, one of his trained animals."

"Yeah, well, you know what they say about first impressions."

"I see a good man in you."

I laughed. "I wish I could frame those words, Lady Volia, and put them on the wall here. Somebody appreciates me after all. Hear that Wren?"

She grinned.

Volia grabbed my wrist. "Rusco, we could use freedom fighters like you. Join us. Come to our haven. There're more than a few rebels down there you'd take a shine to. We need support, your kind of gutsy, off-the-wall leadership."

I smiled. "Sorry, Volia, but think I've about used up my nine lives in this lifetime."

Blest's snort seconded that opinion. No sooner had I acknowledged Blest's dog-eared sneer than a sharp pang hit my heart as I remembered my vow to take down that fucker Mong. Grudgingly, I remarked, "But I'll take you to Baki at least and listen to one of your talks. If you need help flying supplies in, or black market war props, I could help you out—for a price, of course."

She gave a crooked grin. "Always the businessman, eh, Rusco? Consider it a deal. Your services are more than welcome."

Chapter 29

Down on Baki we congregated in a huge war hall at Independence Square. The place held eight hundred or more avid supporters, a mix of Melinarian refugees and Vendecki sympathizers. Volia spoke up in a resonant voice:

"Freedom fighters of Baki, comrades and allies, your enthusiasm and steadfast courage gives me great joy. Though my own planet Melinar fares ill under Mong's occupation, I see you have held out and survived. For that I commend you. Loyalty and unity are the greatest assurances for a brighter future that a leader of the people can ask for."

Her noble presence inspired loyalty. I could see that. First time I'd seen her all cleaned up, her hair shining brilliant hues, bleached pure gold this time under a silver tiara, her cheeks flushed a rosy pink and eyes bright sparkles of fervor, of a nationalism that was, truthfully, one of my least favorite qualities in her. But if it gave these beleaguered people hope…hope against an impossible enemy who I, as much as any, wished to see vanquished and trampled in the dirt, then so be it.

"If not for these brave men and women, I would not be here. Let me introduce my friends—Jet Rusco, Wren Zalan, Noss Brekia, Blest Surok, Zan Vulder and Grild Malsi."

We stepped forward on the low stage in turn and presented ourselves.

Sure enough, we were heroes, even as the deluded Vendecki continued to hold out against Mong's tyranny and the frightfully large number of his attack forces posted at nearby Melinar. Perhaps Mong's crew were thinking twice about advanced Vendecki tech poking up out of nowhere and launching an attack on their doorstep, the same insurgents who had nearly brought them to their knees at Othwan. All the same, I kept glancing out the diamond-shaped panes, waiting for the dive bombers to strike—Warhawks and missiles to come blitzing and dropping on our asses. Maybe even Mong's agents were spying on this little congregation right now. Part of me, did not want to think about that, or even be here. Too close to enemy soil. But I'd promised Volia I'd come and I did not want to live in fear all my waking days…

A standing ovation erupted amongst the gathered rebels for our part in the rescue and daring escape. I had to grin, shaking my head in surprise.

Never would have imagined an accolade like this, nor had I ever been hailed a hero before. The opposite, by many. It felt good, to tell the truth. The others, taken by surprise, laughed and looked around, trading gratifying looks at one another. Though Blest sported his perpetual frown and just shrugged it off in his usual way.

More speeches followed and Phel, the master of ceremonies, the top-ranking war officer of the Melinarians, stepped forward. An olive-skinned man of mixed Melinarian-Vendecki descent, he was all white teeth, a stiff ruff of grey-peppered hair. He launched into a spiel of how Vendecki forces were working with the defeated Melinarians to liberate their sister planet from tyranny. A valiant saga of how the forces were rebuilding themselves, new ships being deployed and manpower raised; they would conquer and turf out the imperial dictators of Jezuan before the next moon.

Yeah, right, dream on, Phel. Pure rhetoric, but it seemed to be what the audience wanted to hear.

Later at a more informal gathering at one of the VIP tables in the bustling war hall, Phel topped off my glass with fine wine and asked me point blank what I thought of the whole Vendecki program.

I shrugged, not knowing how to answer in front of the others.

"Come on, Jet. Aren't you sold yet? Won't you and your crew fly for us? Volia here has spoken highly of you and of your interest in helping us, offering cargo transport of arms for fair market value."

I looked over to the Countess who wore a devil's grin on her flushed face. "They seem to love you," I said.

"Unlike many aristocracies, I believe that leaders are accountable to the people."

Phel added, eager to promote his cause, "We're mounting an assault on occupied Melinar, Jet," he said in a conspiratorial tone. "Our hope is that Mong's forces will take the bait. We'll be more than ready for them this time."

I blinked as would an owl. These people surely had a death wish, or they loved to flirt with disaster.

"We'll retake our home world. This time with a better plan in mind and more allies."

"Are the Vendecki in line with this?" I asked.

"Yes, they're fierce allies."

"To take on Mong will require a lot more than a few allies and some tough talk about general deployment and rah-rah."

"True, Rusco, but we have friends throughout the Larga system. We underestimated Mong's power. We're asking for help from all quarters. Like yourself. Are you on board?"

I hesitated.

"How do you single out his ships with your jammer?" Noss asked, breaking the silence.

"It's complicated," said Phel. "Do you want the long answer or the short? Harg here, our com expert, can explain—" he snapped his fingers, called over a grey-haired man with a tall drink in his hand.

"Never mind," said Noss, "I'll assume you've worked out the deployment issues."

"Our engineers, like Harg here, and other Melinarian experts, are working on a foolproof version of the jammer. A retractable antenna cached to a depth of 500M. Even if Mong or enemy patriots nuke the area, our automated defense system can raise and lower the antenna to changing war conditions."

"Sounds good, but—"

"Where, on Twidor?" I barked, "and that other wasteland moon? How do you manage that? Mong and his rats'll be watching those moons like cheese at a rathole after that last bout on Melinar."

"That's the beauty of it. They'd never guess that we'd employ the same defense tactic twice. We've run cloaked ships in and out and dropped men and equipment down on Twidor to work in the Dusk Caves, digging, burrowing, shielded under the rock from his onboard ship probes and scanners. The antenna'll be the last thing to go up—and only when we need full jamming capacity. When it's operational, enemies can't indefinitely keep firing on it or patrolling the area. We've redundancy transmitters and backup antennae installed in bunkers across both moons."

"It's a better start," said Noss. "Why didn't you think of it right from the get-go?"

Harg, the signals engineer, answered, "We didn't think Mong or any ally of his could track and destroy a transmitter so quickly. If the transmitters had been up longer, we'd likely have destroyed his armada."

"An honest mistake."

"That cost far too many lives. Let's hope it immobilizes them for good this time."

"I'm still not clear on the overall plan." I rubbed the heel of my palm on my temple.

Phel gave an impatient flourish. "We stir up the pot on Melinar, Mong goes in to retaliate and we jam their signals. The plan's success relies upon the fact that Mong hasn't cracked our jammer infiltration codes. I'm worried his enforcers might have fleshed it out of our captive engineers. But the good news is, we never gave any of them a full schematic of the tech. Mong's crew could theoretically piece it together on the fly—but that'd take—"

"A lot of ifs and probables here, Phel," I interrupted.

"I know. That's why time is of an essence." He turned to Volia and flashed meaningful glances at both of us. "So, will you fight?"

"Hold on. I never agreed to—" My mind flashed on the post and tank in the Redemption Chamber then I clenched my teeth. "I'll help you out."

Volia stirred in her seat and set down her glass.

Wren gaped. "Are you sure, Rusco?"

"Not really, but—"

Wren's eyes fluttered. Blest just gave his head a little shake and took a fish's gulp of wine. Grild and Zan seemed indifferent, resigned to whatever fate was in for them, going whichever way the wind blew. By the look of their hollow stares, I could tell that their lives were at an impasse, governed by the toss of the die.

Conflicting thoughts poured through my mind. Not the least, Mong's words drifting back to me, that dim time on *Vulpin's* bridge, *"I never retreat, Balt. Never. I win every battle I fight."* Perhaps the Vendecki ruse was the deadly hammer that would drive steel into Mong's flesh through that chink in his armor.

And then, maybe it wasn't.

* * *

Down in the underground hangar on Vendecki's moon, Hedra, we oversaw the clandestine loading of boxes and assorted cases of rifles, R4s, gauge 3 power packs, land mines, shell absorbers, flamethrowers, anything we could get in the hold of *Starrunner* and other starships to help the rebel cause on Melinar. We wore standard grey Vendecki khakis with Vendecki logos pasted on our breast over high-grade Kevlar. Black boots, crash helmets, refitted R4s at our waist, the whole shebang.

Phel approached me, wearing a moody frown. "New plans, Rusco.

Forget the scheduled arms drop. We need fighters in the air at 0200."

"Say what?" I stared at Volia who'd come by and overhead.

"Conditions on Melinar have turned for the worse," she said in a strained voice. "Mong's amped up his persecutions, accusing Melinarian spies of being the ones who dug up the location of Othwan and brought about the invasion of his sanctuary. I just watched the video feed." She uttered sorrowful croak. "Slave camps, interrogations, brutal torture. Mong's captains have examined all our technically skilled engineers and scientists. They ply them with truth-serums, discarding them like garbage once they've served their purpose. Their minds are fried from drugs and repeated drills. The Vendecki endure no less savage scrutiny. When will it stop? It'll never stop! Not until that madman is put down."

"I agree with you there, Countess. But easier said than done." I rubbed my jaw and looked around at the smattering of ships, pilots, crew and engineers. "You expect to take down a sociopath and a well-greased war machine skilled from day one. You have largely untrained rabble here and some low-tech ships. You don't even have fareons installed. Mong hasn't gotten to where he is without substantial resources."

"You underestimate yourself, Rusco—and us. You had him! *We* had him—we had him worried, and we escaped from his lair right under his nose."

"A lot of luck and diversion there. With more luck to go. How many died?"

Volia sighed. "Our ratio was 4 to 5. That puts us at a 20% total fatality figure. Most of the forces escaped unscathed in that shootout. We decimated Othwan. And we're ready to counterattack."

My eyes could not help but gleam with temptation, unusual for even me. It was an impressive statistic. I looked to Noss and the others who'd been silent this whole time. "So what do you have? What's your plan?"

Phel pushed closer with his teeth clacking. "Mong's fallen for the bait. We've confirmed knowledge of his next attack. Nineteen brave men and women died to bring us that information. We mustn't squander their sacrifice. We'll use the intel for max gain to strike Mong where he least expects it!"

"All fine and nice. A motley crew of disorganized skullbashers. Angry dissidents whose friends and families have been tortured and killed by that mongrel, all fired up to fight an impossible fight."

"Yes, that's what we are, Rusco, you've summed us up all too nicely."

I grinned. "You're at least an honest, pushy bastard, Phel. This rabble is my kind of piss and vinegar folk."

"Great to hear." He brightened. "Because you're going to lead Reaver Party 3."

I let out an explosive breath. "What the fuck? Where did you dream up this hare-brained idea?"

"I know your type, Rusco." Phel narrowed beady eyes on me. "I did some digging on you. You've got nothing else left. Your life's worth shit now, a shambles, debt up to your ears, bounty hunters in every sector looking to cash in, with that alpha dog hounding your heels, nose up your ass."

"Wait a minute! I agreed to run transport, no more—arms in, soldiers out—for pay. An even 5k was our deal."

"It was, but it's gotten bigger than that."

Eyes were on me. I heard the pound of my heart in my ribcage.

"You have the chance to take him down, help millions of people! Why pass that up for some lesser role, playing baggage jockey over here? You and Wren and the others are among the few rare ones in the galaxy who've ever defeated and escaped the Star Lord."

"And we'd like to keep it that way."

"We need you!" he cried, grabbing my shoulder.

I looked at his hand and he licked his lips and withdrew it, realizing he'd overstepped.

There passed a moment when a tense silence passed, when my life flashed before me—all the times I was a little shit disturber, seven, eight? breaking everything in the house, lighting things on fire, playing tricks on the neighbor's cat. Suddenly time jumped and there were shell shots, explosions, my parents and friends fried by flash bombs—then, like the tenebrous haze in the tanks, a zap of light, illumination, I knew after all this searching that I had a real purpose…as if my life leading up to this point had been only prep, paving the way for this one desperate act. It was crazy. But then again, everything in this mad universe was crazy. A big, mixed-up, shit-for-brains soup of craziness.

"It's 10k yols, if you pull it off," Phel said, intruding on my thoughts, "and Mong is taken down and destroyed."

"Well?" I looked at the others.

Wren shrugged, gave me her 'could take it or leave it' look. I sighed, knew they wouldn't go for it.

"10k bonus each," Phel said, realizing he'd have to sweeten the pot.

Wren's and Blest's eyes flickered. I saw a hint of interest there, and a touch of greed in Blest's.

So they were on board. I grinned and nodded. "Okay, Phel, it'll surely fail, badly—but what the fuck."

Phel beamed and slapped me on the back. "Good call, Rusco. You're a good man."

"I keep hearing that," I said with a frown.

Phel spoke into a com. "Team leader, move out. We have 24 hours to pull this caper off."

Chapter 30

The camoed grey moon rock flap slid aside and *Starrunner* burst out of the cave on Hedra. Five convoys at our heels impulse-thrust away from the desolate lunar plains into the deepening blackness of space—older Alpha X's, but capable of speed and looking beat-up and retro enough to pose as beleaguered rebel craft fighting for a doomed cause.

"Team leader to Sparrows," I rasped into the com. "On my signal."

"Roger, team leader. This is Sparrow 1. Give us the word."

I kept an open channel. Once we escaped Hedra's gravity and were in the safe zone, we'd make the jump to Melinar.

Phel's voice came over the encrypted link, his grey-peppered hair tied back in a bun. "Remember, you're bait only. When Mong's defense guard are alerted and paralyzed by our jammers, you turn and attack them. Until then, maintain defensive positions. When jammers are at full capacity, no mercy! Blast those maggots to shit! The bulk of our fighters will warp in and join the slaughter."

"Roger. Over." I signed off with a grim sigh. Grim plans for grim times.

"T-7 minutes. Remember," I told Wren and the others, "we warp in, make it look like a drop off of arms to the Melinar rebels. No land action. The risk is minimal. At the first sign of trouble, we zigzag then warp the fuck out of here. We hope their little jammers do the work. Then in comes their fleet to finish the job. We're just extra change in the overall equation. Remember the payout—big payout."

"Gift wrapped with pretty little red ribbons," quipped Blest. "Wonder what can go wrong?"

"Nothing'll go wrong," I said to him. "Do your job, have your gun on the ready in case we need backup."

"No one can pay me enough for this shit, Rusco."

I ignored him, spoke quiet words into the com then to Wren, briefing her and the others on procedure. It seemed as if this op was all sewn up, almost too clear and clean. That queasy feeling in my gut sensed something havey-cavey and that things would not be so easy.

My hoarse whisper echoed into the com. "Now."

In a blast of brilliant light, *Starrunner* arched through the Varwol tunnel into Melinarian space. We materialized outside the grav danger zone. Melinar hung below us, a distant turquoise disc, its twin moons bright on the far side of their orbits. The five other convoys materialized beside us, dim grey craft, looking very ragged and wary. I loosed a breath of pent up exhaustion. Word had been dropped to Mong's spies that Vendecki sympathizers were planning a run to grant aid to the demoralized rebels in the Jezuan hills. I didn't doubt Mong's watchdogs would be arriving soon. Very soon. Noss readied *Starrunner* and we set a course for Targan, the square continent in the middle of the vast ocean Praxeus on Melinar's far side where the conquered city Jezuan lay on a jagged coastline.

Hulking shapes were suddenly all around us. Fifty Warhawks—dark gunmetal grey predators, cannons locked on us.

Black-hearted Mong had fallen for the bait, faster than I thought, incensed at the piercing thorn in his side at another Melinarian uprising.

The Star Lord himself was there. His ginormous flagship *Vulpin* loomed into view. I'd recognize that bloated hunk of scrap metal anywhere. Its twisted control towers and bullfrog midsection, rear radial boosters and energy thrusters gave me the shakes. Some hundred or more cannons sprawled fore and aft from every angle of its prickly hide. Didn't surprise me. The bigger they are the harder they fall…Well, wonder if they leaked the news that Jet Rusco was on board leading the expedition. Likely, the fuckers.

Fareons arched out at us almost instantaneously in green and violet menace. Our shields dipped to an appalling low. One of our convoys rippled in red, then exploded in ruin, her shields weak or malfunctioning.

I grimaced in astonishment. "Jesus, Noss. What's going on? Now, Phel! Fucker, get those jammers working!"

It seemed Phel wanted to draw out the Warhawks more, lengthen the charade. Perhaps the jammers were fucked? What was one sacrifice? For a second, I thought we'd been had.

But *Vulpin's* fareons did go haywire and stray fire lashed out from her cannons and ignited one of Mong's own lead craft that was firing on us. I smacked my fist in my palm. Wren locked fareons on the nearest ship in the enemy line. Noss kept *Starrunner* on a sweeping tangent over the warcraft's hulls—a risk, even if we avoided their haywire beams, yet maximizing the damage we could inflict on them at such close range. We rained destruction on their hulls, penetrating their mega shields with repeated bursts. I waited for the rest of the Melinarian fleet to show up with their Vendecki scrabblers.

But they did not come. Or at least not too soon. I saw a hundred Warhawks blitz into existence from various parts of the galaxy and they sent flash bombs after us—salvos that had not been affected by the jammers. Our shields would not hold out for long. The rebel fleet materialized at last. The fireworks began. But this was a different type of fireworks. Little glowbugs on the underdog side burning and biting the big blackbirds. From grey, tiny fuselages pricks of red light lashed out and slammed into the larger Warhawks.

Enemy craft lit in orange and yellow and foundered as their shields gave way.

"There!" I cried in triumph. "Target Mong's shitty flagship! Spare nothing! We have no better chance than now. Do it, Wren!"

She opened full fareons on *Vulpin*. The superstructure rippled, a complex metalworks of folds and dark, twisted cannons and com towers. Rebel craft from all angles opened fire on Mong's mother ship along with others of the fleet. We pelted them with all our megavolts could give, and the enormous craft started to list and fall in orbit toward Melinar.

"Hot damn!" I cried. *Vulpin* flared, pitched and rolled and continued her descent toward Melinar and we raced after her.

Phel's voice came rasping over the com, "Do not go in, Rusco!"

"Bring your ships over!" I cried. "Mong is falling. We've got him. We've already got our weapons locked on his rude bastard hide!"

"Can't. We're too busy fighting Warhawks and having a hell of a time of it."

I could see on the ship's holo tactical that the Vendecki craft were taking heavy losses from flash bombs and were prey to Mong's superior numbers. Sparrow 1 ignited to starboard; the last two of our team lay heavily taxed by enemy fire.

"The warbirds have no com," Phel shrilled, "but their limited reserve weapons are still wreaking havoc on us."

Flash bombs and convention torps. I gave a miserable sigh.

Wren hit the override switch for reserve fareon power. "That bastard Mong's going to get away. Too many slimy tricks up his sleeve."

"Not if we can help it," I growled. I peered over at Noss. "Can you bring us in close enough?"

Noss grinned.

Sure enough, *Vulpin* jettisoned an escape craft from the starboard port as she hurtled planetside. I boomed at Noss, "There!"

Wren targeted the shuttle.

Phel grunted in amazement. "A blip has appeared on our scanners. Wait…No, we do not see him anymore. Mong must have curled around the shadow side of the planet."

"No, we're tracking the bogie jettisoned from *Vulpin*."

"Rusco, I forbid you to go down there—"

I cut the channel. Enough of meister Phel for one day. "Fire every volt of fareon juice we have into that bastard's ass, Wren!"

She unleashed full fareons. We streaked after the fleeing shuttle, a dark bottle-green shape with bulbed prow and twin fins. Straight to the dimming planetside the shuttle spiraled. We entered Melinar's atmosphere. Glowering scarlet hue of early evening fell on the rich landscape. We skimmed over the featureless plains in pursuit of the shuttle.

Vulpin nosedived several miles in front of us then smashed into a large paddy field. A bright blue explosion marked the crater of her entry. The shuttle cut through the smoldering cloud and roared skyward, barely saving its hide. Wren's continued blasts hit it square on, shearing off the rear fins and sending the fuselage spinning out of control. Corkscrewing, it crashed at the side of a hill at the edge of an arid field, smoke trailing from its crumpled fuselage.

As the haze cleared, we saw three figures emerge dazedly from the blackened husk. Magnified resolution revealed one hulking shape, garbed in half-scorched leather and furs, staggering out with two of his henchmen. All were disoriented, blood streaming from their faces and arms. Wren's holo screen showed higher resolution and her fingers twitched over the fareon blaster.

I reached over and grabbed her hand. "Wait!" I rasped. "As much as I want to nuke that bastard's ass right now, we can take him alive! To suffer a thousand deaths for the ones he has given to so many others."

She exhaled an exasperated breath, but the others nodded in agreement.

"Give us air coverage, Noss. An eagle-eye's view. We're going in on foot. Keep us apprised of any unpleasant surprises. We don't want any predators biting us in the ass."

"Roger that."

Starrunner settled beside Mong's broken escape craft, at the rising hill to our right. Noss checked shields and disengaged the rear cargo door. We glimpsed the crash survivors struggling up the hillside on the holo display.

"Zan, you stay behind and help Noss with weapons and nav. Your back wounds are still not healed enough to do a land op. Wren, Blest, Grild— come with me. We go in on foot."

We had no need for masks. Intrepid pioneers had terraformed Melinar centuries ago, with big air generators, water synthesizers, and feeding crops and flora liquid nutrients once transplanted from earth-like worlds.

The four of us stepped out, fully equipped, with R4s, Kevlar vests, coms, helms. The air had a dry distinct tang of slightly tart fecundity, but not unpleasant. Bird song was nonexistent here. The smoke from the escape shuttle had frightened off any animal life. A sudden rank, burning waft of melted metal and gas fumes hit us head on. I motioned Wren and the others up the slope.

Mong and his surviving crew had stumbled up the hill into a grove of weird, strangle-branched trees. Though the word 'grove' was a misnomer. Alien flora at best—a petrified forest. Large tracts of thick-boled trees rose up the crumbling slopes, creating a perfect haven for ambush. I weaved among the tan-colored trunks of the broken landscape, urging the others along through the unyielding limbs.

Almost immediately I hunched under the heavier weight of the planet's gravity. I didn't have the same spring and jump in my legs at all.

My boots crunched on the gravel-like soil. I heard the distant shuffle and crunch of boot heels and heavy breathing up ahead. Fugitives, not far away.

I gave the signal. We split up to flank them. Wren and Blest took the east, Grild and I took the west, up a steeper, rougher tract with strange flakes of shattered, mars-red rocks. At one time these trees had been living things, but now they were dead, only dry spiky, spidery remnants of a forgotten past.

The runaways had split up too, judging from the scuffling echo coming back through the alien flora. A shrewd tactic, to limit the chance of getting tagged.

I wanted Mong badly. I rasped into the com. "Noss! Do you have a read on them?"

"Negative. We lost air coverage... Wait. Two pulses. Lifeforms at

A23.61. Sending location…"

"That's them." I firmed my lip. "We see them in our helm scopes. Unless they're indigenous deer, it has to be them."

Mong and his company had no chance. When the rebels blew his fucking, wretched Warhawks out of the sky, neutralized every last one of his killing machines, he'd have nothing. This cat and mouse guerrilla war we were playing then would be pointless. But a nagging uncertainty still tugged at the back of my head. What if those jammers failed? What if Mong's ships came streaking down out of the clouds and incinerated us instead?

I swallowed hard. What mess did you get yourself into, Rusco? Did you think it would be that easy? Your impetuousness may have landed you in a bigger jam than last time.

Voices of doubt. Ghosts of fear. I shook them from my mind and moved ahead, nudging Grild in the ribs.

A deeper feeling hit me, struck now with the growing suspicion that if I didn't catch Mong here, we'd never get him. He was a monster larger than life, an ulcerous cancer armed with an unnatural tendency to escape justice. I could envisage his hulking frame disappearing in the soil forever, like an everlasting termite, hiding, escaping the justice he was due.

I was not going to let that happen.

Like weasels we moved in undulating, semi-crouched positions while the dim light of fading day filtered through the spiny twigs, lending an eerie unreality to the lands around us.

I heard Noss's voice hiss over the helm's com. "They're moving away from you, Jet. But we don't have great resolution up here. Grainy. You've got to cut them off at the next ravine—A25.44. I can't blast the area without taking you out too."

"Affirmative, Noss. Keep scanning. Let us know of any anomalies." I kept my voice to a bare whisper.

The petrified twigs, like crazy fractal patterns, obscured our view. Surreal this landscape. As from a dream I studied the impossible foliage—a massive primordial canopy that blocked out the little light remaining in the sky and left only a dull golden-amber staining the shattered earth floor.

Distant gunfire echoed hollowly through the trees. Impossible to gauge distance with all these stony echoes in this strange geography. The sound bounced off trunks and ricocheted to other places, prompting even a professional soldier to draw false conclusions.

With less confidence than before, we stumbled forward.

We'd gotten no further than a bend in the knoll when fire bit at us from out of nowhere. Grild fell, uttering a moaning cry. He lay face down in a riddled heap.

I grimaced, dove out of the way just as more deadly fire ate into the trunk behind me. I crouched in the dusky light, a wary wolf, my heart pounding. No hits, but I could hear my blood pound in my throat.

Grild wheezed, shifted his gaze toward me. He snuffed out a trickle of blood from his nostrils. He was in a bad way. I motioned him to silence, and to stay still. No way of getting to the man. He was six feet away. Damn it! Mong or one of his gunmen was closer than I thought. He was covering the area with a marksman's expertise. How could I have been so fucking stupid? That fiend moved more stealthily than any predator. Now the hunted stalked the hunters.

Chapter 31

I inched forward, creeping on my stomach at a snail's pace, moving toward shelter amongst the petrified roots. I felt like a foreign grub here, with my R4 trained—hoping it didn't clink on the flaked shingle, alert for any sound or signal.

Grild gasped behind me. Poor bugger. What could I do for him? I'd get my head shot off if I tried to double back and minister to him. What good would that do either of us?

Where the fuck was Mong?

How far I crawled through that rooty hellhole like a miserable worm, I don't know, but it was far, and I could feel Mong's or his marksman's hawk eyes trained on me all the time. Why'd he keep me alive? I knew he could have plugged me anytime. I had no idea where they were. He could be hiding behind the next trunk or crouched behind some shattered boulder, anywhere in the heavy, dusky, growing shadows, waiting like a ghoul for me to slip up. Where the fuck was he?

"Wren," I hissed in the com.

No answer. Maybe she was playing possum too on purpose, staying dark.

A stone turned several feet away to my right.

"Looking for me, Jet Rusco?"

I whirled in the red shale, my gun raised. I sprayed out a stream of fire and Mong leaped back in all his charred, blooded glory, sheltering behind a massive rocky trunk. His rifle pointed out. My fire ricocheted off the rippled bark and took out large chunks of the petrified wood he crouched behind, spewing flakes every which way.

"That's a waste of bullets, Jet."

Closer he limped. I sprayed more fire but missed. He ducked back behind another tree, less wide than the others, but enough to conceal his ape-like frame. He'd timed it so he'd make it. I gave a silent curse. I panted, my eyes darting wildly from trunk to trunk. Maybe the fuck'd already hopped to a new hiding place while I rubbed the grit out of my eyes. I wouldn't doubt that his injured leg was crippled enough, but he could still walk on it. Bloody hell! Didn't surprise me.

A metal barrel spat a few rounds at my heels—just to tease me. I wormed my way more desperately along, the blood hammering in my skull.

My rifle caught on a rock and I heard a grunt of triumph somewhere to my right. That last glimpse of him I saw: his face so placid, untroubled, it unnerved me. As confident as the wild animals that once roamed this forest habitat.

Thirty feet separated me from his last location as I scrambled behind a tree of my own, barely avoiding his return fire. I kept my head and body under cover and my gun low. I dared come no closer. I knew the man's illimitable power. Even maimed, he was a threat. A surge of raw panic tickled up my spine. My mouth felt like a dried prune, a sandpaper desert. Mong was a force to be respected. Any fool could see that. My breath rasped in my throat. The worst stranglehold of fear was on me, having a monstrous tour de force so close. The ultimate psychopathic sadist...

A vision sprang in my mind. The lurid memory from back in the tanks when I experienced that horrible case of deja-vu. I saw myself again on an alien, freaky hillside on a faraway world, facing down Mong. The same as now.

I heard a familiar voice wheeze out a tired breath. "Yes, Jet, one must be careful when he hunts the tiger. Star Lord and con man—here we are—Hustler wanting to be Star Avenger. No need for quiet. My colleagues will keep your friends busy for some time, so we may converse freely."

I peeked an eye out from behind my trunk. I could not see him. I pulled my head back.

"I must commend you for taking down my flagship and shuttle. I don't know how you did it, but I guess you managed to reinstate the Melinar jammer. Very good. Funny how I dismissed that tech. I don't know how you defeated Balt either and liberated the Mentera. But I can guess. You capitalized on my mistake. Kudos to you, Jet Rusco! Ingenious and spontaneous. Perhaps my teachings were not in vain after all. Balt will stay in his glass prison; in fact, he has moved to primary exhibit in my new 'restored' Temple of Light on a different world, far away in the Butala sector that nobody will find. You'll have to visit it sometime. I've renamed it 'The Temple of Wrath'—in dedication to all the worlds of this filthy system who will pay for rising against me."

The man was talking far too much. Why? I snatched a quick look over my shoulder. The gunmen I expected to come leaping out, fry me from behind, were not there.

Mong must have caught the movement for his lips curled in a blood-smeared grin. Double bluff. My head spun. The man was mind-fucking with me. "You don't seem to be in any position to uphold that claim," I croaked.

Mong clicked his tongue. "Armies can be replaced, Rusco. Ships can be rebuilt and amassed. Like the rich man who loses all his money. Within a week, or two, such a man has rebuilt his empire stronger and bigger than ever."

I raised my weapon.

Mong gave a cynical flourish. "Let's dispense with our toys. I propose a duel. A test of strength and will. We compete with only physical and inner components. The best man wins. Are you game?" He tossed aside his rifle in a clatter of metal on stone, his R9, a rare and deadly weapon, smaller and more efficient than my R4.

Why would the sod do that? Was it jammed up or kaput? Or just another mind fuck?

"I'm not that stupid, Mong." I clutched my weapon tighter.

He narrowed his eyes. "Just stupider in other areas. I see you had the fool plan of trying to take me alive." He shook his head, smirked again and clicked his tongue. "That narrow ambition is revealed in your eyes. Hero Rusco captures Star Warlord! Pah! You still have a dreamy sentimentalism to you. Nor have you lost your old crone's desire to get 'one up' on your enemy. Shame on you." He exhaled a long breath. "Let it go, Jet Rusco. It'll only kill you, like a pig with a skewer in its belly." He motioned his right arm, his augmented arm, to unleash some foul telekinesis on me.

But a sharp burst of fire caught him sideways, slamming the other weapon he was trying to draw from his half-burned furs. The R3 vaporized in his hand and I whirled out of hiding and sprayed fire as I looked to see where the flare had come from. Who was it? Wren?

Mong rolled, grunted, and was up on his knees in three seconds, lifting his augmented arm, as if he'd caught in his grip some of that vicious fire flare.

He gave a wheezing sigh. "Do you need a woman to fight your battles? Die, you miserable coward! You're not deserving of my instruction." He flicked up his augmented arm.

I felt a terrible stinging pain course through my bones. Unbearable agony. As if I burned from inside. My fingers could not clutch the gun's trigger. I fell, gasping, clutching at my abdomen, gasping for air as the rifle fell from my nerveless fingers.

The stinging pain reached an apex. I fought nausea and unconsciousness. Blackout and death. All of a sudden, I snatched myself erect, struggling to save myself from falling into that deep abyss, staggering like a straw figure, with the cellular memory of all the times I'd withstood the depths of his torture, hanging in the Chamber of Redemption. I twisted to face him and used my inner force to redirect that hateful burst of energy from his synthetic limb back at him. How, I don't know. It was as if the Jet Rusco of old went away, and another Jet Rusco of the future took his place, some ancient incarnation of a dead, blooded warrior who raged and gave me the power to wield such formidable magic against a primordial enemy. I focused the energy with my mind, knocked Mong backward, sent him spinning on his heels.

His lips parted in soundless cry. "Wha—" It was like a sound a child might make who sees too late the vicious dog come bursting out of the neighbor's yard.

I snatched up my rifle, sprayed him with death-wielding fire. His right limb disintegrated in a ruin of machine parts and synthetic flesh. The limb hung severed from the shoulder.

His mouth dropped into a silent rictus. And yet, a flicker of amazement touched those swarthy lips, triumph even, that his magical teachings on me had worked—but also fear, for the first time in that man's brain, that defeat quite possibly loomed at the hands of his unwilling pupil.

Powers, it is said, come into the body through penance, or out-of-body experiences. Maybe they had?

Mong wheezed out a hoarse gasp and dropped to his knees. "I—sensed it back on Othwan. I gave you that power, Jet Rusco, would you bite—the hand that feeds you?"

"I would cut out your heart and feed it to the crows," I barked at him.

He nodded and sagged, his head lolling on his chest. Broken wires and white plasma oozed from that smoking shoulder socket, the mechanics of his augmentation. "I have trained you well," he croaked. "You've made me proud. But still you are only on the first rung of the ladder."

Bootfall echoed from behind the nearby trees. Wren approached breathless, training her gun on the weaponless, mutilated man.

I reached for her to steady myself. "Glad to see you! The others?" I croaked.

"His point man is dead. Blest is back there scouting the perimeter for the other one. Where's Grild?"

I shook my head. "Grild's not good. Back there too. Shot up."

Wren winced.

The whine of engines buzzed down through the treetops, echoing over our grim, bloody pasture. Not the deep-throated roar of Warhawks, but the higher-pitched thrum of Vendecki fighters. I could have jumped for joy. Mong's world was crashing down on him, his luck turning sour. I was fucking glad. Mong's eyes bulged, with a white flare of disbelief. He could be conquered and lose.

Blest came limping out of the swatch of trees. He stared at Mong and gave a crooked grin. "So, the mighty Master Mong isn't so mighty any more."

"Any trouble with our friends?"

Blest shrugged. "Sorry to say, the last loose runner has offered his body as fertilizer to dandelions."

I breathed a sigh of relief. I croaked into the com, "Noss! get over here, we need backup. Grild is down. I repeat, Grild is down." I turned to Blest. "Blest, run back and see if you can find him. I didn't leave him in a good state." I motioned in a vague direction and tossed him my extra pack of regen. Blest gave a crisp nod and hobbled away.

Wren wheezed out a hoarse breath, her weapon still trained on Mong. "I saw this bastard through the trees and fired from long range. I must have clipped him. I thought you were dead when you crumpled. What happened?"

"Mong fucked up and you and I blasted him." I debated telling her the whole story of how my inexplicable powers had deflected his killing blow but quickly decided against it.

She stepped over and lashed out a boot to smash in Mong's teeth but I quickly pulled her away from him. "Careful, that viper's—"

Even as I spoke, Mong's left hand flashed out and snatched up a long bowie knife from under his furs. The edge caught Wren's shin and drew a thin line of blood. She leaped back with a shriek, whirled and spat fire at him, catching him in his legs. He howled, yelping like a wolf. I surged forward and kicked the weapon out of Mong's last good hand as he tried to use the knife to cut his own throat.

"No unheroic behavior at this late hour, Mong! Die like a warrior, for Christ's sake. None of this hara-kiri shit," I sneered.

In a snarl of rage, he clawed for the knife, blinking back the agony from his ruined legs. "You have not won yet, Jet Rusco. You forget—the Mentera. The ones you let escape from the tanks. They'll bring back others to this world. You revived them from their slumbers—" he choked out a gob of bloody phlegm "—I would bet my life on it."

He half pulled himself upright among the sprawling roots with his twitching arm.

I wanted to plunge that knife into his throat, rid the universe of him once and for all. But my heart sank in my chest, my eyes glazing in horror. Ships blitzed over the sky. I was lost in a daze. A dangerous one. Mong scrabbled before me, seeking escape, looking for some way to end this life, but I would not let him. I hopped back to tower over him with my weapon cocked. He croaked, wearing a grin of lunatic rage on his grime-smeared, blood-dripping face. "Do it, kill me!"

I shook my head and watched him crawl his way toward the cover of trees, like a sick animal that slinks away to die.

I heard the cries of animated figures through the screen of trees, snatches of dim conversations, shapes of villagers emerging with hoes and rakes and shovels, seeking vengeance on the one who had caused them so much misery. Doubtless they'd seen the smoking wreck of Mong's flagship and put two and two together.

Wren lifted her R4 to go after him and finish him off, but I held her back. "Let the villagers have him. It's a worse punishment than the quick death he desires."

Wren lowered her gun and clasped me. "It's about time for that holiday vacation. Didn't you mention a spa on Palm Monterey?"

I held her close. I caressed her lovely, dust-filled, smoke-reeking hair. My eyes glazed over. "No beaches, Wren. Anytime. Nothing near water."

She stared at me. "Okay."

We both looked back with chill horror upon Mong's retreating shape. The man's psi power was flickering out fast with such grave injuries. A blank look of resignation had come over his face as he peered back. Not physical but spiritual. His confidence had withered, knowing his forces were being wiped out and his invincible fleet was teetering on its last legs. My pulse hammered. Revenge was here and now. And yet, such a bitter dessert.

Why did it feel so cheap and savage? Being in those tanks and enduring Mong's torture had opened me to a starker perspective of reality—it had given me powers as yet unexplored. True, my life as it was, would change. For better or worse? Who knew? Time would tell.

Villagers came plodding out of the dimness, yelling, gesticulating, a small army of them. Hundreds. Dust-streaked vindictive faces with eyes glaring in hate, following Mong's slimy trail of blood. I shuddered to think what they'd do to him.

Wren and I looked to the sky, hearing the roar of Vendecki ships blitzing across the darkening dusk-blue followed by more skyslips of the Melinar guard. The Melinarians would not get their revenge today before these villagers took theirs first.

A vague unease stirred at the base of my throat. As Wren and I hustled off to find Grild, I could not dismiss Mong's last grim warning of chittering Mentera skittering through the amalgamator and back to their dead power plant. Who after all, had let the flesh-eating crickets out of their cages? Maybe you need to clean up your mess, Rusco. If those crickety little bastard grasshopper fucks were to get one of their ships running...The disturbing thought faded and became but a grey smear on the fringe of my mind.

I shoved the worry aside, touched Wren's shoulder as we loped through the darkening trees. Live today, Rusco. Live in the moment. Today the living is free and easy...

OTHER BOOKS IN THE STARSHIP ROGUE SERIES:

STAR RUNAWAY
STAR WANDERER
THETIS 3
STAR REAPER
STARHUSTLER

https://innersky.ca/starship

ABOUT THE AUTHOR

Chris is a prolific author of fantasy, adventure, and science fiction. His writing spans many genres: heroic fantasy, sword and sorcery and speculative fiction.

Browse Chris's books at:

https://innersky.ca/books